Do That Again Son and I'll Break Your Legs

DO THAT AGAIN SON AND I'LL BREAK YOUR LEGS

Phil Thompson

First published in Great Britain in 1996 by
Virgin Books
an imprint of Virgin Publishing Ltd
332 Ladbroke Grove
LONDON W10 5AH

Typeset by Avon Dataset, Bidford-on-Avon, Warks B50 4JH
Printed and bound by Cox & Wyman Ltd, Reading, Berks

Contents

Acknowledgements

Special thanks to Linda McDermott, Damien Lepts, Jack Clark, Phil Jackson, Paul Harrison, Ian Cook, Nigel Sands, Gill Crickson, Mal Peachey, Hannah MacDonald, Liverpool City Library microfilm unit, staff at Birkenhead Library, BBC Radio Five, BBC Radio Merseyside, BBC GMR and BBC Radio Lancashire.

Thanks also to Ken Rogers, sports editor of the *Liverpool Echo*, for granting me permission to include extracts from articles that first appeared in that newspaper, and to all the footballers, referees and football journalists quoted in this book. I am indebted to Tommy Smith for his memories and his honesty.

Permissions

Grateful thanks to the following publications for permission to reproduce extracts.

BOOKS
An Autobiography, Pat Jennings in Association with Reg Drury, Willow Books, 1983

Baxter: The Party's Over, Jim Baxter in Association with John Fairgrieve, Stanley Paul, 1984

Docherty: A Biography Of Tommy Docherty, Brian Clarke, The Kingswood Press, 1980

Alan Mullery: An Autobiography, Alan Mullery with Brian Woolnough, Pelham Books, 1985

Ossie: My Life In Football, Osvaldo Ardiles with Mike Langley, Sidgwick and Jackson, 1983

Gordon Strachan: An Autobiography, Gordon Strachan with Jack Webster, Stanley Paul, 1984

Yours Sincerely, Ron Greenwood, Ron Greenwood with Bryon Butler, Willow Books, 1984

Just Like My Dreams: My Life With West Ham, John Lyall, Viking, 1989

Walk Alone: The Craig Johnson Story, Craig Johnston with Neil Jameson, Fleetwood Books, 1990

Beardsley: An Autobiography, Peter Beardsley with Andy Cairns, Stanley Paul, 1988

Macca Can! The Steve McMahon Story, Steve McMahon with Harry Harris, Pelham Books, 1990

Liverpool Greats, Ian Hargraves, Sportsprint Publishing in association with Liverpool Echo, 1989

For Leeds And England, Jackie Charlton, Stanley Paul, 1967

Only A Game: The Diary Of A Professional Footballer, Eamon Dunphy, Penguin, 1979

Give A Little Whistle: The Recollections Of A Remarkable Referee, Gordon Hill, Souvenir Press, 1975

Soccer Round The World: A Football Star's Story From Manchester To Mexico, Francis Lee, Arthur Barker, 1970

The Mavericks: English Football When The Flair Wore Flares, Robert Steen, Mainstream, 1995

Man On The Run, Mick Channon, Arthur Barker, 1970

Soccer The Hard Way, Ron Harris, Pelham 1970

Soccer Rebel: The Evolution Of The Professional Footballer, Jimmy Guthrie, Pentagon, 1976

Strachan Style: A Life In Football, Gordon Strachan with Ken Gallacher, Mainstream, 1991

Encyclopedia Of British Football, Phil Soar, Willow Books, 1987

Mark Lawrenson: The Autobiography, Mark Lawrenson, McDonald, 1988

Stanley Matthews, David Miller, Pavilion Books Ltd, 1989

Sparky, Barcelona Bayern And Back: The Autobiography Of Mark Hughes, Mark Hughes with Peter Fitton, Cockerel, 1989

Inside Anfield, John Aldridge with Brian Woolnough, Mainstream, 1988

Wor Jackie: The Jackie Milburn Story, John Gibson, Sportsprint Publishing, 1990

Revelations Of A Football Manager, Terry Neill, Sidgwick and Jackson, 1985

Clough: A Biography, Tony Francis, Stanley Paul and Company, 1987

Gascoigne: The Inside Story, Jane Nottage, Collins Willow, 1993

Hacketts Law: A Referee's Notebook, Keith Hackett, Willow Books, 1986

Graeme Souness: No Half Measures, Graeme Souness with Bob Harris, Willow Books, 1985

Out Of Time: Why Football Isn't Working, Alex Fynn and Lynton Guest, Simon and Schuster Ltd, 1994

Phil Neale, A Double Life, Phil Neale, Ring Books, 1990

The Best Of Times: My Favourite Football Stories, George Best with Les Scott, Simon and Schuster, 1994

Gazza! A Biography, Robin McGibbon, Penguin Books, 1990

Only The Best Is Good Enough: The Howard Kendall Story, Howard Kendall and Ian Ross, Mainstream Publishing, 1991

Out Of His Skin: The John Barnes Phenomenon, Dave Hill, Faber and Faber, 1989

Manchester United: My Team, Sammy McIlroy, Souvenir Press, 1980

Let's Be Honest, Jimmy Greaves and Reg Gutteridge, Pelham Books Ltd, 1972

The Lion Of Vienna: 50 Years A Legend, Nat Lofthouse, Sportsprint Publishing, 1989

Leeds United And Don Revie, Eric Thornton, Robert Hale Limited, 1970

Soccer: A Panorama, Brian Glanville, Eyre and Spottiswoode, 1969

Never Walk Alone, Gavin Peacock and Alan Comfort with Alan Macdonald, Hodder and Stoughton, 1994

Clough: The Autobiography, Brian Clough, Partridge Press, 1994

Arsenal: From The Heart, Bob Wall, Souvenir Press, 1969

Soccer Refereeing, Dennis Howell MP, Pelham Books Ltd, 1968

Soccer Refereeing: A Personal View, Jack Taylor, Faber and Faber, 1978

Charlie: An Autobiography, Charlie Nicholas, Stanley Paul, 1986

Billy: A Biography of Billy Bingham, Robert Allen, Viking, 1986

Champions Of Europe: The History, Romance and Intrigue Of The European Cup, Brian Glanville, Guiness Publishing, 1991

Oh Ref!, Pat Partridge and John Gibson, Souvenir Press, 1979

Liverpool's Sporting Pages, Phil Jackson, Lechlade Press, 1991

More Than A Match, Lee Chapman, Arrow Books, 1993

Top Mark! An Autobiography, Mark Hateley with Ken Gallacher, Mainstream, 1993

Shades Of Gray, Andy Gray, Queen Anne Press, 1986

Steve Bruce: Heading For Victory, Steve Bruce, Bloomsbury, 1994

Sir Matt Busby: A Tribute, Rick Glanvill, Manchester United in Association with Virgin Publishing Ltd, 1994

It's All About A Ball: An Autobiography, Alan Ball, WH Allen, 1978

Joe Mercer: Football With A Smile, Gary James, ACL and Polar Publishing, 1993

The Match Of My Life, Bob Holmes, Kingswood Press, 1991

Rangers: My Team, Derek Johnstone, Souvenir Press, 1979

The Sash He Never Wore, Derek Dougan, Allison and Busby Ltd, 1972

Soccer At The Top: My Life In Football, Matt Busby, Weidenfield and Nicholson Ltd, 1975

Willie Johnston: On The Wing!, Willie Johnston, Arthur Barker Ltd, 1983

Bobby Moore: The Life And Times Of A Sporting Hero, Jeff Powell, Robson Books, 1993

The Umbro Book Of Football Quotations, Peter Ball and Phil Shaw, Stanley Paul Ltd, 1993

Champions: The 26 Year Quest For Glory, Frank Malley, Simon and Schuster, 1993

Both Sides Of The Border: An Autobiography, Terry Butcher, Arthur Barker, 1987

Viv Anderson, Andrew Longmore, Heinemann Kingswood, 1988

A Year In The Life: The Manager's Diary, Alex Ferguson with Peter Ball, Manchester United Football Club plc in association with Virgin Publishing Ltd, 1995

Alan Shearer's Diary Of A Season, Alan Shearer with Dave Harrison, Virgin Publishing Ltd, 1995

The Seventies Revisited, Kevin Keegan and Norman Giller, Queen Anne Press, 1994

Alex Ferguson: Six Years At United, Alex Ferguson with David Meek, Mainstream Publishing Company, 1992

My Life And The Beautiful Game: The Autobiography Of Pele, Pele, Doubleday, 1977

Three Sides Of The Mersey: An Oral History Of Everton, Liverpool And Tranmere Rovers, Rogan Taylor, John Williams and Andrew Ward, Robson Books Ltd, 1993

So Far So Good, Liam Brady, Stanley Paul, 1980

The Football Man: People And Passions In Soccer, Arthur Hopcraft, Simon and Schuster, 1988

Shankly By Shankly, Bill Shankly and John Roberts, Arthur Barker, 1976

The Cassell Soccer Companion, David Pickering, Cassell, 1995

Venables: The Autobiography, Terry Venables and Neil Hanson, Michael Joseph, 1994

Where Do I Go From Here?, George Best, Futura, 1982

George Best: An Intimate Biography, Michael Parkinson, Hutchinson, 1975

The Good, The Bad And The Bubbly, George Best and Ross Benson, Pan Books, 1991

Everton Winter Mexican Summer: A Football Diary, Peter Reid with Peter Ball, Queen Anne Press, 1987

Winners And Champions: The Story Of Manchester United's 1948 FA Cup And 1952 Championship Teams, Alec Shorrocks, Arthur Barker, 1985

Tommy Smith: I Did It The Hard Way, Tommy Smith, Arthur Barker, 1980

Ian Rush: My Italian Diary, Ian Rush, Arthur Barker, 1989

Life At The Kop, Phil Neal, Queen Anne Press, 1986

Bruce Grobbelaar: More Than Somewhat, Bruce Grobbelaar with Bob Harris, Willow Books, 1986

Michael Parkinson: Sporting Lives, Michael Parkinson, Pavilion Books Ltd, 1992

The Soccer Tribe, Desmond Morris, Jonathan Cape, 1981

You Get Nowt For Being Second, Billy Bremner, Souvenir Press, 1969

Forward With Leeds, Johnny Giles, Stanley Paul, 1970

The Only Game: The Scots and World Football, Roddy Forsyth, Mainstream Publishing, 1990

NEWSPAPERS

The Times

Sunday Mirror

Daily Mirror

News of the World

Daily Express

Guardian

Sunday People

Liverpool Daily Post

Liverpool Echo

Everton FC Freedom Special

The Kop (Liverpool Echo)

Hexham Courant

MAGAZINES

90 Minutes

Football Monthly

Shoot

Illustrated London News

Loaded

Total Sport

Goal

Foreword by Tommy Smith

It took me twelve months to build up a reputation as a soccer hard man . . . and I'm still living it down.

I still can't shake it off, even though I've not kicked a ball since 1980.

It all started back in 1960 as a fifteen-year-old groundstaff lad at Liverpool.

I always got stuck in as a player, even when I played centre forward for Liverpool Schoolboys. I must say the opposing centre half wasn't too happy about it, but you look after yourself in football.

The two men in charge at Liverpool at the time were the legendary Bill Shankly and his assistant Bob Paisley, who later become the most successful manager of all time.

They taught me that if you are going to tackle anybody, make sure you do it with everything you've got. They would say: 'Rattle his bones!'

In fact, the reason I actually got established was because big Ronnie Yeats, another hard man of the time, couldn't kick with his right leg. I became his right leg on the pitch.

Later on, I coined a phrase which became part of Tommy Smith's Anfield Iron image. It ensured opponents knew straight away that I was up for the game in every way.

I would say: 'Come near me son and I'll break your back.' It wasn't so much getting that first tackle in as the first advantage in the mind game that is part and parcel of football. In truth, the saying belonged to a no-nonsense right back named Stan Lynn who played for Birmingham City.

I was just fifteen when I first came across him. Luckily, I took no notice of him, but he still managed to kick me up in the air. The one thing that did register was that I was conscious of him throughout the game. It taught me an important early lesson.

If you can break somebody's concentration from the word

go, you have immediately got an advantage. Down the years, I uttered my little warning to some of the game's greats who reacted in different ways.

Those easily intimidated included Malcolm MacDonald of Newcastle, Clive Woods of Ipswich, Leighton James of Burnley, Gordon Hill of Manchester United and quite a few more. Others were stronger mentally. Denis Law and Georgie Best of United shrugged aside threats, as did Allan Clarke of Leeds United and Johnny Morrissey of Everton. Later Ray Kennedy and John Radford of Arsenal showed steel of their own.

I started playing on a regular basis in 1964 for Liverpool and soon found out that every team had its own hardmen. For instance, Everton had the likes of Jimmy Gabriel and Brian Labone. Manchester United had Nobby Stiles and Paddy Crerand.

Chelsea had Ron 'Chopper' Harris. Arsenal had Peter Storey and West Ham had Billy Bonds. Who could forget Dave Mackay at Tottenham.

I once had the privilege of playing against Dave and not just winning a tackle with him, but coming away with the ball. The next day, picking up one of the Sunday papers, the headline read: 'The king is dead. Long live the king.'

It was a proud moment for me because Dave was one of my heroes as a lad. Having said that, not many people got the better of Dave Mackay. He was a giant.

And then there was Leeds United.

The joke at the time was that they didn't so much have one or two hard men as a hard team. Norman Hunter, Jack Charlton, Billy Bremner, Johnny Giles, etc.

In all of this, one thing stood out like a shining light. As well as being hard, the most important thing of all was that all of these lads could play quality football at European and international level.

There have been many excuses as to why today's game has taken a downwards spiral. They have tried to change the game to protect the so-called skill players, under the impression that the demise of football was the fault of the hard men. The truth is the opposite.

Back in the past, there were far more skilful individuals in the game who not only survived, but progressed in tandem with the hard men. Just look at the European record of our clubs in this era and compare it with today.

Modern referees have been instructed to cut out 'dirty play', but if you don't know the difference between a good tackle and a bad one, how can you police the game without controversy?

Today's game is made up of a more athletic type of player. Sometimes, the game is so fast, it leaves behind all the skills and rules against the physical side of the game. But the fans love a good tackle, just as they love a great piece of skill. Football has got to have balance.

The present trend is threatening to take away an important part of the game – the physical side which has always been so important. Let's hope referees go professional and the game's ruling bodies provide them with the right guidelines to ensure football survives in the way most supporters want it to, with tackling recognised as an art, not something to despise.

Tribal Elders generally, seem so fearful that critical comments may 'bring the game into disrepute' that they feel obliged to present the sport as God's gift to human health, happiness and the pursuit of international harmony and goodwill. Since it is patently obvious that it is also capable of providing its share of human injury, stress and international ill-feeling, their remarks inevitably sound naive and one-sided to an outsider. There is no need for them to be so defensive. All major human preoccupations – not only sport, but also religion, science, art, politics and the rest – carry with them the potentials for both good and ill, for both ecstasy and agony. It is what we make of them that matters, not what they make of us.

Desmond Morris, anthropologist,
taken from The Soccer Tribe

1 Do That Again Son and I'll Break Your Legs

Initiation of the young player into the violent side of football

I'd just broken into the first team at Tranmere and had scored two first-half goals to put us 2–0 up at half-time. Halfway through the second half, Rochdale's centre half sidled up to me and told me in no uncertain terms that my goal-scoring exploits had finished for the day. I took no notice of him and carried on with the game. A few minutes later, however, a kick to the genitals laid me out flat. In an attempt to ease the pain, one of my team mates began to rub them. 'Never mind bloody rubbing them – count them!' I shouted. I ended up in hospital that night. It was my first taste of the rough stuff that I would have to put up with for the rest of my career.

Dixie Dean, on his experience as a young player at Tranmere, 1925

When he was a boy the other players used to look after him. I remember playing in one game when an experienced Scottish player threatened Tommy. He said, 'I'll break your leg.' I heard this, so I went over to the player and told him, 'Listen, you break his legs and I'll break yours. Then we'll both be finished.' He didn't bother Tommy after that.

Bill Shankly on the young Tom Finney,
taken from Shankly by Shankly

My first game for Everton was against Leeds. Everton were playing Manchester City in the Cup Final so they rested a few players. I played against Potts, Milburn, Willis, Edwards, Hart, Copping and they kicked the stocking tops off everybody.

Joe Mercer

All the teams had men who could handle themselves, and there was a certain amount of protection for boys of sixteen or seventeen. The older players couldn't stand by and see a boy kicked around. You would be playing against lions but there would be lions on your side as well. There were a lot of hard men about.

Bill Shankly, taken from Shankly on Shankly

I played the game hard. I gave some clumps and took my lumps. I never cried to the referee or tried to get a man sent off. I had respect for players who were doing their best for their side.

As a young man I learned an early lesson. Alex Ferguson of Queen of the South gave me a few clips, stood on my boots, pulled my shirt and kept swearing at me all through the game. I appealed to international referee Willie Webb time and again. When my face hit Ferguson's boot causing me the loss of three teeth I thought I would take the law into my own hands . . . or feet. But Fergie cleverly rode all my tackles and obvious lunges and taunted me that it was a man's game. Finally Webb came alongside me as we lined up for a corner. 'We're friends aren't we, Jimmy?' I nodded. 'If you keep this up we won't be!'

Jimmy Guthrie, taken from Soccer Rebel:
The Evolution of the Professional Footballer

I was seventeen years old and I'd played about eight games at left back. Major Buckley moved me up to centre half. It was at Bradford and I remember going for a corner. The ball came across and the next minute, bang! I was lying on my back. Their goalkeeper, Jim Farr I think his name was, said, 'Don't you ever come in the penalty area again.' I said, 'I won't, Mr Farr, believe me, I won't.' That was the start of my career at centre half.

John Charles

I used to get stuck in and I was afraid of nobody. I was taught as a fifteen-year-old by Shanks that who have you got to fear? It's a football pitch; sometimes a player can be better than you, but he can have a bad day and if you can get around the situation by telling him that you are going to do something to him that his mother wouldn't, it all helps. Shanks was always football wise and he used to tell us to say a few things. Sometimes it worked, other times players wouldn't pay a blind bit of notice to it. Shanks used to say, 'Just hand them a hospital menu, son!' It's quite laughable when you think about it, but sometimes it worked.

Tommy Smith

I learned most, I suppose, around the ages of fifteen and sixteen, when groups of older lads would sometimes let me join in. On other occasions they would say 'Get out of it' and I did exactly that, I scarpered. If you hung around they gave you a clip. It happened to me, countless times, but it did me no harm to learn when I was or wasn't wanted. When they let me play, my God, was I in my element! They used to whack me all over the place, leaving me on my bum more than I was on my feet. It was a form of bullying, I suppose, but I never looked upon it like that because the pain faded once you scored a goal – and I scored plenty against the bigger guys.

Brian Clough, taken from Clough: The Autobiography

You always knew which way Cloughie was going to turn when he had his back to you – round to his left with the ball on his right foot. It was as regular as clockwork. I caught him with such a crunching tackle he went down like a sack of spuds, moaning and groaning in the mud. I did enjoy it. They called off the practice and carted him away for treatment.

Brian Phillips, a team mate of the young Brian Clough at Middlesbrough, taken from Clough: A Biography

I made my debut for Everton in 1957 against Newcastle at Goodison, and I always remember that game because we were playing against Jimmy Scoular. I was put in as a centre forward, although I wasn't really big enough. Newcastle had an inexperienced goalkeeper named Mitchell, and I was challenging for every ball in the air. Scoular said to the goalkeeper, 'Get your so-and-so knees up,' because the goalkeeper was going up just full-stretch and I was going up and knocking him and the ball was bobbling about. Anyway, the next time I went up to head the ball, the goalkeeper brought his knees up. I caught it right in the solar plexus, and I was flat out. I couldn't breathe. I couldn't get air into my lungs. And I always remember Jimmy Scoular was straddling me, and Jimmy Scoular had legs like tree trunks and always had his shorts pulled up tight. He was straddling me, and he said, 'You asked for that, you little sod,' or worse than that. Tommy Casey was the other wing half, and just after that – I think it was an accident – I went to chest a ball and he came behind me and kicked me on the chin. I had my chin split. Then I got carried off at the end. We won, by the way, 2–1.

Derek Temple, taken from Three Sides of the Mersey: An Oral History of Everton, Liverpool and Tranmere Rovers

In my first Scottish Junior Cup-tie, I'm playing outside left and the opposition is Tranent Juniors. I'm not quite seventeen years old at the time and I weigh about nine stone, soaking wet. But of course, I've got lots of confidence, even if there were some who thought I had too much of that. We're lining up at the start, and I look casually over at the right back. It's not that I was a coward, you understand, but there was nothing wrong with my sense of self-preservation. This man was maybe six feet tall, but he looked like a blend of King Kong, Ernest Borgnine and Bobby Shearer. In fact, he made Bobby Shearer look like Danny La Rue, and Bobby could handle himself very well. You have to say to yourself, 'Ah, but a real player can always make a monkey even out of a gorilla.' That's a good theory. It pre-supposes that you get tackled only when you've got the ball. I've played in dozens and dozens of matches where that theory is nothing better than a poor joke. I've been kicked up in the air when nowhere near the ball and so have plenty of other folk. It's called teaching a lesson and I was beginning to learn that lesson as early as sixteen.

Bobby Simpson, my cousin, was playing in that game against Tranent. He had once played for Rangers and for a couple of the Fife senior teams. I shouted over to him, 'Bobby, what am I supposed to do about this fella? Look at him! He'll kill.' 'For God's sake, keep me out of this. Just concentrate on the other side of the park, all right?'

I don't pretend to remember exactly what happened during

that game, but I do remember having what the scribes would call a quiet match. If I did get the ball in space, I got shut of it again right away and then jumped as high as I could. That's another lesson that has to be learned early; if you don't jump high enough, you're in trouble. Even so, you can jump six feet from a standing start and there are still lads who'll get you on the way down. Maybe they're sent off, but they walk off smiling. Usually, they're not sent off and then they're laughing.

Jim Baxter, taken from Baxter: The Party's Over

I made my debut in the League in a Chelsea–Sheffield Wednesday match at Stamford Bridge on 24 February 1962. Vic Buckingham was the Wednesday manager at the time. Vic, a debonair type, smoothly wished me well in my first outing and, referring to Wednesday's inside forward Bobby Craig, the tricky Scot I was scheduled to shadow, said: 'You'll have no trouble today. You've only got that little so-and-so to mark.'

Out on the park Craig and I came into contact in the opening minutes when I went across to take a throw-in. His opening gambit was: 'What are you doing here – you should be locked up in the zoo.'

There wasn't much more conversation between us for, shortly after that, Craig was carried off on a stretcher. Nothing to do with me – 'Chopper' Harris was not involved.

Ron 'Chopper' Harris, taken from Soccer the Hard Way

I remember playing against Stanley Matthews. I was 20, he was 40. He was like greased lightning. The only way I could get to him was by grabbing his shirt. Stanley stopped the ball dead and turned to me and said, 'Why did you feel that you had to do that, son?' I felt so ashamed and such a twit all I could say was, 'I am very sorry, Mr Matthews.' He gave me a withering look, and was off again with the ball like quicksilver.

Jack Charlton

Goals came easy from the very beginning. I know that sounds rather boastful and I do find it difficult talking about the subject of goal-scoring because, whichever way you look at it, I was good at it! I was never frightened and always kept my eye on the ball. It was the only thing I had in mind and, years later, it was to be my undoing, the element of my game which brought a premature end to my playing career. Once around the penalty area there could be somebody pushing, somebody trying to hack me down, somebody clinging to my shirt. None of that bothered me. I was never, ever, physically afraid. My terms of reference were basic and simple: put the ball in the net. That was my job, that's the way I saw it, and I allowed nothing and nobody to distract me from that purpose.

Brian Clough, taken from Clough: The Autobiography

Bolton were the team then, and they could all dish it out. I remember playing on the wing at Bolton. Roy Hartle and Tommy Banks were the two full backs, and they used to dish it out. The pitch slopes down on to the track at Bolton, and when a ball used to go out, and it was their throw-in, I used to go and get it and give it to Roy Hartle. He'd pat me on the head and say, 'Well done, son.' There's a story, I don't know whether it's true, about Roy Hartle. He was giving a winger some stick, kicking lumps out of him, and the story goes that Tommy Banks shouted over in his broad Lancashire accent: 'Eee, Roy, when you've finished with that lad, kick him over 'ere and let me 'ave a go.'

Derek Temple, taken from Three Sides of the Mersey: An Oral History of Everton, Liverpool and Tranmere Rovers

When he came into the League side as a teenager Johnny was pure gold. Specially that fabulous left foot. Early on he played against Liverpool and went to go down the line. As he went past Chris Lawler, the full back, Tommy Smith came hammering across and knocked him clean over the low wall at Upton Park into the crowd. I thought: 'Jesus, poor little feller. That's the last we'll see of him.' But he picked himself up and came back to run Lawler and Smithy ragged. It was one of the sweetest sights I've ever seen.

Bobby Moore talking about John Sissons, taken from Bobby Moore: The Life and Times of a Sporting Hero

I was perhaps lucky to avoid savage treatment. There is nothing you can do to prepare for that kind of brutality, but I did my best to ensure that I was ready in every other way for each game of football.

Terry Venables, taken from Venables: The Autobiography

We played in the GEC Six-a-Side League. My mates and I were all men. Stuart was tiny – and full-blown guys had to pick themselves up when he tackled them!

Ray Pearce on how his brother Stuart succeeded in dishing out the hard tackles even as a kid

When I joined Liverpool, they had some brilliant young Scots on the staff who could almost make the ball talk. They could lose me for skill so I had to think of something else. I was strong, even at that age, so I started putting myself about. I was soon labelled a hard case and it was not long before opponents stayed out of my way.

When I first got into the first team I was only eighteen, crew-cut and a right tearaway. As soon as I got on the pitch I liked to shake a lad with a good, hard tackle early on. I knew then that most of them wouldn't be in too much of a hurry for another one. They'd be listening for me breathing down their neck instead.

I built up quite a reputation and when I went out at night, you'd get lads coming up and saying, 'So you're Tommy Smith! Come outside and we'll see how tough you really are.' I had to talk more lads out of having a go at me than you've had hot dinners.

The funny thing is, I was only sent off once the whole time I was with Liverpool, and that was for arguing. It was during a game with Manchester City, and I kept niggling away until Clive Thomas sent me off. And even he admitted that I didn't use bad language.

Tommy Smith

We played at Manchester City on 4 November 1960. I never forgot that day. David Wagstaffe was playing on the wing for City. He was at it from the first minute, short pulling, niggling. I kept my head until the last minute. Then Joe Kirkup took the ball off him and pushed me a pass down the touch line. I played the ball forward and some seconds later, as he was running back past me, Waggy kicked me across the back of the legs.

That was me gone mad. I turned and gave him exactly the same treatment. Of course, Waggy went down in a heap, putting on the agony. I got my marching orders. He didn't. I got suspended for a week. He didn't.

I detested that in a player. The niggling, the aggravating, the feigning injury. So-called professionalism. I was due to join an England Under-23 party the next day and it was a great consolation to me when one or two of the lads who were a bit older than me said they had the same trouble with Wagstaffe. But it was a lesson in itself.

Bobby Moore, taken from Bobby Moore:
The Life and Times of a Sporting Hero

I was only fifteen when I first discovered the agony of being really injured and what a boring, frustrating time it can be for any player. It was also my first contact with hard men in the game, harder than I've ever been. I remember a game against Aston Villa reserves. They had a brawny full back called Stan Lynn, who came up to me and threatened to knock my head off. He said he'd knock hell out of me if I came anywhere near him. I thought, 'That's not nice . . .'

Later in the game, a ball came across the box and I dived in to try and put it in the back of the net, and they were both coming at me (Villa's goalkeeper Nigel Sims and the full back). In fact Nigel came off his line with his feet out and nearly knocked my kneecap off. I was on the injured list for months.

Tommy Smith, taken from Tommy Smith: I Did It the Hard Way

My first task on my debut was to mark Peter Brabrook. He was a fast, cunning, outside right who had played for East Ham and Essex schoolboys and was now an England international. Peter gave me all kinds of problems. At half-time I recall Noel Cantwell coming into the dressing room with a few words of advice for me, 'If you don't get a good tackle in, he will run you off the park,' he said.

So, in the first minute of the second half, I slid into him like an earth-moving machine with a perfectly timed challenge. From that point on, as Noel Cantwell pointed out, I was dictating the play in the little duel between us. I felt much more confident after making that challenge. Tackling was always the big strength in my game.

John Lyall, taken from Just Like My Dreams:
My Life with West Ham

I was brought up in a place called Raploch, a tough district in my native Stirling.

There's only one word, really, to describe Raploch, and that's *hard*. You had to be hard yourself, to survive there.

I soon discovered one thing about playing against lads who were twice my size, I had to make up for my lack of height and weight by getting stuck in just that little bit harder. And it's funny, you know, when you come up against a big fellow, and he doesn't realise you've got this streak of steel inside you, he's apt to think you're a pushover. Until the first real tackle – then, he suddenly realises that you may not have brawn, but you do possess bite.

Billy Bremner, taken from You Get Nowt for Being Second

I had first come up against Dave when I was seventeen. The Tottenham side was the double team of 1961, full of quality footballers, and playing with a confidence and skill that left every other team trailing in their wake. I had not played many games for Chelsea at that stage, but had been given a lot of publicity, which Dave had obviously noticed. I was warming up near the tunnel, when Tottenham came out. Dave ran out, holding the ball above his head, looked across at me and shouted, 'Oi, Venables!' He tossed the ball over to me and said, 'Have a kick now, 'cos you won't get one once the game's started.' Sure enough, he was right.

Terry Venables on Dave Mackay,
taken from Venables: The Autobiography

Playing a Swiss Under-21 side, I got knocked out by Ronnie Harris of Chelsea. We'd both gone for a header and he butted me, so I had to come off. I get migraines these days – one of the many legacies of a football career – and I'm sure it started after that collision.

Tommy Smith, taken from Tommy Smith: I Did It the Hard Way

Alex Young, the 'Golden Vision' to Everton fans, was a beautiful player, but he could also handle himself. He put in a particularly vicious challenge on Johnny Hollins when we played Everton in 1963. Fresh to the game, Johnny was an exuberant boy, full of running and smiles. When he went into a tackle with Young, however, Alex really 'did' him. Johnny was lying on the ground, writhing in agony, and Alex just stood there, hands on hips, looking down at him. While our physio was trying to put Johnny back together, I said to Alex, 'Come on, what's your game? He's a great kid, what did you do that for?'

'I know he's a good kid,' said Alex. 'That's why I only gave him half of it.'

Terry Venables, taken from Venables: The Autobiography

The soccer-going public at large probably consider that I've always been a firebrand since the day I first donned football gear. Yet, believe it or not, when I was a youngster playing inside forward, between the ages of seventeen and nineteen, I was never even cautioned.

Billy Bremner, taken from You Get Nowt for Being Second

When I first started out at Walsall there was a player named Alex Dawson, the 'Black Prince'. I was a young rookie goal-keeper for Walsall and I came out for a ball and all of a sudden whack! I was upside down. The next one came over and once again whack! This guy just wouldn't leave me alone. After the game Alex came up and said, 'If you had been a more experienced goalkeeper after the first one you probably wouldn't have come for any more crosses.' I came off the field black and blue.

Phil Parkes

I remember my first experience of appearing with the senior players. Southampton had two of the hardest men I've ever played against in my life, Cliff Huxford and Dennis Hollywood. I went to go between them in a training session. But their motto was: 'You can go past me; the ball can go past me – but you won't bloody go past me together!' That was their law – break it, and they'd have your legs off. Those two gave me some terrible kickings, they could really hurt you, but I learned one of the best lessons of my life, to know what's going on and be aware of other people. I also learned to take my knocks without squealing.

There are certain situations where you just can't win, never mind if you're the best player in the world. But you've got to pick those situations out. As a kid you don't know, until you get a right good hiding. You either learn from it or go back and get it again, perhaps badly. Cliff and Dennis hurt me physically, and mentally it made an impression.

Hollywood was the only person I've known who could look you squarely in the eye, tell an absolutely blatant lie – and you'd believe him. 'I won't kick you, you know I wouldn't do that,' he'd say, or 'I didn't do that, you know I didn't,' just when you could feel the bruises coming up.

Mick Channon, taken from Man on the Run

In January 1969 I first experienced a new and sinister dimension of a footballer's lot – the early bath. In a catch against Falkirk I received the dreaded marching orders for the first time in my career, for retaliating to what I can only describe as actual bodily harm. I had already been through a couple of short suspensions for run-of-the-mill bookings, but this was something entirely different.

We all know that retaliation is pointless and stupid because the consequences are always the long, lonely walk, but I defy any mortal to take kick after brutal kick, then be tossed high enough in the air to catch a lift back down on the space shuttle, and not eventually seek retribution. Not that there should be any need to retaliate, because the offender, who usually escapes punishment, shouldn't be on the park long enough to retaliate against. Nevertheless, the outcome of the affair was a 21-day suspension, at a very important part of the season.

All I have ever wished for is that the kickers be treated the same as the kicked. Otherwise sooner or later it will be all kickers and no players.

Willie Johnston, taken from Willie Johnston: On the Wing!

The physical toughness of league football came as a shock to me. I knew it wasn't a game for namby-pambies, but I always believed that you could play cleanly and still come out a winner. In my first season with Lincoln, we played up at Hartlepool and Percy Freeman, our big centre forward, was hammered within a couple of seconds of starting the game. Percy, who had terrorised Hartlepool in an earlier cup game, kicked off and with the referee following the ball, their right back tore into the centre circle and trod on Percy's ankle. So, within thirty seconds, I came on as substitute and had to play up front. Almost immediately, I was tackled from behind after the ball had gone, and I felt the studs go straight into the back of my calf. I was then punched in the unmentionables by their centre half, when the ball was up the other end of the field. Not long after that, I picked up more stitches in the North East, this time at Darlington, after a guy planted his studs in my knee. As they sponged off my knee in the dressing room the blood started pumping out. Even though I swore to get even with those two defenders, I never caught up with them, and to be honest, I would probably have cocked up my attempts at retribution.

Phil Neale, taken from Phil Neale: A Double Life

I think I came on the Tuesday, and on the Thursday I played for the A team on the B pitch at Melwood. I didn't know at the time but the B pitch is notorious. I've played on it a few times since and there's no way you can play football on it. It's a kick-and-rush pitch. We played somebody's reserves, it might have been Morecambe Reserves. It was unbelievable. I played in the middle of the park at that time and I was used to getting the ball and playing it, and after about 30 seconds this guy – he must have been 26 or something and I'd only been used to playing Under-16s – just came and hit me from about ten yards and I went about twenty feet up in the air. Of course, I'm on the deck and I'm looking for a bit of support and they're just getting on with the game. This went on for 90 minutes. I thought at the time that there was no way you could judge anybody on that sort of game, because I was only a kid of fifteen, but they sent me packing anyway. I didn't know it at the time, but my father kept the letter of rejection, and of course it was funny that seven years later they were paying 100 grand for me.

Alan Hansen, taken from Three Sides of the Mersey:
An Oral History of Everton, Liverpool and Tranmere Rovers

The example I was set by my other defenders dragged me into death-or-glory tackles. Instead of jockeying for the ball like a senior pro.

During this period I picked up most of my eight bookings. I wouldn't let my mates down – they were committed, so I had to stop being just the interceptor, the intelligent reader of the game, it was 'muck or nettles' time.

Phil Neale, taken from Phil Neale: A Double Life

I was still learning the difference between playing football as a professional and playing for fun. My father was a great believer in the traditions of schoolboy football and had brought me up to play as a sportsman. If I knocked someone over, I would help them up and make sure they weren't hurt. When I did this at a professional club people laughed at me. The coaches said I had to be aggressive. But it wasn't in my nature and in practice games I was scared to tackle the first team players in case I hurt them. People like Allan Hunter and Kevin Beattie were my heroes and it didn't seem right for me to go in hard against them.

Terry Butcher, taken from Both Sides of the Border:
An Autobiography

Sam Ellis used to call me a 'stupid schoolboy' because I would leave myself open in the tackle, so that forwards could stamp on me as I lay on the ground. Once, at Watford, I was having a really good game against their right winger, and as I tackled them to sort the ball out of play, he left his studs there and caught me. As I lay on the ground having treatment, my captain (Sam Ellis) walked over to me and said soothingly: 'You stupid boy, when are you going to learn to tackle properly?' I didn't feel you had to kick a player to get the better of them. You have to be competitive, in order to get the ball, but I didn't want to play unfairly. In one sense, I was an amateur throughout my professional soccer career.

Phil Neale, taken from Phil Neale: A Double Life

I was not large for my age, but more often than not it was me who was on the wrong end of a kicking, which taught me how to avoid those lunging boots. The first time I really came across the very physical side of things was as a youth at Tottenham, but especially when we played indoors in the club gymnasium among ourselves. That sort of football is all about bodily contact and it was often a case of knock 'em over or be knocked over yourself. No wonder there were always black eyes, when fights would break out regularly. But even that did not prepare me fully for my first taste of the real rough stuff in the later stages of the Youth Cup. I am a bad loser. Aston Villa were in the process of beating us (FA Youth Cup Semi-Final) and Dennis Mortimer had, as their best player, become a personal challenge to me. In the end the referee had enough of our warrings and, right on the halfway line, in front of both benches, the director's box and the press box, I was sent off. My only consolation was that I did not have far to walk.

Graeme Souness, taken from Graeme Souness:
No Half Measures

I've been sent off twice in my career. The first was at Liverpool, in the Reserves against Derby. I got into a fight with somebody who called me a 'black pig'. It was quite funny, actually, because I was expecting a bollocking when I came off, but the team manager was laughing. He said, 'That's the fastest left and right hook I've ever seen.'

It doesn't happen to me so much now, because people tend to know me more and they give me a bit more respect. It's usually when you're just coming in, a raw young lad. That's when they do their shouting out on the park. Once I got sent off I realised that it was doing me more damage than anybody else. And it just inspired me more. It made me play better, 'cos I knew that scoring goals would sicken the people that were doing it, kicking me or whatever. You just go and score a goal and give them a little wink as you're running past them. That does the job. There's nothing else you can do.

Howard Gayle, taken from Out of His Skin:
The John Barnes Phenomenon

I made my football league debut for Stoke against Southampton in 1979. Within minutes my vision of life at the top was somewhat tarnished. I had challenged for the ball with a Southampton player, Steve Williams, and managed to come out on top. I passed the ball to a colleague and as I turned away, Williams reacted in a way I found hard to comprehend – whether intentionally or not, he spat in my face. Up until that moment he had been someone I had respected for his obvious potential as a player. Any respect for him as a person was wiped away along with the spittle on my face.

Lee Chapman, taken from More Than a Match

I mistimed a tackle on Steve Williams, the Southampton midfield player. It wasn't a bad tackle but he made a meal out of it and started writhing about in melodramatic style. I knew he was nowhere near as injured as he made out, but what really made me angry was the reaction of the Southampton players. They surrounded the referee and were shouting at him to send me off. I couldn't believe fellow professionals would do that, but I could hear it for myself. Eventually the referee emerged from the melée and pointed to the dressing rooms. For the first time in my career I had been sent off. I kept thinking about the people I had let down – especially my father.

Terry Butcher, taken from Both Sides of the Border:
An Autobiography

My debut game for the first team at Everton was away from home at Brighton. I'd only been on the field for ten minutes and my first introduction to English football was to get a right hook off their centre half, who said, 'Welcome to English football, son.' I thought what have I let myself into, getting a right hook on my debut. I don't think I got a kick, just a punch. So it made me stand back and think have I done the right thing leaving Scotland?

Graeme Sharp

Newcastle were a fearsome side then, with MacDonald and Tudor and, to be honest, before the match I was terrified. I went to look at the pitch with the rest of the Forest players and only got as far as the end of the tunnel. I poked my nose out, took one look and then went back to the dressing room. But when I started playing, it was fine, despite being dumped into the hoardings by MacDonald's elbow.

Viv Anderson on his second game in the football League,
taken from Viv Anderson

When I first broke into the team I would go up for high balls like an innocent and was being back-headed and elbowed. I picked up a painful collection of cuts and bruises from pros who never missed a chance to flex their muscles. Allan Hunter taught me how to protect myself and jump with one arm in front to keep daylight between my face and my opponent's head – a trick which has become even more invaluable in Scotland!

Terry Butcher, taken from Both Sides of the Border:
An Autobiography

I'd rear up on players if they said anything and footballers aren't the bravest people in the world, so they used to think twice before they said anything to me and that helped me.

Justin Fashanu

I respond to taunts on the field. If someone says, 'You black bastard' I say something equally as personal and that subdues them.

Bob Hazell

16

I am the first to concede, I was just a soft touch. Too soft at one stage, in fact, to have a hope of making it. When the other street-wise kids got stuck in and I accidentally caught them with a loose boot I used to turn round and apologise! I'll bet they couldn't believe their ears. But I didn't know any better.

With that kind of attitude I was going absolutely nowhere. I had to find the cut-throat meanness to survive in soccer. And it was a footballer that few people at United will now probably remember who helped me make it. For that reason I'll always be eternally grateful to Gary Worrell. He was a tricky, awkward, ball-hugging winger who always made it hard for me when we were both still wet behind the ears, attempting to break through as teenagers.

One day, in a bloody-minded mood for once, I decided to do something about it. Put short and not-so-sweet, I decided to become a bit nasty and aggressive. I really got stuck in to him. It worked, too. I loved the physical contact and, just for a change, ending up with the ball. It was the major turning point in my life. From that morning kick-about I was a changed man. I got stuck into everything that moved, legitimately of course, and suddenly I started making progress through the United ranks.

Mark Hughes, taken from Sparky, Barcelona, Bayern and Back: The Autobiography of Mark Hughes

Before long I was playing for my first men's team, my brother's pub side – The Fusilier. I was pushed out on to the right wing because I was so small. Inevitably I found it tough at times and I used to get the occasional kick from opponents who were bigger, older and more experienced than I was. My brothers were prepared to let me grow up the hard way. They took no notice when I was on the receiving end of some rough stuff, and it was up to some of the other lads to come to my defence when the fists and boots really started to fly.

Peter Beardsley, taken from Beardsley: An Autobiography

We had a match at home against Newport County. Their attack was led by a tough old professional by the name of Tommy Tynan. He had been in the game a long time and had played for different teams, scoring goals wherever he went, but on this occasion he did not score. We were 2–0 up by half-time, after I had scored the second goal from the penalty spot. In the second half, Tommy Tynan hit me with his elbow in an off-the-ball incident. It was all of 30 seconds later that the ball was thrown in to him in the 18-yard box and bounced in front of the two of us. He had just hurt me and, for the only time in my career, I tried to hurt him, aiming a kick at him. He saw me coming, he lifted his leg and I got a glancing blow on the ball but followed through to kick straight on to the bottom of his foot. I knew my leg was broken as soon as I went down.

Steve Bruce recalling his early days at Gillingham,
taken from Steve Bruce: Heading for Victory

When I arrived at Highbury the tackle from behind had been outlawed by the referees, but that ruling had not been adopted north of the Border. Up there they could whack you from behind for the full ninety minutes and get away with it.

I was given a lesson in that when I was just sixteen years old. The two strikers in possession of the first team places at Celtic Park were Frank McGarvey and George McCluskey. One day I was called over by manager Billy McNeil to join the first-team training at Barrowfield. They had an exercise worked out in which the midfield player pushed the ball up to the strikers, who were being tightly marked by the two central defenders. The object was for the striker to get the ball back, allowing the midfield man to come up in support and possibly get in a shot at goal.

I'd seen the lads working out from the other end of the training ground where the reserves and the ground-staff lads did their work, so I knew what was wanted. But I didn't realise how hard Billy made it for the strikers. For two weeks he had me taking part in this particular exercise. And for those two weeks big Roddy McDonald tackled me from behind. Every time the ball reached me, *whack!* I was up in the air. God, I was sore. I doubt if I've ever been kicked with such consistency in all my career. I took terrible stick and all the players felt sorry for me – I felt sorry for myself.

Later on I clocked what was happening. Billy was telling big

Roddy to give me a kick. He wanted to give me a hard time in training because it would prepare me for what I would have to face when I played in the Premier League. It was shrewd thinking because it taught me to take my lumps without retaliating or squealing too much.

Charlie Nicholas, taken from Charlie: An Autobiography

I do instinctively take exception to intimidation. Early in my United career, about the fifth or sixth senior game it would be, I got my first taste of it. All I was guilty of was trying to make myself useful and put myself about in a battle with Spurs. Little Stevie Perryman and his mate Paul Miller didn't appreciate my style at all. Soon they were into the verbals. Threatening to break me in half, and that sort of thing. They were probably thinking they would put this young whipper-snapper in order before he got too big for his boots. I just ignored them. In turn they got more angry with me by the minute. That was the first lesson I learned at the top. Keep your mouth shut because the people doing all the talking are really the losers.

Mark Hughes, taken from Sparky, Barcelona, Bayern and Back: The Autobiography of Mark Hughes

I was playing against the Everton B team at Borough Road, Birkenhead. The match was about ten minutes old and I received the ball on the wing. Within a split second Bang! the Everton full back was in on me and took me from behind. As I lay on the ground he said: 'There's more of that where that fuckin' came from.' I'd heard all this stuff before. Also, we are taught not to retaliate at Tranmere. If you do you might get a fine taken from your wages, which don't amount to much as it is.

I looked at him and smiled. He was a big, ginger-haired lad who looked a bit like Stuart Pearce, with legs like tree trunks. Later in the first half I received the ball and he took the legs from under me again. This time I was hurt. His parting shot as he ran away was to inform me that he was 'going to fuckin' kill me after the game'. The referee called him over and took his name.

The Tranmere coach gave me some treatment and told me

not to let the full back see that I was hurt. This was easier said than done. I struggled on until just after half-time and then had to go off. Basically I was kicked out of the match.

A Tranmere Rovers youth player, 1995

I have been watching youth games lately and it's not a football match, it's a war. It's a battle. I've never seen such bad fouls, so much aggression. With the long-ball game, that's what it is, a war.

Malcolm Allison

2 He'd Kick His Own Granny

Hard men and skilful players 1930–1960

There was one fellow at Liverpool who used to try to break my toes. He used to jump on them – and he used to brag about it. In those days when you were injured you were injured. It was genuine. When you went down, you stayed down – you weren't able to hop up and take a free kick like some of them do today. They'd try all sorts of things to stop me getting to the ball. In a match against Sunderland I had two pairs of shorts pulled off me inside the first twenty minutes.

Dixie Dean

Dixie Dean's greatest secret was that he would never retaliate. They would push him out, he would stand there. If he'd had pockets in his shorts he would have put his hands in them. But when he moved a goal was on the way.

Joe Mercer

Dixie Dean got into the bad books through a rather wild idea against Hapgood, and Stevenson had the misfortune to have his name taken for clogging the ball against Beasley's legs. There was no justification for this, as both went for the ball at the same moment, and Beasley was merely unfortunate. Beasley was carried off to have stitches inserted in his shin. It was a grand match, albeit the crowd took exception to Dean's foul on Hapgood!

Everton v Arsenal, *Liverpool Daily Post*, 3 November 1934

He put your heart in your boots every time he had the ball, but he was a great sportsman and was never nasty. He took a terrific hammering, we were all at it trying to cut him down, but I never knew him to moan or retaliate.

Sir Matt Busby on Dixie Dean, taken from Soccer at the Top:
My Life in Football

I would always send Elisha Scott, the Liverpool goalkeeper, a package on the eve of derby day. It would contain a bottle of aspirin with a note telling him to get himself a good night's sleep because I'd be there tomorrow.

Dixie Dean

To play against Dixie Dean was at once a delight and a nightmare. He was a perfect specimen of an athlete, beautifully proportioned, with immense strength, adept on the ground but with extraordinary skill in the air. He was resilient in the face of the big, tough centre halves of his day – and I cannot think of one centre half today to match up with that lot, though it was often the unstoppable force against the immovable object – and he was a thorough sportsman.

Sir Matt Busby, taken from Soccer at the Top: My Life in Football

No one like him ever kicked a ball. He had a most uncanny and wonderful control, but because this was allied to a split-second thinking apparatus, he simply left the opposition looking on his departing figure with amazement.

George Allison on Alex James

Alex James used to mesmerise his opponents with a feint that said: 'Now I'm here, now I'm not,' and Hughie Gallacher used to paralyse them with a dribbling run and power of shot and a line of pertinent or impertinent patter to go with it. In the magnificent Arsenal of the early thirties, James was the great creator from the middle. From an Arsenal rearguard action the ball would, seemingly inevitably, reach Alex. He would feint and leave two or three opponents sprawling or plodding in his wake before he released the ball. Alex James sent more opponents 'into the tube station' with a little feint than any other man who ever shook a hip. I remember a couple of wags shouting to me before a match in which the great Alex was in the opposition. One of them bawled out: 'Don't worry, Matt, we've just locked James in the toilet.' (Spectators didn't use naughty words in those days.) Gallacher seemed unrobbable. If the ball had been tied to his boots with string it could not have been more adhesive. Incidentally, James and Gallacher took as much stick from tough nut defenders as any modern 'great' does. I saw their bruises.

Sir Matt Busby, taken from Soccer at the Top: My Life in Football

Hughie Gallacher was more demonstrative than Alex James, always talking, arguing and swearing to rile the opposition. He would say to big centre halves, 'How did you get on to the field? You won't get a kick of the ball today!' Everybody would be chasing him, trying to kill him!

Bill Shankly, taken from Shankly by Shankly

It was always lively travelling with the big club teams. Even in the twenties, too, by what I've always been told. And no wonder with such types as Harry Storer around. The old cricket and soccer star was always up to his tricks.

This was the way it went one day. Derby, for whom Storer was then playing, were due to meet Arsenal in an end-of-season game of no importance to either club. Joe Hulme, then in the Gunners' line-up, was, like Storer, preparing to move over to county cricket for the summer. He to Middlesex, and Storer to Derbyshire.

Well, Harry said to Joe, just before the start: 'We can have a nice friendly game, because neither of us wants to get hurt just before the cricket season begins, so if we find we're going for the same ball, one of us had better shout "yours" or "mine", and then the other can let it go.'

Joe seemed happy with the idea until 80 minutes had gone by, and then he called out to Harry: 'When do I get a shout?'

Bob Wall on the humour of football before the Second World War, taken from Arsenal From the Heart

In his first appearance for Scotland at Wembley against England in 1938, Shankly encountered the fearsome Arsenal half back, Wilf Copping. Shankly recalled: 'I was a hard player, but I played the ball, and if you play the ball you'll win the ball and you'll have the man too. But if you play the man, that's wrong. Wilf Copping played for England that day and he was a well-known hard man. The grass was short, the ground was quick, and I was playing the ball. The next thing I knew, Copping had done me down the front of my right leg. He had burst my stocking – the shin pad was out – and cut my leg. That was after about ten minutes, and it was my first impression of Copping. He was older than me and he had a reputation. He didn't need to be playing at home to kick you – he would have kicked you in your own back yard or in your own chair. He had no fear at all. What Copping did stung me, but I didn't complain about him. I said to him, 'Oh, you're making the game a little more important.' Copping had been after me and had caught me and I never contacted him again during the match. He also caught me on my right ankle playing against Arsenal at Highbury on a Christmas Day. For years afterwards, I played with my ankle bandaged and to this day my right ankle is bigger than my left because of what Copping did. My one regret is that he retired from the game before I had the chance to get my own back.

Bill Shankly, taken from Shankly by Shankly

Wilf Copping never shaved before a match to try to frighten the forwards. He was very dark – and he was tough. Great to have him on your side. You can't have eleven gentlemen in a team.

Stanley Matthews

At Huddersfield one day, coming back from a training session to the stadium, he detailed nine players to come with him. 'Right! You five, white shirts: England! Us five, blue shirts: Scotland!' The flower in Huddersfield's buttonhole at that time was the very young left winger, Mike O'Grady. Shanks played for 'Scotland'. O'Grady glided past him twice, and scored. The third time it happened, Shankly hacked him down. 'Do that again, and I'll break yer bloody leg!'

Brian Glanville on Bill Shankly, taken from Champions of Europe: The History, Romance and Intrigue of the European Cup

Bill Shankly was a marvellous competitor, but he was always yapping. It was generally when you were about to take a shot, he'd start yapping and put you out of your stride.

Tommy Lawton

Before the 1933 FA Cup Final (Everton v Manchester City) one
of the members of the Everton board came into the dressing
room and began to give me a lecture about the Manchester City
danger man Eric Brook. Dixie Dean stood up and told him that
I knew all about Brook. The bloke left the dressing room with
his tail between his legs. When the game started I hit Brook
with a hard tackle in the first few minutes. That was the last we
saw of Brook for the rest of the Final.

Billy Cook

I came home for one game. I played outside left and Billy Cook
was right back for Everton at that time. I received a throw-in from
our wing half on the wing, and the next minute I was laid out flat.
Billy Cook came up behind me and put me in hospital. I don't
know what the unit thought about it by the time I got back, but I
was hospitalised for a week. I know Billy Cook, of course. We
were the best of friends. At the same time, I never forgot that.

Phil Taylor, taken from Three Sides of the Mersey:
An Oral History of Everton, Liverpool and Tranmere Rovers

As a player I specialised in tackling, which is an art, and I was
never sent off the field or had my name in a referee's book. The
art of tackling, as with many things, is in the timing – the
contact, winning the ball, upsetting the opposition, maybe even
hurting them. You're in, you're out, you've won it and you've
hurt him and left him lying there, but it's not a foul because you
have timed everything right. I played it hard but fair. No
cheating. I'd have broken somebody's leg maybe, with a hard
tackle, with a bit of spirit, but that's a different story from
cheating. Cheats will always be caught in the finish. Punishment
is sometimes a long time coming, but it comes. If you've done
something really vile, you will be caught in the end. There was
one player I remember who, from the age of sixteen, built
himself up as football's answer to Billy the Kid. This fellow had
all the dirty tricks in the trade. He would cut people in the

windpipe with an elbow, kick at ankles, take a swipe at heads when he could. You name it, he did it.

He got me in the diaphragm and really sickened me, so I joined the growing number of players with scars on their bodies who were looking for him. There were people who would have crippled him. It was like turning an army against himself. He got away with it for a long, long time, but he got what was coming to him in the end.

I hurt him myself in one game – and he was hurt a few times before he was finished. I got him in a tackle. It looked legitimate, but it wasn't. If you're a good tackler you can hurt people, and I made sure I got him. He was finished for that day. He was being repaid by player after player and in the end he got a bad injury.

Bill Shankly, taken from Shankly by Shankly

As we broke away after the presentations, Tom Rowe said, 'They're scared stiff', and a blow up came in the first minute. Rowe got his knee in the way of a boot and there was some verbal between Westcott, Dorsett and myself. Then the ball went out to Maguire. I timed the tackle well and he went down hard. I picked him up and muttered, 'Next time you finish in the Queen's lap.' Maguire took another ball on the touchline and down he went again, appealing to referee Tommy Thompson. 'Take it easy, Jimmy,' said Tommy, signalling a throw, and the Wolves' winger had to take some stick from Lew Morgan our right back. We were not troubled again by Maguire and began to knock the ball around.

To be honest, I did bend the rules when we beat Wolves in the Final.

Jimmy Guthrie on the 1939 FA Cup Final Portsmouth v Wolves, taken from Soccer Rebel: The Evolution of the Professional Footballer

It was more rugged. There was more physical contact. We always had what we called the killers in the game, players who went deliberately over the ball to get the man. They were all known, and you took special precautions against them. The play was rougher and dirtier than it is now.

Stan Cullis

I had no trouble with referees, but I think I had as much heart as the next man and tackled opponents as determinedly. Unquestionably a player who goes half-heartedly into a tackle will not only fail to win the ball, but will make himself vulnerable to injury. If a fair and determined tackle is met fairly and determinedly seldom is either player injured. Determined is a clumsier word, perhaps, but that is what is meant when football people talk about 'hard' tackles.

There are bound to be some unfair tackles, many of which, however, are perpetrated by players who have not mastered the art of tackling. They do not time the tackle properly and therefore they arrive late with it, the ball is gone and the leg of the opponent is tackled instead. There are players, happily not many of them, who are unscrupulous, who, for example, will go 'over the ball' as a last resort, contacting the opponent's legs. There is no excuse for any tackle that sets out to get the ball at the calculated risk of injuring an opponent.

Bill Shankly, taken from Shankly by Shankly

I was playing at Seaham-Harbour for Sunderland Reserves in a League game. It was a very cold day, and on my left hand side the wind was blowing a gale off the North Sea only 50 yards away and at my back was the local graveyard.

I was a goalkeeper, and when I was in the second team I never had much to do and on this occasion we were winning 9–0 with only ten minutes to go.

My colleagues knew I was perished so they were knocking long back passes to me to keep mobile. Suddenly the Seaham centre forward began to chase these long back passes and twice he jumped at me like a wild man and I said nothing.

When he came the third time I went out for the ball and timed it so that I would be picking up the ball when he would be about three yards away then I crouched down to his size and met him with my shoulder – I am six foot tall and twelve stone.

The full backs knew what was going to happen and they were enjoying the situation. He bounced off my shoulder for about three yards and I just walked all over him.

He was flat on his back, and I stopped and said, 'You little b**ger, you asked for that, you could have put me out of the game for weeks if you had caught me.'

When I got washed and dressed I was standing outside the dressing room when a little fellow came out and said to me, 'I am sorry about jumping at you.' I looked at him and he had a collar on; it was the local Catholic priest, and I apologised for swearing at him, but he said he had learnt a lesson this day and he got what he deserved.

Jack Clark

The game was much harder and dirtier than it is now. There were a lot of dirty tricks practised. Going over the top was the worst thing. You had to be very skilled, very well practised to really be effective at this sort of thing. And ankle-tapping. And going in to head a ball where you'd miss it deliberately and get a fellow in the face instead of getting the ball. Look at that nose of mine.

T. G. Jones, taken from Three Sides of the Mersey:
An Oral History of Everton, Liverpool and Tranmere Rovers

I remember once receiving a painful and deliberate kick to the base of the spine from Arsenal's Joe Hulme. Furious, I took the next opportunity to send Hulme sprawling across the touchline. With a diplomacy that I applaud to this day, the referee commented, 'You've got your own back, Milne, now get on with the game.'

Jimmy Milne

I always remember a bloke called Syd Bycroft who played for Doncaster Rovers. He was 6ft 3in, raw-boned, couldn't play, thick as two planks, and it's like he used to say to me, 'I can't play and you're not going to.' I was the England centre forward when Everton were drawn against Doncaster Rovers in the cup, and this Bycroft knocked on our dressing room door, opened it, and said, 'Is this Lawton playing?' Little Alex Stevenson says, 'Yeah, why?' 'Where is he?' he says. Alex said, 'You'll see enough of him when you get on the park. You'll see the back of him. Close the door on the way out!' This was Stevie, you know, he was quick. 'Run him ragged,' he said to me. 'Run him ragged today.' I got four, and we licked them 8–0.

Tommy Lawton, taken from Three Sides of the Mersey: An Oral History of Everton, Liverpool and Tranmere Rovers

I was not a battling centre half, although I was always ready to tackle hard: the ability to mix it is often essential. Basically, though, I avoided contact just for the sake of it. I was convinced there was more than one way of winning possession and was only hard when there was no alternative. I was more concerned with the ball than with my opponents. I tried to read the game intelligently, holding back to mark space rather than a man, to win the ball by thinking first and moving first. My game was all about anticipation.

Ron Greenwood, taken from Yours Sincerely, Ron Greenwood

I was once attacked by a spectator, which is why I will not pass judgement on the Manchester United player, for I do not know what the Crystal Palace fan said or did to Cantona – but it must have been very nasty for him to act in the way he did.

In my own case, it was a bad decision by the referee which led the man to come on to the field and lash out at me with his walking stick.

I was in goal for Sunderland at Feethams, the Darlington FC ground and 'Argus', the *Sunderland Echo* sports reporter, wrote that the Darlington game was like a cup-tie, for the visit of Sunderland was a big enough attraction to provide the season's richest harvest, a gate of over 11,000 spectators.

What happened was that my team-mate Jimmy Gorman handled a shot, but the ball still went into the net. Most referees would have given a goal, but the official on this day awarded a penalty – and I saved the spot kick.

After saving the penalty a man jumped over the fence from behind the goal and began lashing out at me with a walking stick. The only place I could go was into the net, which protected me until my colleagues jumped on his back and disarmed him. He was taken away, but I never got an apology off the Darlington club.

In the second half of this thriller my head was split with
something thrown from behind the goal.

Jack Clark

I always remember that my first League match was for Bourne-
mouth against Walsall. It's only a small ground with a wall
around it and there was an old West Brom player playing full
back against me. At that time I used to show the full back the
ball and go past him. I went past him a couple of times and he
said, 'Son, don't do that again.' I said, 'I beg your pardon?' He
said, 'Don't bloody do that again.' I thought, 'What's he talking
about?' Then the next time I gets the ball and goes past him and
suddenly I'm into the wall. I thought every bone in my body
was broken. I thought, 'I know what he means now.' Going off
at half-time my father said, 'Son, hit him back, he won't hit you
any more if you hit him back.' In the second half he had a go at
me and I had a go at him and hit him back and stopped him . . .
and it always stuck in my mind that if someone clobbers you,
you clobber them back.

   The game isn't as physical as it used to be. You can't even
look at a player now but it's a foul. When I played if a goalkeeper held the ball on the goal-line he went in the back of the
net.

Jack Rowley, taken from Winners and Champions: The Story of
Manchester United's 1948 FA Cup and 1952 Championship Teams

The Midlands League team had started the game rigorously and
had kicked several Barnsley players over the wall when Skinner
decided to exert his authority. He stood with foot on ball and
beckoned a challenge. Three of the opposition accepted. When
the dust had settled Skinner was seen still with foot on ball while
the three defenders were stretched out on the turf.

   The referee ran over, pulling out his notebook, whereupon
Skinner held up a hand in a placatory gesture and said: 'Tha'
needn't bother, ref, I'm going.' And then he left the field.

**Michael Parkinson on Barnsley hard man Sidney 'Skinner'
Normanton,** taken from Michael Parkinson: Sporting Lives

On 14 November 1943, there were 24,241 spectators. The limit on the stadium was 25,000, but it felt more like a full house of 40–50,000.

Newcastle were winning 2–1 after 65 minutes when Albert Stubbins broke through and Gorman obstructed him. Stubbins got a hold of Gorman and threw him to the ground. Jimmy said to me: 'I thought St James' Park had turned upside down.'

The referee sent them both off, but as they went, a Newcastle supporter hit Gorman's eye with a stone. At the subsequent hearing, Stubbins got a warning and Gorman was suspended for five games.

'Argus' wrote in the *Sunderland Echo*: 'I hold no brief for Jimmy Gorman but on this occasion he was sent off for defending himself. Gorman was not the aggressor.' There is no justice with the FA.

Why 'Argus' wrote about Gorman and having no brief for him is for something that Gorman was alleged to have done coming back from the 1937 FA Cup Final. Players were celebrating on the train, and someone pulled 'Argus's' bowler hat over his ears, and Jimmy got the blame.

After that Jimmy would be sitting on the train coming home from away games and he would say: 'My ears are burning – 'Argus' must be writing his report in the next carriage!'

Bad decisions by referees cause a lot of trouble in the game.

Jack Clark

He was a hard boy who had a big heart and never shirked a tackle. I wouldn't mind four or five Tommy Dochertys in my team.

Bill Shankly

There was a two pound bonus for a win in the early fifties and I remember when we were playing Blackburn away: Joe Harvey had come into the dressing room beforehand and said, 'I want that two pounds, my kids need some new shoes.' Early in the game Joe thumped Bobby Langton, their left winger, a couple of times. The next time, Langton side-stepped him and Joe bellowed at Bobby Corbett, 'Thump him, Bobby, or I'll thump you.' Bobby caught him all right; and poor Langton had to go off. He'd got two broken ribs. We won 2–1, and Joe got his shoes.

Bobby Cowell, taken from Wor Jackie: The Jackie Milburn Story

There were three in particular who always gave me a hard time: Stan Cullis of Wolves, Neil Franklin of Stoke and Manchester City's Dave Ewing.

I could always understand my problems with Franklin and Cullis. They were clever players, read the game well. They seemed to be one step ahead of me all the time.

Dave was different. He was a big man, a pure stopper. And when you ran into Big Dave you stopped! Every time we played City I'd say: 'I've got to beat this devil today.' But I never did. I'd play like a real donkey. Dave always came out on top.

Nat Lofthouse, taken from The Lion of Vienna: 50 Years A Legend

Don't be under any illusions, the fact that he was a delicate player; small like a ninepenny rabbit as the man used to say. He took stick like everybody else did, they clattered him like everybody else got clattered, and when Billy Liddell broke his jaw (Scotland v England) in Scotland, he stood all the way back home on a train, 'cause there were no seats.

So that was his strength, he could ride tackles, he could get around people, he'd go one way then the other and send defenders the wrong way and that was the way he was.

Brian Clough on Wilf Mannion

Nobody ever got near him to kick him. He didn't have to be tough. When people tackled him he seemed to ride everything. He just floated over the turf.

Alan Peacock on Wilf Mannion

People try to tell you Stanley Matthews wouldn't get a kick these days but don't believe it. Nobody succeeded in booting Stan into the crowd because the ball was laid off quickly until he got the upper hand. He had the skill and confidence to operate in confined spaces and get past people. Where are the players today who can do this? John Barnes and Mark Walters, young Ryan Giggs? There aren't many.

Vic Buckingham,
taken from The Umbro Book of Football Quotations

Stan was one of the game's greats but was less effective in pre-war games than later. His image for the sport was so important in post-war days that, although he was closely marked, no full back ever gave him a whack. In the thirties Stan was treated as just another player and we knew that he did not like the rough stuff. He was brave enough, but would have no part in the tough, hurly burly. One strong shoulder charge, within the rules, would lessen Stan's effectiveness and this was well known in the game.

Jimmy Guthrie, taken from Soccer Rebel:
The Evolution of the Professional Footballer

Once playing at Chelsea with Blackpool in the mid-1950s, his team was 2–1 down and on the receiving end of some rough treatment. McFarland, the left back, had put his knee in Stanley's thigh; and after giving him a long hard look, Stanley had limped off the field. Ten minutes later, following treatment, he was back on the field. Jimmy Armfield, his own right back, asked him if he was all right, with his thigh heavily strapped. 'Yes, keep knocking it in quick,' Stanley replied. There were twenty minutes to go, during which time McFarland was twisting and turning until his boots nearly fell off. Blackpool won 4–2. For the last goal, Stanley ran through from an inside right position, beat two men and tapped the ball past the goalkeeper. The grandstand crowd rose to its feet. Professional footballers came to learn never to expect the handshake of friendship from Stanley if they had deliberately fouled him. That was the world of the hypocrite.

David Miller on Stanley Matthews, taken from Stanley Matthews

When he was clogged by some full back, the most he would say afterwards was: 'He wasn't nice at all, was he?'

Nat Lofthouse on Stanley Matthews

Playing Stan is like playing a ghost.

Johnny Carey

There weren't many who could hold him. The only way to counter him was to hit him hard, which wasn't me.

Ron Burgess

If I'd been kicked in one match, it didn't run in my mind in the next.

Stanley Matthews

Eddie would give him a warning, and afterwards would say in one breath, 'I looked after you all right, didn't I?'

Stanley Matthews on his minder at Stoke, Eddie Clamp

Some young full back whacked me in a charity match, he followed me everywhere. I suppose trying to make his name, and wouldn't lay off, even when I pointed out that we were only playing for charity.

Stanley Matthews

Over the years, I've seen him [Stanley Matthews] tripped, charged in the back, flattened in the mud, almost have his shirt pulled off. Yet I've never heard him say a wrong word or retaliate in any way. If there were 22 Matthews on the pitch, I would be out of a job.

Referee Arthur Ellis, taken from Stanley Matthews

I noticed in England training sessions that Stanley Matthews concentrated almost entirely on 10-yard bursts. This was the secret of his tremendous acceleration.

Henry Cockburn

Stan Cullis was as strong as an ox, he hurt you in the tackle.

Stanley Matthews

Playing against Charlton at the Valley on his fortieth birthday, their turn back had made it known in the local papers that he was intending to make it an unhappy birthday for Stanley. That was like a red rag to a bull, and he put on a one-man show in a 4–0 victory.

Jimmy Armfield

Don't ask me to describe it. It just comes out of me under pressure.

Stanley Matthews on his famous body swerve

There was no secret, I knew that once Stanley had the ball and a bit of space in which to work you hadn't got an earthly chance. He was as tricky as a wagon load of monkeys, and you never got a clue which way he was going. So I reckoned the only sensible thing to do was to mark him very closely and be on him like a shot as soon as the ball was coming his way, never giving him the opportunity to fasten on it. It seemed to work all right, anyway.

Everton full back Norman Greenhalgh, who generally had a good game against Matthews

I never saw Stan Matthews or Tom Finney have a good game against Roger Byrne. He read the game brilliantly and took the whole field of play into his perspective, always knowing where he should be.

Sir Matt Busby, taken from Soccer at the Top: My Life in Football

Birmingham left back Jack Badham was mesmerised, hood-winked and pulverised by science all afternoon, yet never put a boot wrong against the master.

John McAdam on Stanley Matthews

The only similarities between Matthews and Finney are that both were great and both were murder to play against. I speak with some knowledge. I had the doubtful pleasure of playing against Stanley Matthews and the real pleasure of playing with him for the Combined Services. He would come to you with the ball at his dainty feet. He would take you on. You had seen it all before. You knew precisely what he would do and you knew precisely what he would do with you. He would pass you, usually on the outside, but as a novelty on the inside. If you went to tackle him it was merely saving time for him. He then simply beat you. If you didn't he would tease you by coming straight up to you and showing you the ball. And that would be the last you would see of him in that move. If you were covered he would do the same with your cover man and his cover man and so *ad infinitum*. Then, in his own good time and not before, he would release the perfect pass.

People were as aware of him as they are of any player today. They set out to stop him as they set out to stop the best today. But the best can't be stopped just by setting people on them.

Sir Matt Busby, taken from Soccer at the Top: My Life in Football

Matthews and Tom Finney were the two finest wingers I ever played against. Each were geniuses, and of the two I reckoned Finney the more dangerous. He wasn't a better footballer, but he could beat his man in almost as many ways as Stanley, and, unlike Stanley, was also dangerous with his head. You daren't give Finney any more scope than Matthews. If you did you were asking for trouble.

Norman Greenhalgh

Even the tough guys felt guilty about putting the boot into such a unique talent as Tom Finney.

Jimmy Armfield

I got clobbered a few times. I won't mention any names but there were quite a few who used to try and rough you up.

Tom Finney

If Tom was tackled unfairly you never heard him complain or retaliate. He was a gentleman on and off the field and an inspirational captain. I became a much better player watching him and listening to him. His enthusiasm for the game never wavered. He had a genuine love for football.

Tommy Docherty on Tom Finney

Tom Finney was deceptive with his physical strength and possessing great strength of character when opponents tried to kick him into submission.

Henry Cockburn

What more can you give a player than everything, plus this wonderful temperament and humility, an absolute gentleman. You couldn't buy him today. I would say he is the finest player that I ever saw in my life. For fifty games a season I would have Finney in my team before Pele, Cruyff and Di Stefano. Both on and off the pitch he is an absolute credit to his profession.

Tommy Docherty on Tom Finney

He was fearless in the tackle and gave all-out effort. I knew after his first tackle on me that I was in for a tough game. He was very hard but always fair.

Roy Clarke on Tommy Docherty, taken from Docherty:
A Biography of Tommy Docherty

He was a tremendous player and never pulled any punches, even on the training ground. It was like a juggernaut behind me in the team. He was a relentless competitor throughout a game and a man to have on your side.

Tom Finney on Tommy Docherty, taken from Docherty:
A Biography of Tommy Docherty

At Crystal Palace, I was a fish out of water; we were playing Millwall. I dummied the Millwall hard man Neary, put a sweet pass through their backs and then whack! Neary fells me. Just like an ear of corn thrashed by a reaper and binder. This was professional football lad! and welcome. Feeling like Ruth amid the alien corn, I moved my skills, an artist among artisans. At full-time a solitary voice said, 'Well played Hall.' I received the ten shillings in expenses, returned to my cosy middle-class house and turned my back on pro-football to embark on a proper job.

Stuart Hall, radio and television broadcaster

Those matches against the Scots were always hard. I was up against men like big George Young, Willie Woodburn, Tommy Docherty, Willie Cunningham and the rest. Hard men. You could expect to take a few knocks. But there was never anything dirty. If you had a bruised ankle it was because you'd got a kick from someone going for the ball. On balance, he probably had a few bruises himself.

We'd shake hands after the match and they'd come into our dressing room. Big George would say: 'Come on, Lofty, get your coat on, we're going for a pint.' We'd played our best, done our job and now the fun could start. There was always a banquet in the evening. A really good do.

Nat Lofthouse, taken from The Lion of Vienna: 50 Years A Legend

During a particularly tough match Baily was shouldered 'into the crowd', as he put it, more times than he could count. Eddie did actually finish up standing next to a spectator against whom he had crashed after being bowled over the touchline. Eddie shook the man's hand before going back to the field, saying, in a stage whisper, 'It isn't often you get the chance of rubbing shoulders with a really great player, is it?'

Spurs' Billy Walker on his team mate, Eddie Baily

After a series of rough games at the Valley, during which I narrowly escaped injury, I was persuaded to try out a crash helmet specially designed for goalkeepers.

If anybody at the time had called me big 'ead, I should have been inclined to agree with them. I never felt more awkward, nor more unbalanced, and I knew at once that the risk of getting a kick in the head was preferable to wearing the top of a diving suit – which was what it felt like!

Sam Bartram

I've come across more than my fair share of keepers who knew my reputation and were prepared to 'get the first one in'. I often used to get a thump on the back of the head as I went for an early cross and a reminder from the keeper. 'There's more where that came from, Lofty!' But it didn't stop me going in just as hard next time around.

Big Sam Bartram, the Charlton keeper, was a larger-than-life character. Like a lot of goalkeepers Sam enjoyed the centre forward's challenge. He was never averse to mixing it . . . but all in the best possible spirit, of course.

Nat Lofthouse, taken from The Lion of Vienna: 50 Years A Legend

Sunderland attracted another large crowd when we visited Hartlepool. Gorman and I were glad to get away safely for I heard some of the crowd plotting to get Jimmy after the match.

Jimmy had made what could have been a fatal mistake, about an extremely drunken man in the crowd. Jimmy turned to me and said: 'Jack, I thought they had hung the monkey – but he's here at the match!'

(This is a reference to the famous tale of a ship sinking off the coast, from which a monkey somehow survived and landed on the beach at Hartlepool. Locals reputedly thought it was a French spy, and are supposed to have hung it.)

I told Jimmy that the outraged fans were plotting to sort him out after the game, so in the final minutes, Jimmy went on to the wing and Hughie McMahon came to full back. When the whistle went he ran straight up the tunnel to safety – and I was not far behind him!

Jack Clark

I always remember the first game I played at Wrexham and there was a centre half called Bill Tudor. Bill had legs bigger than me. He was massive. He used to head the ball further than I could kick it. He came up to me and said, 'Get past me, and I'll break both your legs.' I just looked at him. I was *giving* him the ball.

Harold Atkinson, taken from Three Sides of the Mersey: An Oral History of Everton, Liverpool and Tranmere Rovers

Before the 1950 FA Cup final, Tom Whittaker, the Arsenal manager, reminded Alex Forbes that Liverpool's greatest threat could come from Billy Liddell. Before the match Tom said to Alex, 'Liddell is one man who can win the match for Liverpool. It's up to you to see that he doesn't.' In the eyes of the Liverpool club and their supporters, Alex took these instructions a bit too literally. He set out to destroy Liddell's chances in their infancy. He thundered into his tackles and never allowed Liddell a moment's respite. I have seldom seen a more devastating wing half display.

Bob Wall, taken from Arsenal From the Heart

They had a lad there, Forbes, who did his job on Billy. He just hammered Billy everywhere he went, because he was just that type of player, this Forbes.

Ray Lambert on Alex Forbes' treatment of Billy Liddell in the 1950 FA Cup Final

It came after Les Smith, our winger, had made a run down the right. He had put in many throughout the season and would usually follow with an excellent cross. I would come in from the other wing to capitalise and I was doing that and just picking my spot for this one. Over it came and I wanted to hit inside the far post from outside the six-yard box. Unfortunately, I didn't hit it quite right and sent it straight at Wood. He caught it. But he was moving forward as he did so and I followed up in case he dropped it. I was sideways on to him and was preparing to charge. Now he was a keeper who was not afraid of being hit and in we went.

The trouble was that on impact our heads clashed, the side of my head with his cheek-bone. I was hurt, too, and lay there on the ground with the stadium spinning around me. Luckily, I recovered, but Ray had to go off. I felt very sorry that a fellow player had been injured in the Cup Final. The United fans gave me some stick, but our trainer Bill Muir had told me: 'There's only one way to shut them up.' He did not have to tell me what it was.

Peter McParland on his clash with Ray Wood, 1957 FA Cup Final, taken from The Match of My Life

I now believe that Ray Wood was targeted, deliberately put out of the game. It was the way it was done. I watched him, he went right for him, he head-butted him. It was too obvious because Ray had the ball in his hands for seconds before McParland came in. His head went straight into his face and he was out of the game. That cost us the Cup. Now I wasn't a dirty player – I'd go in hard, but I'd go for the ball. If that had been anywhere else but Wembley, I don't think MacParland would have lasted the game. My first reaction was, 'Right, you're going out of the game', but it was Wembley, so you had to restrain yourself. If it had been at Aston Villa he'd have got it. And what was worse, referees in those days were strict, but the ref didn't even speak to McParland.

Bill Foulkes, taken from Sir Matt Busby: A Tribute

I remember I was playing against Hull Beach. I went past their full back, I nearly left him for dead. I went past him again and was making him look a bit of a fool. He came over to me and whispered, 'If you do that to me again I will stop you the only way I can which is by breaking your leg.' It frightened the life out of me. The guy was built like a tank. He said to me, 'I probably won't get the ball, but I'll get you next time.' I didn't go too near him for the rest of the game. I thought, 'I don't really need this.' Maybe I was a bit chicken. I don't know.

Entertainer Des O'Connor, a semi-professional with Northampton Town

He was nearly frothing at the mouth and getting us worked up about tackling, about getting stuck in, saying, 'I want BITE in the tackle.' Danny Blanchflower suddenly looked up and said, 'Peter, they're bringing a new boot out next month which will suit you; they're having false teeth built into the toe-caps.'

Jimmy McIlroy on the Northern Ireland manager, Peter Doherty, taken from Billy: A Biography of Billy Bingham

Dennis Stevens fired in a shot from the left-hand side of the box that Harry Gregg stopped but couldn't hold. Perhaps he was surprised by the pace of the ball. I don't know. But I was following in at top speed. I saw Gregg turn to catch the ball and then I hit him, the ball, the lot into the back of the net. A foul? Looking back, yes. Today I would probably have been sent off. But in those days you could challenge the keeper. That's what I did. I didn't go in to hurt Gregg. I went for the ball. And that's how the referee saw it. When I looked round he was pointing to the centre circle. Goal. I don't argue with referees! Harry always says to me, and I see him quite often – we're still friends, and he said, 'I'd have done the same to you, Lofty.'

Nat Lofthouse on his clash with Harry Gregg in the 1958 Cup Final

I had initially stopped the ball, didn't keep hold of it, I turned to catch it and that's all I remember. I remember waking up and kicking about and somebody putting an ammonia pad up my nose. I didn't really realise what had happened until I saw it on television. I went to dinner about two years ago when everybody was paying compliments to Nat, telling him what a wonderful fellah he was and how much he had done for the game. Then it was my turn as a guest and I just basically said, 'What a load of rubbish! You were a hooligan! Had it happened today you would have been done for GBH,' and all Nat did was laugh.

At the time I never made any comment on it, even today I haven't said it was a foul because I'd given a few smacks in my time, sometimes intentionally and sometimes unintentionally. So when it comes to your turn you don't cry about it. But for a long time afterwards, I used to pray quietly – this was at one stage when the press said Nat was going to retire, and being the religious fellah that I was, I used to pray every night, 'Please, God, don't let him retire until I get one smack at him.' It stayed that way until the end. Nat's a nice fellah, who was a very good player; he's one of the greats of the English game and we are to this day very good friends.

Harry Gregg

It could be that one reason why there seem to be more violent tackles now is that the fair shoulder charge seems virtually to have been banished. This is sad, because fair shoulder charging used to be part of the entertainment and seldom caused more injury than the wounded pride of the charged one, who added to the exhilaration by getting his own back with a charge later on. On the other hand I hate to think what some of the play-acting characters – those who are one second seen writhing in agony after a tackle and the next second running 50 yards in even time – would do if a good, healthy, bone-shaking shoulder charge should hit them.

Sir Matt Busby, taken from Soccer at the Top: My Life in Football

They used to say that if you kicked one man in the side you had to kick 'em out. This was a tremendous team in the true sense of the word.

The full backs were that legendary pairing of Roy Hartle and Tommy Banks. They had a reputation of being hard men. Let's put it this way . . . I used to wear my shin pads at the back of my legs and I was on their side. Hard. Yes. But fair. Good men. Good players.

Nat Lofthouse on the 1958 Bolton team,
taken from The Lion of Vienna: 50 Years A Legend

What a Jekyll and Hyde character he was. On the field he had the reputation for being as hard as nails and wingers would bounce off him like peas off a tin roof. But off the field you would think you were speaking to a university professor, and in fact he was a Conservative councillor for the Halliwell ward of Bolton.

Roy was a true professional. He would play hard against anybody and I don't recall anybody giving him a chasing. As Cliff Jones once remarked: 'The bloke who gives Roy a chasing ends up with a gravel rash.'

Malcolm Allison tells the story of the time he told Mike Summerbee to push it past Hartle and run. Roy might not have had the legs to match Mike at the end of his career, but he scythed him down as he was going past. And Mike still remembers it. But Roy was never booked or sent off in his career. His famous words were: 'But I played the ball referee.'

And Roy would always get up, dust his opponent down and walk away without another word.

Francis Lee on Roy Hartle, taken from Soccer Round the World:
A Football Star's Story from Manchester to Mexico

I was only booked once in my career. Once in over 700 games for club and country. It was such a silly incident. I ran on to a through pass that put me in the clear and was just thinking in terms of another goal to add to the tally when the whistle blew. Offside. To prove it there was the linesman's flag. I don't remember what colour it was but I know I saw red. I picked up the ball and threw it at the linesman.

My only booking . . . but generally bookings were few and far between in my day. There were no red cards and yellow cards, of course, and although the game was every bit as hard as it is today there weren't as many bookings. Why?

I think the referees saw a booking as a last resort. They were reluctant to bring the book out.

Nat Lofthouse, taken from The Lion of Vienna: 50 Years A Legend

The only time John ever got nasty was when Wales played Austria at Wrexham. One of the Austrian players came up and kicked me from behind. That's how I got my first cartilage problem and John did get a bit nasty then. He just picked the bloke up by the throat and slung him.

That was the only time I ever saw him being nasty; he always looked after the younger brother.

Mel Charles on his brother John

I thought I was dying. It came into my mind that I was going to die and I still had £200 in the dressing room that I hadn't spent.

**Malcolm Allison, after a collision with Derek Dooley of
Sheffield Wednesday that left him flat on his back,**
taken from Venables: The Autobiography

3 The Beauty of the Beast

Don Revie's Leeds United

Every team had a hard man. We had Nobby Stiles, Chelsea had Chopper, Arsenal had Peter Storey, Liverpool had Tommy Smith. Leeds had eleven of them!

George Best

Make no mistake – at Leeds, every player is taught to put side before self. Above my peg in the dressing-room there hangs a motto: 'Always keep on fighting.' That motto means exactly what it says . . . and there is a hidden message, as well. It means that not only do you keep on fighting, you keep on fighting for the whole *team*, not just yourself. So it's side before self, every time. And all the hard, unrelenting work we have to slog through has this as its aim.

Billy Bremner, taken from You Get Nowt for Being Second

We were learning to play it hard – because the Second Division was a hard school. It is true that manager Don Revie always told us to give 100 per cent effort for everyone of the 90 minutes – but never at any time were we encouraged to 'put the boot in'. Often, indeed, it was our opponents who, perhaps, fearsome of our reputation or aiming to snuff out the so- called menace, went in first for the taunting – and, of course, at times that brought retaliation. And so often in football it is the player who retaliates who gets marching orders, or whose name goes down in the referee's little black book. There was a period when we were all concerned about this 'dirty team' stage – it even followed us up to the First Division for a spell. But the truth is that we never intentionally set out to play any other way but hard and fair. Perhaps Billy Bremner was the biggest sufferer, for he knows no other way to play his football but with the intention of winning the ball every time he goes for it. And this whole-hearted effort, which was so good for the team, sometimes rebounded upon Billy. But, believe me, I have often seen Billy more sinned against than sinning. And there have been occasions when, having realised that opponents were deliberately setting out to needle him, I have had a quiet word with Billy, and told him, 'Watch out – they're trying to get you in lumber.'

Jack Charlton, taken from For Leeds and England

As is so often the case when there's a lot at stake, these matches were all bitterly fought, and produced numerous explosive incidents.

In this respect the worst clash was the one against Sunderland four days previously and, not surprisingly, all the bad feeling in this match was carried over the return fixture.

Leeds were no angels – far from it. But I honestly believe we were more sinned against than sinning.

As I said earlier, we were a young and inexperienced team – and Sunderland knew only too well that we would be suspect to physical and verbal provocation.

Billy Bremner was repeatedly scythed down, and Jim Storrie was carried off twenty minutes before half-time after a tackle.

In addition, some of Sunderland's players successfully managed to intimidate Leeds players with such jibes as: 'You're a bunch of scrubbers' or 'That was a rubbish tackle', and so on.

I am not condemning them for this, as I have done it myself. After all, taunting of opponents is commonplace in professional football.

However, Leeds tended to allow this to affect their game in those days.

Johnny Giles, taken from Forward with Leeds

He never gave us a minute, because he was always telling us to do this and do that, and do something else, and go fight there, and give it plenty of room in another place, and then get everybody running and running, and, of course, we were all 'a load of bastards' at the time.

Billy Bremner on Bobby Collins

Bobby Collins made an impact on everyone because he was such a smashing player and a tremendous competitor. If you stepped out of line in training, then he would do you, no danger, but having said that you looked up to him because of his ability.

Everton's Colin Harvey on Bobby Collins

Leeds United were being driven by this midget human dynamo, and every one of Bobby Collin's team mates was responding with a will. So much so that the team spirit became as good as a goal to us; we seldom thought about the danger of defence – we thought much more of what we were going to do to the opposition!

Jack Charlton on Bobby Collins, taken from For Leeds and England

I remember once, when we were staying in a Harrogate hotel just before a game with Burnley, and a plate-glass door accidentally got broken. Bobby's arm was split badly, it was an injury which would have caused lesser men to cry off, and not without good reason. But Bobby played, and scored two goals in our 5–1 victory. I shall always remember him as we clamoured around him to congratulate him on those goals. He was trying to get away from us as he shouted: 'Mind my arm! Mind my arm!'

Billy Bremner on Bobby Collins, taken from You Get Nowt for Being Second

I knew it wasn't going to be a garden party, but I didn't expect it to be like first night at Madison Square Garden either.

As the two teams walked down the tunnel at the start of the game, I felt a terrific pain on my right calf as someone kicked with brute force. I turned. It was Bobby Collins. 'And that's just for starters, Bestie,' he said.

From the kick-off it was mayhem. Leeds came at us like something possessed, kicking and hacking any United player who came their way. Only twelve minutes had gone when Bremner brought me down for the umpteenth time. As referee Arthur Luty struggled to impose his authority, I decided I was going to try to give as good as I got. I set off in pursuit and gave

Bremner a taste of his own medicine by dumping him on the cinder track that encircled the pitch. The first half progressed the way it had begun. Some of Bobby Collins' and Billy Bremner's tackles were outrageous and a threat to a fellow pro's livelihood. Collins patrolled up and down our right-hand side, dishing out one crude tackle after another. After I had been sent sprawling by a tackle that caught me somewhere around the midriff, I dusted myself down, and Nobby Stiles appeared by my side. 'Don't worry, George,' he told me, 'I'm going to put a stop to this nonsense. Forget about Collins, I'll sort him out for you.' As soon as Bobby latched on to the ball, Nobby took off. There was a sickening sound of bone on bone. Bobby Collins was flying through the air, flattened against the concrete wall that separated the fans from the pitch. 'Every time you come down our right-hand side and kick George, you filthy bastard, I'm going to friggin' well hit you like that, only harder.'

George Best, recalling United's first visit to Elland Road after Leeds had won promotion from the Second Division, taken from The Best of Times: My Favourite Football Stories

Don Revie produced a team of outstanding players at Leeds who would give 100 per cent effort for the whole 90 minutes, home or away, which, I grant, made us the hardest team in football . . . but not a dirty one.

Jack Charlton

Yes, we did have a reputation once upon a time of being a 'dirty' team. The Everton fans at Goodison reminded us of that a few seasons ago when trouble flared there, and the game was held up for ten minutes to allow tempers on both sides to cool down.

At first, in our early days in Division One, we had to get used to hearing people say we had kicked our way out of the Second Division. It just wasn't true, of course, but because we all went in hard for the ball we became tagged with that 'Dirty Leeds' label. Today, I'm happy to say, that tag is a thing of the past. More and more people are coming to respect us for the way we do play the game; we *are* hard – and courageous. But not dirty. We can match any team in the world for sheer endeavour; and we can meet most of them on equal terms, when it comes to pure footballing skills.

Billy Bremner, taken from You Get Nowt for Being Second

In the sensational Everton match the tension reached boiling point after only five minutes due to an incident between the Merseysiders' Scottish left back Sandy Brown and myself.

We collided in challenging for the ball on the edge of the Everton penalty area and our legs accidentally became entangled as we fell to the ground. Then Brown wriggled free, leapt angrily to his feet, and aimed a punch to my head.

Everton became rattled when Leeds went ahead after fifteen minutes through Willie Bell, and their desperation to get back into the game only led to more niggling incidents.

The tackling got fiercer and fiercer, and Everton's fans started demonstrating against Stokes for a number of free kicks against the Everton players. In the 39th minute the crowd was whipped up into a frenzy when Bell and Derek Temple crashed into each other on the halfway line on Leeds' right flank.

Referee Stokes promptly halted play, and when he got to the touchline he was pelted with rubbish by Everton supporters.

That was the most frightening moment I have ever experienced on a soccer pitch. I had the feeling that, at any moment, the fans – all 55,000 of them – would invade the field, just as they try to do in some parts of South America, where players have to be protected by moats, barbed wire and riot police!

Stokes had the same fear, for he immediately signalled for both teams to return to their dressing rooms.

Don Revie did most of the talking as the Leeds players sat waiting for the game to re-start, stressing how important it was for us to keep our heads. Stokes came into the dressing room to confirm that he had taken us off because of the behaviour of the fans. 'Don't worry, lads, I've got the club to broadcast a stern warning over the tannoy,' he added reassuringly.

Everton were down to nine men when they came back on to the field, Temple having sustained a leg injury in that clash with Bell. However, the crowd had calmed down, and there was no further trouble in that direction . . . even though there was still a lot of ill-feeling among the players.

Temple returned two minutes before the interval, and immediately afterwards Rees earned a stern lecture from Stokes for bringing down Bobby Collins.

The free kicks continued to flow freely throughout the second half, with Norman Hunter being booked for a foul on Roy Vernon, and Vernon extremely lucky to escape the same fate for a similar foul on Billy Bremner.

Not surprisingly, all this provided our critics with fresh ammunition in their campaign against the club – although of the 31 fouls in the match, which we won 1–0, Everton committed 19 to Leeds' 12.

Johnny Giles, on the Everton v Leeds game that resulted in both teams being taken off the field by the referee to cool down

It was not the attitude of the players which was causing so much concern, but the attitude of the crowd. I'll make no bones about it – the Goodison Park crowd is the worst before which I have ever played. And I'm not alone in voicing that opinion. Players of other teams have expressed that view to me in no uncertain manner. The particular game to which I refer had been a niggling sort of match, with a few rugged fouls thrown in. And probably both teams were equally to blame for on-field incidents. I take the view that if you let people know that you are not going to be put upon, it is half the battle . . . and Leeds United have certainly never allowed themselves to be put upon. But the crowd behaviour and their reaction to that game at Goodison reflected no credit upon the Everton fans. Our goalkeeper, Gary Sprake, was picking up so many coins from the pitch – coins thrown from the crowd – that at full-time when we asked him how much he had got, he turned round and said, 'I don't really know – I could have got more, but I only picked up the silver.' With the Everton fans there always seems to be a threatening attitude, a vicious undertone to their remarks. You never feel this is a football atmosphere – it creates more a sense of fear.

Jack Charlton on the same match, taken from For Leeds and England

I've been called a firebrand, a hooligan, a thug, a dirty player and so on. It's the absolute truth that talking out of turn has been the cause of most of the 15 bookings I have had. Not to mention the fact that I have suffered the indignity of being sent off twice, and fined and suspended on four occasions.

I say this not with pride, but because I have no wish to wrap anything up and because, I hope, I *have* now learned the lesson which, from manager Don Revie down, everyone at Elland Road has been hammering home to me for several seasons. At last, I believe, I have finally got the message. And believe me, I intend to go straight from now on. By keeping that BIG MOUTH SHUT. TIGHT...

Billy Bremner, taken from You Get Nowt for Being Second

The most frequent accusation against Bremner was that he tried to referee matches. That was rubbish at least when I was around. Sure, he yapped away all the time and he challenged decisions you made but never in a way which you could send him off. It was all down to respect – if he had that for you it was all right.

I remember driving away from Anfield after a Liverpool-Leeds match, which were always highly competitive with both teams superbly talented and as hard as nails, and Alan Hardaker was speaking on 'Sports Report' on the radio. 'At least we had a referee today who treated men like men and let them get on with the game,' he said. That was what Billy Bremner liked.

With that mop of curly red hair and fiery temper he was the player the fans loved to hate but I'll tell you something ... those same fans would have loved their club to have bought him.

Referee Pat Partridge, taken from Oh Ref!

It was a victory we paid for. Leeds were as cold as ice, a team and a club without heart or mercy, when we played them over the next few years. They always saved up something special for us and even carried the 'cold war' into the boardroom. We did not beat Leeds again until 1972.

Ron Greenwood recalling the effect that beating Leeds 7–0 in the mid-60s had on them, taken from Yours Sincerely, Ron Greenwood

Ralph Brand, who was no great respecter of reputations, in one game against Leeds indulged himself with a couple of sly digs at big Jackie Charlton. Predictably, he chose the wrong man. Jackie looked at him, picked him up, lifted him into the air, and threw him down on the deck. The referee either didn't see anything or decided that justice had been done.

Jim Baxter, taken from Baxter: The Party's Over

My appeal for a penalty fell upon deaf ears, and as I rose from the mud, I looked at the player who had clobbered me and said 'you so-and-so', whereupon he walked past me and spat in my face. By this time, I was ready to hang a punch on his chin, but as the referee was nearby I managed to restrain myself.

So instead of swinging a nifty right upper cut, I turned on my heel and with the spittle still clearly running down my face – said to the referee: 'What about this?' The answer I received was: 'Don't moan about things like that. Get on with the game.' So there is a clear case of one player having instigated trouble ... and the player who flared up and was provoked being promptly choked off by the referee.

Jack Charlton, taken from For Leeds and England

By the early 1960s, Chelsea had become a good side and a tremendously exciting team to watch, playing some fabulous football.

Yet it was also a time when the game was getting very dirty, with 'over the top' tackles almost a routine. It was not always easy for a bystander – or even a referee – to spot if the tackle was deliberately vicious or just an innocent, mistimed effort, but the effect of 'showing six' – the six studs on the sole of the boot – and kicking or stabbing downwards over the top of the ball into the shins, would put ball-players off their game, and could even put them out of the game altogether. Talented players, who wanted to play football, spent a lot of time being carried off, because the others spent most of their time stopping them from doing so.

Chelsea were not the worst side by a long chalk, but we were by no means entirely blameless. I was about four yards from Leeds' Johnny Giles, when my Chelsea team mate, Eddie

McCreadie, launched himself at him and went straight through his shin pads. Giles was carried off. After it had happened to him a few more times, Johnny said that it would not happen again; he was going to protect himself in future, and many of the talented players decided that they were going to have to be tough, just to survive.

Terry Venables, taken from Venables: The Autobiography

During my time as a player the team which stood out as arguably the best of the lot was the one assembled at Leeds United by Don Revie in the late sixties and early seventies. It is often said that Revie's famous side was cynical, sly and ruthlessly uncompromising and while it is true that they gave a whole new meaning to the term professional, nothing should be allowed to detract from the quality of their football.

Leeds were good but, my word, they were a hard bunch. I remember once going into a tackle with Giles and bundling him on to the dirt track which used to surround the pitch at Elland Road. I didn't go over the top or anything like that; it was a good, solid challenge. After Giles had picked himself up and dusted himself down he walked back on to the pitch and just glanced at Charlton, Hunter and Bremner while nodding in my general direction. It was like having a contract put out on you.

You had to have eyes in the back of your head when you played against Leeds in those days. People talk about one-touch football but, believe me, when you played them it was down to half a touch. It was a case of getting the ball and then releasing it as quickly as was possible. It was just the way Revie's players had been brought up but, to be fair to them, they were so good that they didn't really have to resort to intimidation.

Howard Kendall, taken from Only the Best is Good Enough:
The Howard Kendall Story

Against Leeds United I had to be on my guard for the whole game. They were a terrible side to play. They were always niggling and complaining to the referee and 'giving you the verbal', which means questioning the sexual behaviour of your mother, your legitimacy, the mental health of your children. They would say anything to provoke you. And they were dirty.

Leeds was the only team I ever wore shinguards against. And they had Paul Reaney. Reaney was the toughest player I played against. He was at you the whole 90 minutes, using every dodgy trick in the book.

It was a shame because Reaney did not have to play like that. He had a lot of talent. He was capable of playing good football. He chose instead to subvert his talent. But that was the way Leeds played under Don Revie. And that's why, no matter how many Cups or Championships they won, nobody liked them. The fans on the terraces could see what they were up to and they hated them for it.

George Best, taken from The Good, the Bad and the Bubbly

Most people thought Johnny Giles was a dirty bastard. Yeah, Leeds were dirty, but they were professional about it. I admired them for it. They had it down pat, the way Revie organised them. If there was trouble it wasn't one player involved it was all fucking 11 of them. I loved that.

Charlie George on Don Revie's Leeds United

You knew that if you didn't compete with Leeds you were going to get kicked off the park. So you geed yourself up before you went out. It was out-and-out war.

Ian Hutchinson on Don Revie's Leeds United

Obviously some players are tougher than others. The names of Graham Roberts, Remi Moses, Graeme Souness and Paul Miller come to mind as recent examples but the hardest side I ever played against was Don Revie's Leeds United. They were undoubtedly a very good side; they could play football but they were also extremely physical and everyone was wary of going into a 50–50 ball against any of them. In those days Peter Storey, Tommy Smith and Norman Hunter were known as the 'hard men'. I remember Norman with great affection as he was a delightful character off the field and that pro- bably influenced me in one of my early games against Leeds when I could have had Norman sent off. He was booked for a late tackle against me and, just a couple of minutes later, he sent me tumbling again. Norman could see the referee striding purposefully towards us and he urgently bent over and said: 'For God's sake, Steve, get up.' I know that if I had made a fuss about it he would have been on his way to an early bath.

To Norman's obvious relief and the doubting referee's satisfaction I jumped to my feet only to walk straight into a severe dressing down from my team mate Tommy Jackson for not behaving professionally. He maintained that I should have stayed down and rolled about a bit which would have had Norman sent off and reduced the powerful Leeds side to ten men. I did not because it is not in my nature.

Steve Coppell on Leeds

Leeds United? Most people imagine us as an evil-looking bunch of characters with black capes and handlebar moustaches!

For years we were cast as the 'baddies' of British football; looked upon as a rough, ruthless team which achieved soccer success through physical violence and gamesmanship.

But perhaps this is not surprising when one considers that in the Club's first season in Division One in 1964–5 the Football Association took it upon themselves to produce a report which suggested to some people that Leeds were the dirtiest team in football. This slight did irreparable damage and it took us some years to break down the prejudice against us.

Leeds didn't have one first-team player sent off during the period in question, while Manchester United, who weren't mentioned in the report, had *five*!

It is a fact that Leeds courted controversy in Division Two, and that a number of rival managers and players accused us of dirty play. And I am not claiming that we were completely guiltless.

As I explained earlier, we were a young and inexperienced side, and I possessed a burning determination to do well. So there were bound to be times when our sense of values became entangled – when our keenness led us over the borderline between the fair challenge and the foul.

But there is a difference between players who foul by design and those who do so in the heat of the moment. There was so much skill in the Leeds team that we didn't *need* to clog rivals in order to achieve success.

Sadly the FA's 'evidence' created so much prejudice against Leeds that our bid to win friends was doomed right from the start. To build such a false picture of the side was bad enough. To present it to the public was even worse.

Johnny Giles, taken from Forward with Leeds

My memories of the Leeds United team of the 1960s are not pleasant ones. Leeds were a nasty lot. Don Revie, though a friend of mine, has a lot to answer for. His team, admittedly, were a poor lot at first. He built them into one of the most successful in the land, but his methods left a lot to be desired. For sheer ruthlessness there was nobody in their class, nor had there been previously, so far as I know. Certainly there hasn't been anybody since.

All other clubs hated to play Leeds. To them, the rules of the game were a nuisance, merely worth a gesture of lip-service before being ignored. They got up to all sorts of tricks, all sorts of gamesmanship. If you tried to take a free kick against Leeds you'd have three or four of them standing on your toes. It wasn't that they hadn't heard of the ten-yard rule. They simply didn't believe in it. At corner kicks Leeds would be digging away before the ball had even been placed for the kick. If they knocked you down and picked you up, they'd pick you up by your hair. Every one of them could kick, and I don't mean the ball. Of course, one of the great Leeds players before the title-winning team was built, was Bobby Collins. Bobby was a genuine artist on the ball, but he could slice your leg off at the knee and take the bottom bit home before you knew anything about it.

That was the irony of Leeds. Every man could play. Think of names like Norman Hunter, Paul Madeley, Johnny Giles, Billy Bremner, Jackie Charlton and Mick Jones. They didn't have to be assassins. They didn't have to intimidate. Or did they? Did Don Revie insist on such tactics? Did ruthlessness become an ineradicable habit?'

Jim Baxter, taken from Baxter: The Party's Over

During his pre-match brief, Jack got on to the subject of professionalism in clubs. Jack intimated that he believed Don Revie knew all his strengths and weaknesses as a referee, and he added, 'You'll notice one thing today. If Leeds go a goal ahead, all the ball boys will disappear from around the pitch. It is a little ploy they have at the club which wastes just that extra bit of time. There will then be nobody to retrieve the ball when it goes out of play.' Leeds went a goal ahead and, sure enough, the ball boys disappeared.

Referee Keith Hackett on Jack Taylor's brief before a Leeds United game, taken from Hackett's Law: A Referee's Notebook

Leeds were pulled to pieces in the 1960s and early 70s because of the physical element of their play. From goalkeeper to outside left they had fantastic players. But there were one or two in their team who were told to clog. They didn't have to clog. They did it because they were told to do it. But they didn't have to clog because they had outstanding world-class players. That was a great side.

Tommy Docherty

Football is a physical game and I took probably more than my fair share of knocks. I never got uptight about it because I accepted good, hard tackling as part and parcel of the game I played. That Leeds side, however, were over the top. The midfield contained three players who thought nothing of kicking anything that moved. Johnny Giles, Billy Bremner and Bobby Collins were all under five feet seven, but big trouble on the park. Bobby was only five feet four inches tall. We used to joke in the United dressing room that he was the only player in the League who had to have turn-ups on his shorts, but for all his diminutive size, he was a tough nut on the pitch.

George Best, taken from Where Do I Go From Here?

The outstanding team were Leeds, and though I admired their efficiency I thought they could have entertained more. They carried the possession principle too far. Arsenal had some fierce encounters with them, usually coming out on the losing side.

Johnny Giles took on Peter Storey – what a battle that was!

Terry Neill on the Leeds team of the 1960s and early 70s

Like many older people in the game who remember Leeds during the Revie era, I have often wondered if they sold themselves short by trying to be too clever; whether they might not have been even more successful if they had been a bit more lovable. I know the policy at Elland Road was to win points rather than friends but, believe me, the side was oozing with talent. Johnny Giles and Billy Bremner were both great players and although Norman Hunter was noted for his reputation as a hard man he had tremendous skill, far more than most spectators probably realised.

Pat Jennings, taken from An Autobiography

One date I'll never forget is Wednesday 17 April 1968. That night at Elland Road, Leeds, my name went into the referee's notebook for the first and – so far – only time. Matches between Leeds and Spurs were never kid gloves affairs. Leeds in those days had an exceptionally good team and when we met there was no quarter asked or given.

You had to be at your strongest, for the Leeds lads under Don Revie were noted for their gamesmanship. In fact, I always got the impression they were proud of it. The two clubs had clashed at White Hart Lane five days earlier on Good Friday, and Spurs had won to end an unbeaten Leeds run of 26 games. When we travelled up to Yorkshire we knew they would be seeking instant revenge for that set-back. I certainly got a quick reminder, for a Leeds player ran into me on the first occasion I went to gather a cross from the wing – and that treatment was repeated five or six times in a tough but goalless first half. I kept my cool until the 63rd minute when I jumped up to fist the ball away and Leeds striker Mick Jones cannoned into me. We both crashed to the ground. The trouble started when I tried to regain my feet. Jones used his legs to keep me pinned to the turf. When I eventually struggled free, we both jumped up and glared at each other. Mick must have thought I was going to have a swing at him and decided to get in first by planting a right hander on my chin. That was too much! I lashed out with my foot and kicked his behind. It was a natural reaction, even if a foolish one, and I was spotted by a linesman. The referee not only booked me but added what I regarded as insult to injury by awarding Leeds a penalty. Lorimer beat me all ends up with his penalty and that was enough for Leeds to win 1–0. It hardly cooled any Spurs tempers and ten minutes later another incident saw Alan Gilzean sent off following a clash with Leeds full back Terry Cooper. Bill Nicholson gave me a real rocket when I got back to the dressing room. He told me that Leeds' gamesmanship was no secret and that I should have known better than to rise to the bait.

Pat Jennings, taken from An Autobiography

Arsenal recently held Leeds to a 0–0 draw at Elland Road in a match littered with bad fouls and ill-feeling. The Londoners, who had three players booked, made little attempt to play constructive football – they were determined to get a point at all costs.

Their tactics raised such an outcry in the press that many people must have got the impression we at United were preparing for the return clash at Highbury the following week by sticking pins into wax effigies of the Arsenal side. Nothing could have been further from the truth! I have a lot of respect for them as professionals. Therefore, the so-called Battle of Elland Road didn't dissuade me from going out for a drink with the Arsenal players later that evening.

Johnny Giles, taken from Forward with Leeds

Gary was warned beforehand that Bobby Gould would try to intimidate him, as he does so many goalkeepers, and before we left the dressing room the Boss made a special point of impressing upon him to keep his temper. Yet Gary's powers of self-control snapped after only four minutes. As I remember it, Gould challenged Gary for a high ball through the middle and as it ran out of play he appeared to flick up his heel and catch Gary in the stomach. Gary immediately scrambled to his feet, landed a short vicious left hook to Gould's jaw and then slumped to the ground again, holding his leg. I was certain he would be sent off – he certainly deserved to be.

Luckily, however, Worcestershire referee Ken Burns, who you may recall was the centre of controversy when he disallowed Leeds' equalising goal against Chelsea in an FA Cup semi-final in 1967, let off both players with a booking and a lecture. Gary's flash of temperament could easily have cost United the match . . . and the Championship. No one was more aware of this than Gary himself. He was almost in tears in the dressing room at half-time, staring disconsolately at the floor as Don Revie gave us our instructions for the second half. The Boss didn't say a word to Gary; he didn't have to. You only had to look at the expression on his face to see he was being sufficiently punished by his own conscience.

Johnny Giles on the clash between Arsenal's Bobby Gould and Gary Sprake, taken from Forward with Leeds

In all honesty there has never been anything underhand in Leeds' use of the goal-line tactics. Jack is perfectly within his rights to take up these positions, as long as he plays the ball. And that's exactly what he tries to do.

When Leeds developed the ploy of having a big man on the goal-line at corners it took referees a few games to realise how he was impeding the goalkeeper. When they did, attention tended to concentrate on Jack Charlton, who had scored a number of goals that way. But by then Big Jack was just the decoy, and as often as not it was another player who would do the harassing unnoticed.

Johnny Giles, taken from Forward with Leeds

I had a lot of fun with Jack Charlton as well, especially in the days when he had this ploy of standing on the opposing goal-line, in front of the goalkeeper, for corner kicks. Many teams claimed that he deliberately impeded keepers in these situations, and he himself challenged me to take up all sorts of positions to judge whether or not they were justified. I even finished up standing behind the goal! I thoroughly enjoyed the repartee between us during a match. For example, when I had to chase after a big clearance by him, I'd say something like: 'Give us a flipping chance' and Charlton, laughing like mad would reply: 'You're too old, Hill. You can't make it.' It was like that all the time – great.

Gordon Hill, taken from Give a Little Whistle: The Recollections of a Remarkable Referee

Bob Wilson often used to moan about Big Jack whose stock answer was 'Aye, I push him all right – usually with both his hands in my back.'

Referee Pat Partridge

The replay at Old Trafford eighteen days later was not as skilful as the Wembley tie and was spoiled to some extent by niggling incidents and some tackling in the X-certificate class! I expected this.

For one thing, Wembley has a magic all of its own, and taking a Cup Final away from this stadium is like taking the All-England Tennis Championships away from Wimbledon and the Grand National from Aintree. In other words, Old Trafford, with its more enclosed, intense atmosphere made our clash with Chelsea more like a semi-final than a final.

Another point to consider is that there is bound to be the odd flash of 'needle' in matches between hard-tackling, determined sides like Leeds and Chelsea.

Johnny Giles, taken from Forward with Leeds

Leeds had many so-called 'hard' players in their line-up, the most celebrated of which was Hunter. You couldn't wish to meet a more polite and friendly man off the pitch but once the whistle went he was a totally different person.

During one game at Elland Road, I sent a pass fully 30 yards to Johnny Morrissey and the ball had actually arrived at his feet before Norman clattered into me.

If you were scheduled to meet Leeds, you had to make sure that your girlfriend of the time was a very understanding woman because it was inevitable that you would turn up for your date on Saturday night covered in plasters and bruises.

Like most of the Leeds players, Norman was hard – very hard – but usually fair. The thing is that no matter how tough you are, you simply cannot survive in the First Division unless you also have a great deal of talent. It is a pity that Leeds' reputation for occasionally accentuating the physical side of the game overshadowed their great qualities, for they had some really marvellous players.

Howard Kendall, taken from Only the Best is Good Enough:
The Howard Kendall Story

Norman nearly kicked Gerry Francis straight over the top of the stand. Afterwards, I told him: 'One day, you and I are going to sit down and we're going to have a talk about what motivates you on a football field. I couldn't see what the hell provoked that foul.' He grinned, and said: 'Put it down to a rush of blood to the head, Gordon.'

OK, it was a diabolical tackle, but to accuse this man of malice, of being deliberately brutal, is very unfair. I could have refereed players like Norman Hunter for ever. They are so open in their belligerence.

Referee Gordon Hill, taken from Give a Little Whistle:
The Recollections of a Remarkable Referee

The real hard men don't see danger, men like Reaney and Jones, but there are times when I go in for a ball and wonder just how I'm going to come out of it.

Norman Hunter

Playing against Leeds for Middlesbrough, I often felt isolated in that midfield battle. My goodness it was hard. Take Johnny Giles, a small man, but how he could look after himself. I am not suggesting he was dirty but he was one of the craftiest and most difficult opponents I have ever encountered. He was a gifted passer of the ball but he also had had to learn to look after himself. I cannot even remember getting in a good tackle against him for he was quick and nippy and if there was the slightest chance of him being hurt you would suddenly be confronted by a full set of studs. He knew I was after him and, once, after nipping me, Johnny gave an impish grin and said, 'You will learn.' I did.

Norman Hunter was always fair and honest when I played against him and a lovely fellow away from the Park. Billy, nearing the end of his career when I played against him, was easier to catch and not as cute as Giles while Terry was as slow as me. It was Johnny who made enemies and upset people – just like me. But playing against players like him and his team mates showed me what an awful lot I had to learn about some aspects of the game. I started to look after myself and learned not to be so stupid as to pick up injuries like the one I suffered against Terry Yorath. I tried to be more selective in the balls I went for but, on no account, to go in half-hearted. All or nothing, that is the way it was to be.

Graeme Souness, taken from Graeme Souness: No Half Measures

Stoke's Harry Burrows hit a very hard ball, around the middle of the park, which hit Norman Hunter on the side of the head. The ball bounced fully twenty yards back into Burrow's path, and he went through and scored a delightful goal. I awarded the goal, and turned round to find that Hunter was flat out. As he was coming to, he was saying: 'What happened, what happened? Did they score?' I said: 'Yes, sorry, they did.' Norman was ranting and raving to himself, really showing absolute anger, and then quite obviously he went looking for Burrows. I didn't leave him for ten minutes. Wherever he went I went with him, talking to him all the time. 'For God's sake, Norman, forget it, it's all over,' I told him, trying to talk him through this aggression he was feeling at that moment.

Referee Gordon Hill, taken from Give a Little Whistle: The Recollections of a Remarkable Referee

I was never subtle about kicking people in the way that Johnny Giles, for example, could be. I used to watch Leeds United in their glory days when I was at university, and I always thought that Billy Bremner was the hard man act. Giles just stroked it around pulling out the strings in midfield. Then we played against him in the FA Cup, a few years later, and as soon as I came on as substitute, he tackled me over the ball and caught me on the shin deliberately. He could certainly look after himself, something I never managed to do.

Phil Neale, taken from Phil Neale: A Double Life

God gave you intelligence, skill, agility and the best passing ability in the game. What God didn't give you was six studs to wrap around someone else's knee.

Brian Clough to Johnny Giles, taken from Clough: A Biography

Giles was the finest passer of a ball I have ever come across. I used to marvel at him. He enthralled me. He was so accurate that it was like using a billiard cue. He made passing a simple exercise.

Referee Pat Partridge, taken from Oh Ref!

I was involved in a ding-dong with Billy Bremner and Johnny Giles and was going in to challenge Billy when Terry Yorath came in on my blind side and took me at knee height. It was some tackle and I knew straightaway that it was a bad injury. In fact it was my knee ligaments and I was in plaster for three weeks and out of action for almost three months.

All I could think of was getting myself fit and ready for the return match against Don Revie's team. I was going to gain my revenge on Terry Yorath at all costs and I told anyone who wanted to listen that, if necessary, I would feed him a knuckle sandwich off the ball. It led to suggestions in the press that there was a vendetta between us. It must have looked that way but it wasn't true. We had terrific respect for each other and he would take it as well as give it. Sure he would moan to referees, that was the Leeds style, but he never moaned in public.

Graeme Souness, taken from Graeme Souness:
No Half Measures

My visits to the Victoria Ground enabled me to form my first impressions of Leeds United. Leeds had a reputation for arrogance, ruthlessness and downright dirty play. If you were not a Leeds supporter it was fashionable at the time to dislike them intensely. I was not a Leeds supporter.

Talk to any old professional who played against them and he will talk of the 'nasty' players the Leeds team contained. The midfield area in particular provided the hard element; Billy Bremner and Johnny Giles were renowned as players not to be trifled with. The universal dislike of the team made them even stronger as a unit.

This strength was emphasised in their reputed policy of looking after each other on the field. If, for instance, Allan Clarke had been badly fouled and injured, the offending person would have been noted by the Leeds players. Shortly afterwards the offender would, so I was told, be on the receiving end of the same treatment, by a player other than Clarke.

Lee Chapman, taken from More Than a Match

You just can't afford to be an individual at Leeds, because people play together instinctively in the Leeds team, and now it's the only way I know how to play.

Allan Clarke

The likes of Allan Clarke at Leeds and Terry Paine of Southampton were sly. There was always one or two sneaky ones. They were not up front about it.

Tommy Smith

I had nobody to blame but myself for getting my marching orders in what was supposed to be a show-piece match at Wembley. I allowed myself to be provoked by the infamous Leeds tactics, first an off-the-ball whack from Johnny Giles followed soon afterward by a crafty dig from Bremner that brought on the red mist of temper.

I went after Bremner and we were both ordered off after swapping wildly aimed punches. To this day neither Billy nor I could explain why, as we walked off, we both pulled off our shirts in disgust. It was an incident seen by millions on television at a time when the game was under the microscope because of increasing violence on the pitch and the escalating hooliganism problem. It was the disrespectful shirt-stripping more than the swapped punches that upset the establishment and they were determined to make an example of us. We were both punished with what was then a massive £500 fine plus a five-week suspension which meant missing eleven matches. I vowed to keep my shirt on in future.

Kevin Keegan, taken from The Seventies Revisited

Gentlemen, the first thing you can do for me is throw your medals in the dustbin because you've never won anything fairly. You've done it by cheating.

Brian Clough's first team talk on becoming Leeds manager, taken from Clough: A Biography

That hurt. No collection of players had worked harder to create success. The physical emphasis in our game had gone. We'd matured into a very good footballing side.

Peter Lorimer's response to Clough, taken from Clough: A Biography

If he [Don Revie] had one chink in his armour it was that he probably paid teams far more respect than they deserved. He should have just told us to go out and beat 'em. Just left it to us.

Norman Hunter

I hate managing them but what can I do? They're filthy and they cheat. They've got it off to a fine art. If the pressure's on, someone goes down in the penalty area to give them time to regroup; then one of them gets boot trouble, which is just an excuse for the trainer to pass on messages from the bench. You wouldn't believe what they're capable of.

Brian Clough on managing Leeds, taken from Clough: A Biography

My wife used to hate Norman Hunter. Every time we played Leeds it was always a battle. Sometimes the football went by the board. She used to say: 'I hate that Norman Hunter. If I could get hold of him I'd kill him!' Norman and I now do after-dinner speaking together and she has got to know Norman and she can't believe that Norman Hunter is such a nice fellah. It's the same with Nobby; once you get to know them they are great lads.

Tommy Smith

4 Steel Toecaps or Carpet Slippers, the Pain's Still the Same

The 1960s

One of the strangest things, and the funniest, that I ever saw on a football field happened during a semi-final of a Youth World Cup that I played in during the early 1960s. I was a spectator watching Northern Ireland play an East European team and the East European goalkeeper kept shouting at his centre half; it was reminiscent of the way that Schmeichel screams at the Manchester United defenders nowadays. The centre half turned around, walked up to the goalkeeper and knocked him out cold. We couldn't believe it.

Tommy Smith

There are a few brave players around, chaps I look at and think 'He's as tough as me!' But players I admire and respect for that asset.

Norman Hunter and Billy Bremner, of Leeds, are two of the bravest. Then there is Liverpool's Tommy Smith, I've never had any clashes or bother with that trio. We seem to respect each other, like fast bowlers do in cricket. I used to play in the same England youth side as Tommy Smith, so perhaps I learned a healthy respect for his bravery.

Ron 'Chopper' Harris, taken from Soccer the Hard Way

I was a reserve standing in the tunnel at Upton Park one day when Bolton Wanderers came down with a team of hard nuts. They were all saying, 'We're going to wipe the field with you pansies.'

Every team seemed to feel the same. Wherever we went they seemed to want to get stuck into us; got all steamed up about giving West Ham a kicking. We were everybody's London hate team.

Maybe we brought it on ourselves. In midwinter, we'd get to

some of those tough cold grounds in the north and we'd upset the locals by going out to play wearing gloves. They just thought we were a bunch of fairies. It was like a red rag to a bull with their players. They couldn't see the sense of it. Ron used to say, 'Put the gloves on; you can't concentrate on playing football when you've got cold extremities.'

Bobby Moore, taken from Bobby Moore:
The Life and Times of a Sporting Hero

As a boy, I loved watching Tommy Banks playing for Bolton Wanderers at left back. When Tommy went into the tackle, the winger would end up on the running track, but there was a sort of basic integral honesty in the challenge.

These are not the villains of football, these are honest men. They'll take both ball and man, but 99 times out of 100 will do so openly without recourse to underhand measures. This is certainly true of the likes of Tommy Smith and Norman Hunter.

Referee Gordon Hill, taken from Give a Little Whistle:
The Recollections of a Remarkable Referee

In the first minute Gerry Byrne got in a hard tackle, and Bob, who was sitting fairly close to me, lost his temper. 'It's bloody happened again,' he said. 'It was an accident,' I said. 'Go on, you so-and-so,' said Bob. 'Shut up,' I said.

'Do you want to fight or something?' said Bob.

'Let's go to the back of the stand – the quicker the better,' I said. We were carrying on like a couple of children, but fortunately, sanity prevailed. Bob and I are very friendly. He's my type of man – he's a bad loser!

Bill Shankly on the then Bury manager Bob Stokoe

I'm not suggesting I'm a soccer angel. Far from it – and I've got the 'crime sheet' to prove the fact that I have learned a few lessons the hard way. I reckon that every class side needs the 'Chopper' type to achieve the blend with class and finesse that spells success. There are a few iron men around in the top flight these days, not only in England but on the Continent and in

South America as well, and there are far more who play the game hard than there are angels.

I've got the scars to prove that it has not been one-way traffic so far as I'm concerned when the going has got tough.

Ron 'Chopper' Harris, taken from Soccer the Hard Way

They were very physical, very hard and not always sporting. They could be vicious at times – but only for the ninety minutes. As soon as the game was finished you'd see Ron Yeats and Tommy Smith, and they were the nicest fellows of them all, people I count as friends. But when they had that red shirt on, they wouldn't let anyone beat them.

Joe Royle on Everton v Liverpool derbies

Calvin Palmer of Stoke City once butted me at Anfield in front of the Kop. He cut me above the eye, he was only a little fellah so he had to jump up to do it. Mind you I did get him back when we were down at Stoke a couple of months later. It wasn't a case of an eye-for-an-eye but it was definitely a case of a tooth-for-a-tooth, I can assure you.

Tommy Smith

I'm not that high on the list of hard players I have known. At Chelsea in my time we have had Frank Upton and Cliff Huxford – and they didn't come much harder than those two. Frank and Cliff were hard and fair; I was glad they were in my camp though.

Ron 'Chopper' Harris, taken from Soccer the Hard Way

Shanks brought him down from Scotland to seal up the middle and, really, he frightened half the country out of playing by his sheer presence. A very, very good centre half and certainly the hardest that I had to play against.

Joe Royle on Ron Yeats

I've discussed foul play several times with retired players, and they tell me what they used to get away with. I know that if anything the modern game is cleaner.

Simply because referees have been clamping down more often and harder. We are often penalised for things that would have been overlooked a few seasons past.

Ron Yeats

I couldn't tackle a fish supper. I think I only made one tackle in my life; that was in a Scotland v England game when I tackled Jimmy Greaves – that sticks in my mind.

Jim Baxter

I was the guy who kicked an opponent if he hurt John.

Alan Mullery on being Johnny Hayne's minder

In our time, you'd get sent off for the sort of tackles from behind we see nowadays.

Tony Waddington

He was playing superbly, totally tying up his opposing full back, who was being made to look a bit of a fool by Douglas' skill. Then, midway through the first half, the young full back clearly decided the only way to stop Douglas was by illicit means – kicking hell out of him. Douglas was sent sprawling by a clumsy foul but, after treatment, was able to continue. Despite my flagging vigorously, the referee took no notice of me. A few minutes later Douglas was kicked even more violently. Again he continued and again the referee ignored me, the linesman. After the third foul, Douglas decided he had had enough and limped back to the dressing room. The referee took no action against the young full back.

Referee Keith Hackett on the frustration of being a linesman when former Blackburn and England legend, Bryan Douglas, was receiving a kicking, taken from Hackett's Law: A Referee's Notebook

He never shirked a challenge in his life and hated to see any player 'bottle' a tackle, even if he was on the other side. Dave just couldn't understand it because it was foreign to his nature.

Not that many Spurs players were guilty of such evasive action if he was around. I knew a few who would jump out of a tackle, but once Dave was at their side they seemed to forget their own fear and draw strength from his presence. Dave inspired his own team mates and intimidated opponents, many of whom went strangely quiet after being on the receiving end of a Mackay blockbuster. He believed football was a man's game and expected no favours on the field, yet he never got out to hurt anybody and had no time for a player who went 'over the top' with a tackle. Not that many tried it on him. Because of the strength of his tackling, Dave had a reputation as a hard man which I felt caused him to get less than the credit he deserved for his skills. And he was one of the most skilled players I've seen. Right foot, left foot, fierce volley or cunning job. He was such a talented all-round performer he could have played in any position.

Pat Jennings on Dave Mackay, taken from An Autobiography

One of the things that has gone from football is give and take. I tackled Rodney Marsh once; he came in like a rocket. Whoff! it was like hitting a brick wall. I'm tackling him, I'm coming in at speed and I just stopped dead, I ran into him. The foul was against me. He lifted me up. He didn't lie there squealing, trying to get me sent off. It was accepted; you've got to accept it; you give it and you take it. I don't go out to deliberately kick anyone. I want to play football. I love great footballers. I know people who are supposed to be hard and kick people. I don't like them. I like football players. I like people who can play.

Dave Mackay

In Nicholson's era Spurs always had a five-a-side match after training in the old ball court at White Hart Lane. It was run by the physiotherapist Cecil Poynton and the rules were that anything went, tackles, shoves, kicks, anything.

Before his first experience I took Terry Venables to one side and explained the rules and told him that if anyone had a go at him, he must have a go back. Terry had a habit of shielding the ball with his back to an opponent and sticking his backside out and in the first minute on this particular morning he was trapped in the corner by Dave Mackay. Out went the backside and up went Dave's left boot, right between Terry's legs. Venables went down like a sack of potatoes, picked himself off the floor and threw a right-hander at Mackay. All hell broke loose as players from each side jumped in and threw punches. The crazy thing was that Cecil Poynton loved to see the players knocking each other about.

'Go on lads, get stuck in. You're not going to let Dave get away with that are you, Terry,' he shouted at the top of his voice.

Mackay and I were always kept apart during five-a-sides because Cecil Poynton knew that the short fuse that the two of us had guaranteed a competitive training session.

Alan Mullery, taken from An Autobiography

On my very first day there, I clashed with Dave Mackay in the gymnasium. As I tried to go by him, Dave hit me right in the balls with his fist. I folded over in agony and fought to get my breath, but when I had recovered, I thought to myself, I won't make a big deal about it, that could have been an accident.

The next time I got the ball, I slid it past him again as he came in to challenge me, and once more he whacked me in the balls. This time I was sure it was not an accident; I turned round and punched him smack in the face. Unfortunately, I had a ring on my middle finger and it sliced his cheek open and damaged my knuckle. He had a scar on his face for a few days and it was quite a while before I could get the ring off my finger, because the knuckle swelled up so badly.

All the boys jumped in to break us up, but by then honours were about even – he had belted me in the balls, but I had punched him in the face. Things remained a little strained between us for a couple of days, because we were both strong characters and he was obviously determined to sort me out and find out what I was made of, but we went over the road to the pub for a shandy after training one day, had a chat, and were fine from then on.

Terry Venables, taken from Venables: The Autobiography

I can still see him lifting Billy Bremner, Leeds' tough little captain, off the floor with one hand and clashing over the incident when he threatened former top referee Norman Burtenshaw.

In another match against Bristol City, an opponent went right over the top in the first minute, Dave reacted angrily and the referee sent him off. Mackay just looked him between the eyes and said: 'You bastard, the game has been going one minute and you are sending me off. There are 60,000 Spurs fans watching this and if you want to get out alive I suggest you change your decision.' The referee changed his mind!

I don't know how he got away with things like that but he did and everyone, team mates and opponents, loved and respected him for it.

Alan Mullery on Dave Mackay, taken from An Autobiography

It was my first game for about eighteen months. I had broken my leg twice. It was a throw in for Leeds and I'm marking Billy Bremner. They threw it to Billy and I pushed him in the back. I never knocked him over. It was a foul. He came right round behind me and kicked me on the left leg. It was more fear than anything else; for my leg, it was instinctive. I didn't say, 'I'm going to do this.' I didn't whack him. I just grabbed him. I was so shocked, he didn't kick me on the right leg, he kicked me on the left leg. It was shock, fear and me being aggressive. Nothing nastier than that. There were no slaps or pushes, no punches. But Billy was a hard guy. He got kicked and he kicked back. If I got kicked I kicked back. But you've got to be careful that you don't get sent off. It turned out a very good picture, probably Billy wouldn't agree with that.

Dave Mackay on the fracas that led to the famous photograph with Billy Bremner

Dave says that I caught him from the back. Well, if you've ever seen Dave Mackay play there's only one place to catch him and that's from the back. You're certainly not going to go head on with him. Dave must have taken exception to it and he grabbed me around the throat and told me exactly what he was going to do to me if he ever got the opportunity in the next thirty or forty minutes of the game. Fortunately for me he never got that opportunity. I never allowed Dave the opportunity. I played anywhere away from Dave for the rest of the game.

Billy Bremner on the Dave Mackay incident

Ron Greenwood and John Lyall shied away when you mentioned putting some stick about. The emphasis was on skill. That was also the thought in our minds.

I look on tackling as a skill. Any time I see a defender just whacking through the back of a forward's legs to get at a ball, that to me is ignorance. You can't win the ball if you've got a body in front of you. You don't have to go around kicking people up in the air to be a good tackler. The art is to deny a forward space and force him to knock the ball away.

Bobby Moore, taken from Bobby Moore:
The Life and Times of a Sporting Hero

Somebody would come and kick a lump out of him, and he'd play as though he hadn't noticed. But ten minutes later... whoof!... he had a great 'golden boy' image, Moore. But he was hard.

Geoff Hurst on Bobby Moore

I admire teams like Liverpool and Leeds. They have players who get stuck in and fight for the ball. They are hard, but they are prepared to work for the Cause – to win.

Ron 'Chopper' Harris, taken from Soccer the Hard Way

The diminutive winger Albert Johanneson who played in the 1965 Cup Final against Liverpool, was a quick, slight, delightfully skilful player but he had a reputation as a faint-heart. Chris Lawler, who marked him for Liverpool at Wembley, recalls being instructed to put Johanneson under physical pressure early in the game, to mark him closely and stop him getting the ball: That's what I was told to do, you know. Cos if you did let him play, he *would* play – he was very quick. But if you put pressure on him, he'd pack in. He did get abuse from other players. It was too much for him. This, added to the tension of the occasion, made the South African crumble. The other Leeds men did little to assist Johanneson. They just moaned. There were no substitutes in those days and Johanneson's broken spirit effectively reduced them to ten men.

Dave Hill, taken from Out of his Skin:
The John Barnes Phenomenon

Albert was quite a brave man to actually go on the pitch in the first place, wasn't he? And he went out and did it. He had a lot of skill. A nice man as well . . . which is, I suppose, the more important thing, isn't it? More important than anything.

George Best on Albert Johanneson

I was once caught by Johnny Giles, and it could have ended my career. At the start of the game he said to me, 'Why can't you be like Bobby Charlton? He's a gentleman.' I ignored that. Those kinds of remarks didn't bother me. Then, about an hour into the game, he came in over the top. An over-the-top tackle is when a player brings his boot down on the shin bone of his opponent. When done at speed and with enough pressure applied the shin bone breaks. The tackle, needless to say, is completely illegal. Because we were playing Leeds I was wearing shinguards. If I hadn't been wearing them my leg would most probably have been broken. As it was, Giles' studs tore through my sock, split the shinguard and cut my leg open. And then Giles had the nerve to say to me again, 'Why can't you be more like Bobby Charlton?'

I was hurt. But I wasn't going to stay down. I wasn't going to let him know that he had hurt me. That would have been belittling myself. The way I played made soccer like a combat sport and I certainly wasn't going to let my opponents know that they had harmed me. And they only rarely did. Instead I raised my performance to meet the challenge. I used to love playing against teams like Chelsea, Liverpool and even Leeds, teams with recognised hard men, because I usually played well against them.

George Best, taken from Where Do I Go From Here?

It became policy to pay special attention to the genius in the opposition. Until nowadays he has to be a genius indeed to survive a match without a scratch. The theory is, and it is a very effective one, that two ordinary players, or three at a pinch, can counter one genius.

This is all very well. But we have to be careful we do not drive individuality out of the game altogether.

This two-ordinary-players-on-to-one-genius idea is in fact a policy of negation. It is based on the premise that the first rule is to stop the other team instead of being to get on with the job of winning straight from the kick-off. And if football is to be a game of not losing instead of a game of winning there is something radically wrong with it.

Sir Matt Busby, taken from Soccer at the Top: My Life in Football

George Best was very, very hard. Bestie played with some horrendous injuries that no player should have played with. He was a brave little fellow. He was ten stone wet through, he could ride tackles, he got a lot of stick, he was tremendous. In those days the referees were different as well. The referees would sort out the so-called hard men immediately. The player got a certain amount of protection. But Bestie could give it as well, Bestie could dish it out.

Tommy Docherty

Basically, Best makes a greater appeal to the senses than the other two. His movements are quicker, lighter, more balletic . . . he has ice in his veins, warmth in his heart, and timing and balance in his feet.

Danny Blanchflower comparing Best with Matthews and Finney

Our right back, Paul Reaney, doesn't stand on ceremony when he comes up against George Best, and he is determined to do the best he can to stop the Irish wing genius. The Stretford Enders don't like Paul, and they don't go much for me, either, because I'm not frightened of tackling Big Jack's brother, or Denis Law, or any of 'em.

I can say that, normally, the games between the two Uniteds

are hard-fought, but fair; they don't usually end up as kicking matches, as some folk seem to think every game in which Leeds played was meant to finish.

Billy Bremner, taken from You Get Nowt for Being Second

George Best had been felled by a full back who was noted for his ability to get in a really tough tackle. The referee gave the defender a ticking-off. The culprit answered back: 'What else do you expect me to do? He's making me look a right idiot!'

Alex Stepney

I had nothing but contempt for the so-called hard men. For hard men I always read, men who couldn't play. Because if you do have the skills, the real talent, you're not going to squander them in spending the afternoon trying to kick an opponent. You're going to play football. That's why I always made it a point to try and stick the ball through the legs of my markers the first time they came in and tried to tackle me. I did it against Ron Harris of Chelsea, Paul Reaney of Leeds and Liverpool's Tommy Smith, though it was dangerous trying it against Smithy – it used to aggravate him and made him more determined to kick you into the stands – but I still always tried it.

In a way they made it easy for me. I always knew that Harris and Smith and Reaney, or Reaney's team mate Norman Hunter, were going to be snapping around my legs during a game. I knew they were going to be climbing all over me. And because I knew where they were – I could hear them, I could smell them – it gave me an advantage. I was always expecting them to come in on me – and if you're expecting it you can get away from it.

George Best, taken from The Good, the Bad and the Bubbly

I don't doubt that many referees would have had Best back in the dressing room after 34 minutes for what seemed a blatant attack on Yeats. Those who seek to minimise the offence say Best pushed rather than punched Yeats and a booking was adequate. That was not my view. If it was just an innocent push Best should not have been booked at all. Best's explanation is that off balance, he fell into Yeats. The Liverpool skipper says,

'Best's hand grazed my jaw, I was off balance and down I went.'

Best is gifted with football genius in far greater measure than most present day players, but the temperament failure to which he is suspect is a weakness which must be remedied now if his talents are to reach full maturity. Undoubtedly his tantalising cleverness brings on more than usual provocation, but this is a price of fame that did not stop men like Matthews, Finney and now Liverpool's Peter Thompson from getting on with their game.

Horace Yates on the occasion when George Best punched Ron Yeats to the ground

Great players are individualists. That's what makes them great players. They do not conform readily. They do the unexpected. That is also why they are great players. If they did what was expected they would be ordinary players.

Greatness is doing things that are different, things the ordinary player cannot do.

Sir Matt Busby, taken from Soccer at the Top: My Life in Football

You couldn't frighten him. Plenty tried. He used to be kicked all over the park. When he was younger, he would just get up – if he could – shrug his shoulders, and get on with tormenting the opposition. Similar to Willie Henderson, in that respect. When he grew a little older, and started getting bruises on the bruises, his temper grew shorter. Can you blame him?

Jim Baxter on George Best, taken from Baxter: The Party's Over

There was an Arsenal defender named Peter Storey. Every time I played against him he would tell me, before the kick-off, that he was going to break my leg, and worse. I used to look forward to my confrontations with Storey and men like him. I used to love it when players said they were going to do that to me. At the first opportunity I got I would run straight at them and slip the ball through their legs and run around them. Sometimes I would then bring the ball back and do it again. I took particular pleasure in turning Storey inside out and leaving him on his backside: in other words, humiliating him.

George Best, taken from The Good, the Bad and the Bubbly

You think of the Liam Bradys, Frank Stapletons, Malcolm McDonalds, the classy players at Arsenal. But now, all these years later, I can be honest. The most important thing, from a manager's point of view, was a player like Peter Storey. You look at, say, the Manchester United midfield and Peter Storey would take three of them out in the first few seconds. Liam Brady and Trevor Ross would think, 'Good boy, Peter, we'll now get on with scoring a few goals.' Players like Peter Storey allowed their team mates to play without fear of retribution from the opposition.

Terry Neil on Peter Storey

I sprint across to our left wing. Glancing up I see Ron Harris moving in for it too. We both have about the same distance to cover to reach the ball but I fancy my chances. I reach the ball first, flick it forward with the outside of my right boot and just as I'm taking to my toes, Harris' tackle hits me. It's lower than usual, just above knee level. I crash to the ground as a searing pain shoots down the right side of my knee. Old Jack Crompton has tottered out of the dugout, sprayed my knee with PR spray to deaden the pain, washed my face with a sponge and shuffled back into the dugout before Paddy Crerand has spirited the 10 yards to see if I'm OK. From the resulting free kick Best scores and United win the game.

George Best, taken from The Best of Times

Another booking, and one I reckon a bit harsh, was in a game against Manchester United. The newspapers headlined the incident the next day – and millions more saw for themselves on television. I tackled George Best and he rolled over on the ground apparently in agony. The United trainer came on and gave him treatment and I was booked.

When the game restarted, a short free kick sent Best racing off from right to left of the pitch and a backheel led to a goal. The crowd booed George, but the fact was that the goal stood. And I was in the referee's book. George's recovery, to my mind, was amazing.

The referee had spoken to me a minute or two earlier after a tackle on Best and the question that will long remain in my mind is; 'Did George play it up because of this?'

Ron 'Chopper' Harris, taken from Soccer the Hard Way

I don't really mind that I'm only remembered as a bloke who went in hard. It's better than not being remembered at all. But I was never what you'd call a gifted player so I had to play to my strengths.

And that involved stopping the other teams playing at all costs.

One of my early managers said to me: 'When you get out on the park, I want you to kick seven shades of s*** out of anyone who gets near you.'

It just went on from there. They'd say to me: 'If Bestie goes off for a s*** you stay with him.'

But I never saw myself as a dirty player. I'd always go for the ball. Quite often, I'd take the man as well.

But that was more a case of bad timing than anything else.

Ron 'Chopper' Harris

I haven't mentioned George Best as a player I admire because I have had a few dust-ups with him in our time. Yet, in fairness, I must say that, when Chelsea beat Manchester United 4–0 at Old Trafford in the 1968–69 season, I had an after-the-match drink with him and am prepared to concede that my previous opinions of George may have been wrong. He was as nice as pie on that occasion and, with one or two of our lads fraternising with one or two of theirs in a friendly way after the game, I got an entirely different conception of him. He seemed so different off the field to the Best I have marked in the past and have had the brushes with.

Ron 'Chopper' Harris, taken from Soccer the Hard Way

Bobby Charlton comes over to me. His face is strained and concerned. 'You watch out for Ron Harris today, George,' he says as I tie my stockings with strips of bandage.

'Why?'

'Because I know what he's like. When it's a line ball, he'll come across and hit you around the waist and try to send you flying into the concrete wall. He doesn't give a toss what he does to you.'

I have no regrets about anything I have done in soccer, apart from a few foolish bookings from referees. I've thought to myself afterwards: 'What a mug – fancy getting into trouble for something as silly as that.'

I've been booked for dangerous play, for late tackles, once even for what a referee described as an 'over robust' tackle. That was on Bobby Charlton when we played Manchester United and, although Sir Matt Busby, the United manager, and George Best, wrote letters on my behalf, the tackle earned me a suspension.

Ron 'Chopper' Harris, taken from Soccer the Hard Way

Fans love to argue about who was the hardest hard man, and though Norman Hunter and Liverpool's Tommy Smith were particularly famed in my own playing era, I thought that Chelsea's Ron Harris was the toughest of the lot. Ron was extremely quiet when he played. He never said much, and kept a poker-face whatever happened, but he was very, very tough. I do not think that Jimmy Greaves ever played well against him, and not many did, in fact. Rodney Marsh played in a Cup quarter-final for QPR against Chelsea, at a time when Rodney was playing particularly well, but he got snuffed right out – he never had a kick all match, except from Ron, who kicked him a couple of times, which did not please him very much.

As a rule, Ron was not a dirty player, he was just a tough one. He would not disappoint you; if there was a hard man coming towards him, he would get the better of him every time. Roy Barry came to Coventry with the reputation of having been the hardest man in Scotland. They played Chelsea in his first game and what he was not going to do to Ron Harris was nobody's business. When he tried it, he ended up on the floor, and for good measure, Ron walked all over him, treading on his hand and his head.

Terry Venables, taken from Venables: The Autobiography

The one player Jimmy Greaves didn't like playing against was Ron Harris, Chelsea's tough captain who had the formidable nickname of 'Chopper'. Spurs were due to play Chelsea in an important game and on the Friday morning Jim told Bill Nicholson: 'I don't know why you are playing me, Harris never gives me a kick.'

Nicholson dismissed it as a joke but after one game when Jimmy had a stinker he tore into him. But Greaves just said with a shrug of the shoulders, 'I told you not to play me.'

Alan Mullery, taken from An Autobiography

Jimmy is a perky character and I have earned something of a reputation for shadowing him in our meetings and keeping him off the goal standard. Greavesy never moans. Plenty do – not him. Just watch the way he rides his knocks and, as you know, a forward of his type gets plenty of close attention. Once or twice I have been over-robust with Jimmy, but he has accepted it as part of the game. He may have the 'needle', but we always seem to part the best of friends.

A pal of mine told me that he saw Jimmy Greaves just before we played Spurs at Easter, 1968. 'What a holiday,' groaned Jim. 'Norman Hunter twice and Ronnie Harris.' I think I know how he felt.

Ron 'Chopper' Harris, taken from Soccer the Hard Way

I was up against Jimmy Hill, and he was up there towering above me. Every time I went up for the ball there he was, just leaning over the top of me. I thought, 'Right, I'm not having this all the game. Next time we go up I'll have his shorts off him.' Well, up we went, and I shoved me hand out and I missed 'em. Instead I caught him right between the legs. He screamed the place down. But he kept with me afterwards, all over the field. I went to the ref. I said, 'Hey, ref, look at this maniac with the beard. Look at the way he's after me.' It worked.

Tony Kay, taken from The Football Man:
People and Passions in Soccer

There was one lad called Johnny Morrissey who played at

Everton. Johnny was an outside left and he was compact. A good player. He was at Liverpool in the early days when I joined and I can remember him going over the top in five-a-side games. I thought, I'm not having this. So I started going over the top on him. What happened in the end was that he got transferred to Everton; behind Bill Shankly's back actually. Shanks wasn't too pleased with this. When we played Everton, and if John was playing, it was a tough game. Shanks would say to me, 'If you get sent off, Smithy, make sure they end up with ten men as well.' Which meant that I was to cripple John. But John could give it and he could take it.

Tommy Smith

I remember Tommy Docherty at Highbury. Like Alex Forbes before him, he was designated 'a hard fellow' by my companions on the terraces, but he was certainly a good and industrious player.

At the Bridge he would often take me on one side. 'If you get a chance to have a tackle in the first minute, let the fellow know he has been tackled,' he advised me.

'Reputations mean nothing in football,' insisted The Doc. 'If you've got to pull them down to size do so, but use only fair means to do it.'

Ron 'Chopper' Harris, taken from Soccer the Hard Way

Derek Dougan was the most difficult opponent I ever played against. He was quick, unorthodox, tricky and good in the air.

I first played against him when he was 21 years old and playing for Blackburn Rovers. He was like a bat out of hell. He's one of those fellows you'd like to meet again, just so you could catch them and kick 'em.

Brian Labone

If you ever saw him play, you wouldn't forget him. If you played against him he was a nightmare. I don't know who labelled him 'The Rhino', but I can tell you that when he charged in on goal, he looked as if only a bazooka would stop him. I'm not saying he was a great footballer. If I did, he'd probably sue me. But he was some asset to his team, if only for the panic he spread amongst his opponents.

Jim Baxter on Don Kichenbrand,
taken from Baxter: The Party's Over

In March 1967 I was involved in a personal feud with Jim Baxter in an FA Cup fifth round tie against Sunderland at Roker Park. I remonstrated with Baxter after he had committed a foul on Peter Lorimer. He called me a 'Catholic *******' and I replied by calling him a 'Protestant *******'. Baxter then fouled me, and was promptly booked by referee Ray Tinkler. Leeds forced a draw in that match, and on the day of the replay Baxter launched a scathing attack on me in the press. 'Giles was definitely going to do me . . . it was either foul or be fouled.' I am sure that if I met Baxter now he would have forgotten all about that feud.

Frankly, I have never come across a player who has refused to speak to another player on account of a bad foul or heated argument during a match. I am not denying that there are vendettas between certain clubs and individuals – but my point is that these are quickly forgotten at the final whistle.

Johnny Giles, taken from Forward with Leeds

Soccer is a mixture of good and bad, but few feuds survive the moment. A rush of blood can cause a moment of heat that is almost instantly forgotten. Two players can spend 90 minutes attempting to kick lumps out of one another, then leave the field arm in arm. The good pro respects the good pro – even if he'd like to smash him at a given moment.

Ron 'Chopper' Harris, taken from Soccer the Hard Way

People used to knock on the front door. It might be someone who had come to do a bit of decorating or the milkman. When I opened the door they would take a step back. They thought I was going to assault them or something. Off the pitch I have never been in trouble in my life.

Tommy Smith

Nobby and I have always been extremely close, which has prompted a number of people to ask what goes through my mind when I have to make a tackle on him, or vice versa.

We rarely come into contact on the field as he generally plays in the back four against Leeds. But we did clash in the tie at Villa Park . . . and I hope I never experience such a moment again.

Nobby had previously made only a handful of first-team appearances that season due to a cartilage operation on his right knee, and would probably not have played against Leeds had United's centre half Ian Ure not been ruled out through injury.

Nobby had a superb first half, and as we trooped off at the interval I remember feeling delighted for his sake that his knee had not given him any trouble. But then, fifteen minutes into the second half, we went into a strong tackle for a 50/50 ball just outside United's penalty area, and Nobby slumped to the ground clutching his right leg.

Afterwards, he admitted it was his own fault as, instead of making a block tackle in an effort to win possession, he had tried to kick the ball away. This meant that his foot jarred against mine.

As he lay there, motionless, I was convinced that he had sustained a serious injury. I felt sick, and started to cry.

No words can describe my feelings of relief when, after receiving attention from the trainer for a few minutes, Nobby sat up and smiled. I heard United's right half Pat Crerand shout: 'Don't worry, John, he's OK,' and then Nobby rose to his feet and signalled to the referee he was fit to carry on.

Johnny Giles on his brother-in-law Nobby Stiles,
taken from Forward with Leeds

Every team needs a man with his capacity for work, and the willingness to hustle and tackle in midfield. In this capacity he did a fabulous job for England in the World Cup and I certainly would rather have him on my side than against me.

Francis Lee on Nobby Stiles, taken from Soccer
Round the World: A Football Star's Story from Manchester
to Mexico

Nobby Stiles a dirty player? No, he's never hurt anyone. Mind you, he's frightened a few.

Sir Matt Busby

I can remember playing against Nobby Stiles in a Liverpool Reserves against Manchester United Reserves game. I was inside left and Nobby was right half for United. I remember kicking hell out of him and him kicking hell out of me. When I see him now he says, 'I remember you, you was the first forward to kick hell out of me.' Generally it was the defenders who kicked the forwards. Nobby said it was the first time a forward had kicked him.

Tommy Smith

I remember writing in my weekly newspaper after the first leg: 'I was sorry Nobby Stiles could not come to the England training session this week . . . it would have been a good chance to give him the stud back he left in my leg in our League Cup tussle.'

After a sickening succession of injuries that looked like finishing him in the game Nobby had come back to the United side just in time for their League Cup semi-final game, and he had done a fantastic job. If he couldn't tackle you he would throw his body in front of you as though he was a human battering ram.

Nobby was magnificent. I certainly felt the rough edge of Nobby several times in the match, and although my article about giving him his stud back was written humorously it was not far off the truth. Certainly Stiles is not really a vicious player, the sort that goes for you rather than the ball. At the same times he is a hard tackler and he does let you know he is there if he is marking you.

Francis Lee, taken from Soccer Round the World: A Football Star's Story from Manchester to Mexico

The Manchester United team I played in could also look after itself, of course. We had Paddy Crerand. And we had Nobby Stiles. He was the man the other fans came to boo. It was

Nobby's style. He had a reputation for being hard but it was the way he played that made him hard to get the better of. He would be assigned on specific occasions to do a specific job and he did it better than anybody I have seen. We rarely marked man for man, but if we played a team like Benfica and Eusebio was playing it was Nobby's job to stop him.

He was once assigned the task of stopping me. It was in an England-Northern Ireland game at Wembley. Nobby came up to me before the start and said, 'Sorry Bestie, I've got to stick to you. I've been told not to leave your side.'

I said, 'Fine, that's your job – let's see who wins.' He was very difficult and it's debatable who came out on top. I scored. But they beat us 2–1. And I had Stiles on my back the whole game.

He didn't take any prisoners but he was more awkward than malicious. He was niggly, like a terrier, always at your heels. You couldn't knock him away. And if you did get past him he came right on after you. He also couldn't see. He was as blind as a bat. He wore contact lenses but he kept losing them, they kept falling out, and he spent almost as much time looking for his lenses as he did looking for me. That made it harder, not easier, because, without his lenses he wasn't able to judge distances properly and he kept clattering into me.

George Best, taken from The Good, the Bad and the Bubbly

There's no disputing the fact that some players do over-exaggerate when they are fouled or tackled and some of the histrionics deserve an Oscar. It's as much a temptation for a player to make a fuss when he is having a rough time from an opponent as it is for the opponent to shirk a tackle for fear of falling foul of a referee.

Ask England's Nobby Stiles his views on this subject. Or Tommy Smith. There isn't an Iron Men of Football Society, but 'Chopper' Harris is ready to subscribe his membership if the other lads think it's a good idea. We alleged tough guys are often more sinned against than sinners.

Some players are 'branded' as trouble makers or dirty players, but so often the fans don't know what is going on and the provocation and gamesmanship that exists in soccer.

Ron 'Chopper' Harris, taken from Soccer the Hard Way

Since the 1966 World Cup, no player has been more maligned than little Nobby Stiles. Like me, he hasn't always been a gentleman on the field but, again like me, he has suffered some outrageous treatment from fans and opponents, even when he hasn't deserved it.

Nobby Stiles, Denis Law, Alan Ball . . . they are my type of players. What I call truly dedicated professionals. I know that Nobby Stiles has been booed before the game has even started – in this country as well as on the Continent. The Stretford Enders would be the first to argue that a man should be given a fair chance, and that this wasn't being given to Nobby; and I would be the first to agree with them. So why not accord the same fair treatment to players who are in opposition at Old Trafford? It cuts both ways.

Billy Bremner, taken from You Get Nowt for Being Second

Playing against England at Wembley in 1967 Alan Ball kept on confusing my shins with the ball. He was running about, demented, like a fart in a bottle. Billy Bremner had told us before the match that Alan was nicknamed Jimmy Clitheroe, because of his high, squeaky voice. Alan resented this, so naturally, that's what we shouted to him throughout the match. He wasn't the only Englishman to go daft that day. Jackie Charlton wasn't in the best of moods either, and Nobby Stiles, minus those front teeth, looked as if he could cheerfully have killed us all. But only Ball kept on kicking, maybe Bremner shouldn't have asked him, 'D'you think you'll be a player when your voice breaks?'

Jim Baxter, taken from Baxter: The Party's Over

I'm very placid most of the time, but I blow up very quickly. I shout and wave my arms, and my lip twitches. I become incoherent and I swear. All at the same time.

Jack Charlton

There was a time when I actually ordered another player to deliberately go out and kick him (Alan Ball).

It happened after I'd left Nantwich and worked my way back into the Football League as chief coach with Stoke City. Of course, the inevitable clash arrived when Stoke met Everton, for whom Alan was then playing.

I had always wanted him to do well in every game he has played before or since, but on that day he was the one player in the Everton side that I knew could give Stoke problems – and, like the professional I have always prided myself on being, I decided that if there was any way of stopping him I was going to use it.

I knew Alan had a bad ankle which needed strapping in order for him to play. I told him a few days before the match: 'If you play with that ankle you'll be carried off before the game is half over. I'll make sure one of our lads never leaves you alone and kicks that ankle at every opportunity.'

As cocky as ever he replied: 'Tell your lads what you like, they'll have to catch me before they can kick me.'

The man I nominated to do the hatchet job on Alan was a tough defender named Eric Skeels. 'Go out and get him,' I ordered. 'But he's your son,' said Eric.

'I don't care. If we don't stop him he'll murder us. He's got a dodgy ankle already, a few whacks and he'll be off.'

And sure enough everything went exactly according to plan. Skeels kept kicking Alan and long before the end he was carried off with his ankle swollen to the size of a balloon. What was even more important Stoke won the match and, at the time, that was all that mattered to me.

But although Alan accepted my tactics as part of the game and never reproached me for it, I had a terrible time with his mother. She was furious with me for, as she called it, 'stooping so low just to win a football match as to order your own son to be deliberately injured'.

She was so furious in fact that she left home and went to stay with her mother. It was three days before I could persuade her to return, and I had to take a bunch of roses and make a lot of apologies to achieve that. I'm glad to say it's the only time I've been on the opposite side to Alan.

Alan Ball senior, taken from It's All About a Ball

Billy Bremner told me that when they played against Bally they used to call him Jimmy Clitheroe. So I can remember going out, standing in the tunnel and Bally was right beside me. I meant it when I said it, I said, 'Congratulations, Alan, on winning the World Cup.' Alan said, 'Oh, thanks very much big man, have a good game, we'll have a few drinks after the match.' We gets on the park and after about two minutes I sidled up besides Bally and said: 'Is it true that Jimmy Clitheroe is your daddy?' The next thing he says, 'Yer fucking Scotch —, yer think yer a smart arse.' I said, 'Wait a minute, I want to ask yer a question.' I said to Billy Bremner, 'Billy, he said it's a load of lies.' Billy Bremner shouted back. 'Jimmy Clitheroe is his daddy right enough.' So people keep asking me why Bally wanted to kick me at Wembley? That is the reason. He had no sense of humour, the man.

Jim Baxter on the goading of Alan Ball at Wembley 1967

Candidly, I believe such players as these have been at least as much sinned against as they have sinned – for the simple reason that many of the incidents which have brought official wrath down upon their heads have been caused by retaliation.

And, frankly, there are other players who have kept out of trouble when they deserved to be suspended for life – because these are the real guilty parties, the ones who put the boot in first. If you're ruthless enough and cunning enough, you can weigh up the situation when you're playing against someone who is known to have a fiery temperament. You can bide your time, sat on the referee's blind side – and give your opponent such a vicious, yet well-concealed blow . . . with boot or fist . . . that he is bound to flare up. That's when the referee spots the trouble. Your low cunning has enabled you to adopt the air of an aggrieved party: your opponent, whose ire you have deliberately aroused, gets it in the neck. And the more he knows he was provoked, the more righteous is likely to be his indignant appeal to the referee . . . and the more likely he is to suffer.

Jack Charlton on Stiles, Bremner and Ball,
taken from For Leeds and England

The football picture of me as a snarling thug, chopping down the opposition, should give me a Jekyll and Hyde complex.

Not at all. Off the field I am an ordinary sort of bloke. On the park I play to win, and I reckon I play the game hard but fair. Soccer's a bit like marriage – you need a fair amount of give and take.

Ron 'Chopper' Harris, taken from Soccer the Hard Way

You knew that if you didn't compete with Leeds you were going to get kicked off the park. So you geed yourself up before you went out. It was out-and-out war.

Ian Hutchinson

Southampton's Terry Paine and Brian O'Neill were constantly talking at Bremner, and to me about Bremner. They were trying to antagonize him by saying things to me like: 'Oh come on, ref, he's refereeing the game. Sort him out.' But he just kept turning a blind eye to it.

I suppose the relationship Bremner and I had was that we could bollock one another and still have respect for one another. In that match against Southampton, for example, a Southampton defender was giving Mick Jones a bit of stick, and Bremner complained to me about it. Bremner wasn't nice about it – he was angry and he showed his anger. But I could take it because I know it was honest criticism and not meant in any way to belittle me nor as an attempt to control the game.

Gordon Hill, taken from Give a Little Whistle:
The Recollections of a Remarkable Referee

Nobby Stiles is not a dirty player . . . a player who sets out to injure or intimidate opponents. Why, then, has he been branded a soccer villain?

This is partly explained by the fact that he is too honest. His excitable nature makes him an obvious target for those players who try to goad rivals into retaliation and therefore get them sent off or booked by the referee.

I have seen many cases whereby a player has been sent off while the man responsible for starting the trouble has escaped punishment.

Players like Stiles are not given enough protection by referees against this and are therefore forced to take the law into their own hands. The sad truth is that the game's stars would not survive if they did not hit back.

This is the only way to stop an unscrupulous rival. He has to be made to realise that his opponents are as tough as he is.

Most players have been guilty of retaliation at some time or another, but the ones who land in trouble are those who make the mistake of retaliating openly – in front of the referee. This is what I mean by being *too honest*. It is not in Nobby's make-up to bide his time and get his own back on a player through professional cunning. When he is badly fouled he reacts instantaneously – he shows his anger and resentment.

I am not suggesting Nobby is some kind of soccer angel – far from it. My point is that any fouls he does commit are due to his determination and emotional involvement in a game, not premeditated skullduggery!

All the top teams have fiercely combative, rugged personalities like Stiles for the simple reason that creature players cannot operate effectively unless they have possession of the ball. For this reason I have always considered that Nobby has played a bigger part than anyone in the success of Bobby Charlton at club and international levels.

Charlton is not very good at winning the ball in midfield and has leaned heavily on Stiles in this respect. To put it another way, Stiles provides the bullets for Charlton to fire.

Giles on Stiles (his brother-in-law), taken from Forward with Leeds

He was very hard, very aggressive and very skilful. If he couldn't give the full back a chasing he used to give him a clobbering.

Francis Lee on Mike Summerbee

I once travelled 200 miles to play in a testimonial for QPR's Frank Sibley. Frank's team mate, Tony Hazell, was not a person who could play in charity matches. He kicked me, so I returned the compliment and was sent off.

Mike Summerbee

Just before Manchester City signed him from Doncaster he

knocked a referee out in a game. The referee sent him off and called him a name. T. C. turned around and stuck one on his chin. He only got a four-match ban!

Francis Lee on Tony Coleman

For my money Mike Summerbee was the best of the lot. He had all the skills – and he was hard, really hard. No defenders fancied their changes against Mike.

Tommy Booth

Mark Lazarus, the East Londoner who has been around with Orient, QPR, Wolves, Brentford and Crystal Palace, has talked to me about his 'crime sheet'. Mark admits he is no angel but, as a Jew, he has taken some severe provocation in his time in remarks from opposing defenders.

I have seen a player land a right-hander on an opponent when the referee has his back turned following the play, but a return punch has earned the first victim his marching orders. Of course, I am not defending retaliation, but the first 'crime' is often the more serious and how many times does the provoker escape?

I've been kicked and fouled hundreds of times, but I pride myself that I don't moan unless it is what I consider a diabolical stroke. I would hate to get a fellow professional sent off because I bleated to a referee.

Ron 'Chopper' Harris, taken from Soccer the Hard Way

Whenever West Ham have been successful at home they have had a strong man, a battler at wing half.

In the mid-sixties we had Eddie Bovington. In the mid-seventies they came up with Billy Bonds. Its been loosely talked about as adding steel to the West Ham team but that's too simple.

There was plenty of bite about West Ham if you knew where to look for it. Even Martin (Peters) had a nasty streak in him if something made him angry.

Bobby Moore, taken from Bobby Moore:
The Life and Times of a Sporting Hero

I would say Denis Law was the most difficult opponent I played against in the English game. He was a very, very tricky player and he didn't stand for fools. He'd get stuck into you, he was a bit sly as well. He used to have a go back and he used to try and scare people to death to get rid of them.

Tommy Smith

The one who I reckon is in a class of his own in the Football League is that fellow Denis Law. I admire him because he is always in the thick of a game and can take care of himself. You can't talk Denis off his game or get away with any of the usual pro tricks.

He's got a reputation for being tough so get in first before he strikes. It's like boxing. You weigh each other up, you feint and you parry – but the first blow is vital. My policy is to let them worry about me or my reputation.

I've handed out a bit of 'stick' to Denis the Menace in the course of a few games over the years – but he's given me back as good as I've given and got on with the game. Denis plays the game the way I like – he doesn't moan every time he gets kicked.

Ron 'Chopper' Harris, taken from Soccer the Hard Way

As a stirring game progressed and as Everton's position became more and more desperate, so Denis Law, whose act is not so much mime as pantomime, got under the crowd's skin by his propensity for not wanting to play the game, but to referee it. Finally he finished with a crack on the shin at outside right, nobody's friend, occasionally not even the friend of his own team mates. One may ask with good reason – 'What makes him do it?' The answer is natural volatility. If he weren't so volatile and temperamental with referees the chances are that he wouldn't be half the player he is.

Leslie Edwards

I was a particular fan of Denis Law, whom I thought was terrific, and rated him even ahead of George Best, though there was very little in it. Denis would play football and score his goals, whether it was a battle on a wet Thursday night in Oldham or a sun-drenched Saturday at the San Siro. He was a footballer for all seasons, an exceptional player.

Terry Venables

Denis once kicked me at Wembley in front of the Queen in an international. I mean, no man is entitled to do that, really.

Bobby Robson on Denis Law

Denis wouldn't think twice about giving you one. You would tackle Denis and all of a sudden it was like a needle in the side – whack, take that one! You had gone to make the tackle but you were the one who ended up hurt.

Emlyn Hughes on Denis Law

I went for a 50-50 ball with him and I thought I'd take it easy because Denis was my big pal. Christ, he nearly killed me. And I says, 'Den, what are you doing?' 'No friends on the park, son,' he says. 'The only friends I've got are in these red shirts for Manchester United.' So that was a lesson I learned and kept throughout my life.

Billy Bremner on Denis Law

Bobby Collins was a good footballer, but an extremely aggressive one, part of a team, including Norman Hunter, Paul Reaney and Billy Bremner, that, to put it mildly, was famous for its aggression. Every era has its hard men, of course, but whether every team needs a hard man is questionable. It really depends on what players you have. If you have a number of skilful players, you may need a hard man to win the ball for them, just as Nobby Stiles used to do for Law, Best and Charlton at Manchester United.

If you have three midfielders who are willing to do their bit in defence, even if all they do is close down space and work to win the ball, you may not need a hard man. It is important to have a blend of skill and hardness, and if you can find players who themselves are a blend of the two, then you are very fortunate. Denis Law, for example, was one such player, and

Desailly of AC Milan, who had such an outstanding European Cup Final against Barcelona in 1994, is another, but it is unusual.

Terry Venables, taken from Venables: The Autobiography

The biggest bone of contention among strikers is the tackle from behind. Of course, they are more prone to receiving these tackles than most because they are forced to play the ball with their backs towards goal and with defenders virtually breathing down their necks.

Nevertheless, without wishing to incur the wrath of the Geoff Hursts and Jeff Astles, I feel that if a striker is tackled from behind, it is invariably his own fault due to taking up a bad position to receive the ball.

Johnny Giles, taken from Forward with Leeds

Clogging is another matter. A player putting his boot 'over the top' of the ball and chopping down an opponent is becoming worse. These fellows are known throughout the game, yet they seem to get away with it every week. Some referees, it seems, don't honestly know the difference between going 'over the top' and a tap-dance. A bit of arm-waving and even a four-letter word should not be encouraged, but it's kid's stuff compared to the clogging that goes unpenalised. The first sign of a stud shown in a tackle and the offender ought to go off – for good.

It takes boldness by a referee to send a player off and too few of them will do it for the right reason. Somebody argues and he'll probably get the finger-waving bit or even sent-off. Yet a fellah can take a diabolical kick at a forward just going into the box and he often gets away with it. Maybe, referees have been brain-washed, like so many players, that putting the stick about is part of the modern game. I'm not advocating that forwards should be given a free run at goal and the tough tackle must be faced, but unless something is done to stop or, at least, curb the blatant clogger the game will die as a spectacle. There's not much fun in being kicked sky-high when going for goal.

Maybe the so-called Refs' Revolution and rule clamp-down

that started the 71/72 season will save the game. I sincerely hope so. The pity is it didn't come two or three years earlier.

Jimmy Greaves, taken from Let's Be Honest

Jim never seemed to take football seriously and never appeared to do any practice, although he must have done a bit somewhere along the line to have acquired that level of skill. When it came to matches, Jim really delivered. He was a natural ball-player and the game just seemed to come easily to him. Nothing seemed to bother him on the pitch. He would never query referees' decisions. Jim would just say, 'Leave it, Terry, it doesn't matter. Forget it and get on with the game.' It was only much later in his career, when he was a part-timer at Barnet, that he began to get into a great deal of trouble with referees and other players.

Terry Venables on Jimmy Greaves, taken from Venables:
An Autobiography

He could lose defenders by stealth and psychic game-reading. He took the ball-player's lion's share of the rough stuff without complaint, though he had the knack of placing himself away from it and had the facility for making the offender look like a big clumsy oaf. Which was not his intention, because gentleman Jimmy Greaves had not an ounce of venom in him. Typically he drifted out of the game with no great noise. I wish he had stayed longer.

Sir Matt Busby on Jimmy Greaves, taken from Soccer at the
Top: My Life in Football

A number of players dislike playing in advanced positions because of the bruising physical contact involved, but I personally found that my slight build helped me to overcome this problem to a certain extent.

Small players are inclined to be more mobile and possess better ball control than those who are tall, and well built, so they can evade physical contact more easily.

A classic example is West Ham's Jimmy Greaves, surely the greatest goal poacher of all time in Britain. Greaves, who is 5ft

8in tall and weighs just over 10½ stone, rarely gets 'clogged' by defenders because he is so quick off the mark.

Johnny Giles, taken from Forward with Leeds

The wee man deserves a great deal of credit for his sheer bravery because he would go at a player, be chopped brutally, receive a free kick and go at the same player again, knowing what was coming. It takes a very brave man to do that because he drove at players very quickly and, if he was brought down in full flight he could receive some very nasty blows time after time.'

Jim Craigh on his team mate Jimmy Johnstone

There have been a few occasions, of course, when I went beyond the mark and got away with it. Tommy Docherty has said to me more than once: 'Be careful' or 'You've been a wee bit silly'; one bit of advice was, 'Don't do it so openly.'

Dave Sexton, who succeeded The Doc as manager at the Bridge, likes people to tackle hard, but he insists on us keeping within the rules. His last words before each match are: 'You are a team. Look after each other and make sure no one's hurt.'

Managers split players into categories. At meetings they say things like: 'Give so-and-so a couple of hard tackles early on and he's finished for the game.'

Ron 'Chopper' Harris, taken from Soccer the Hard Way

Too many people think the big hammer is the magic wand for success in football. I'm afraid that a lot of what goes on during play makes me cringe. I am often appalled at what I see and I want no part in thuggery and gamesmanship that reaches a point of cheating.

Leicester manager Matt Gillies on the day of his resignation, November 1968

It was a match we thoroughly enjoyed because we played so well, but it caused a tremendous uproar in the Midlands press over the running battle Doug Fraser had with me. It is no good mincing words. Fraser used me as a punching bag.

Francis Lee on the Manchester City v West Brom League Cup Final 1970

5   I Always Went for the Ball but If I Sometimes Took the Man So Be It

The 1970s

Ray Kennedy came to Liverpool as a centre forward, Bill Shankly's last signing. At his first training session at Melwood, which was the First team against the Reserves, Larry Lloyd was playing centre half for the Reserves with Ray Kennedy centre forward for the First team. Big Larry wasn't too happy with what was going on and he butted Ray. Larry was actually sent off! Ray wasn't too keen to play centre forward after that in training sessions and Bob Paisley in his wisdom moved him back to midfield. Ray eventually became one of the greatest left halves who ever played the game. Larry was sold to Coventry.

Tommy Smith

The way things are going alarms me deeply. Hard men are nothing new in football. In my young days there were quite a few killers about, men who went in for rough play and intimidation . . . What is new and frightening about the present situation is that you have entire sides that have physical hardness for their main asset. They use strength and fitness to neutralise skill and the unfortunate truth is that all too often it can be done. George Best survives only because his incredible balance allows him to ride with the impact of some of the tackles he has to take. Because of their heart and skill, he and other outstanding players in the League can go on giving the crowds entertainment. And it's true that there are still a few teams who believe the game is about talent and technique and imagination. But for any one you'll find ten who rely on runners and hard men.

Sir Matt Busby, taken from Soccer at the Top: My Life in Football

Until the last few years this kind of thing was quite foreign to the First Division. But it has crept in at a remarkable rate. In my early days the teams with the greatest skill were the most consistently successful. As for the smaller fish, what they lacked in ability they made up for in guts coupled with determination, which, however, could turn too near violence. When I went to Peterborough I realised how much the physical factor mattered in the lower divisions, especially when one played away from home. In some games it was, almost literally, a battle from start to finish. But the experience of two years in the Third Division has physically stood me in good stead. I have developed a resilience which enables me to cope with physical assertion or aggression. Since this experience I have not missed many games through injury received from fouls.

First Division football was and still is thought to be light years away from that in the Third and Fourth Divisions. There teams relied on physical force (or 'physical contact'), hoping that this would make up for what they lacked in skill. There were different elements in this kind of play – late tackling, going over the top, kicking from behind, threatening gestures and language. There could be heard from time to time: 'I'll break your bloody leg!'

Derek Dougan, taken from The Sash He Never Wore

I don't believe in the tackle from behind rule. I think it's a man's game and should be played by men.

Rodney Marsh

I remember playing against Preston Reserves. We won the game about 5–0. A lady and a man approached me after the game. They said, 'Excuse me, can we have a word?' I said: 'Sure, what do you want?' They said: 'We would just like to shake your hand and thank you for not kicking our son!' Their son was playing inside left for Preston.

Tommy Smith

There were worse fates than being fouled, especially for George Graham, who saw himself very much as a man-about-town. In one game, George was involved in a mix-up in the opposition goal mouth, and next thing, he was flat on the deck, blood gushing down his face, as he groaned and twisted in agony. I ran over and said, 'Is it bad, George?' He just gasped, sounding as if he was going to breathe his last at any moment.

'You've got a kick in the head, George,' I said.

'Where?' he moaned.

'Just above the hairline.'

He opened his eyes and asked, 'Can you see it?'

'No, it's above the hairline.'

He sighed with relief: 'Thank Christ for that, I'm going dancing tonight.'

Terry Venables, taken from Venables: The Autobiography

Wingers were scared of him. He was to United what Tommy Smith was to Liverpool in his heyday at Anfield – and, like Smithy, Fitz could turn on some quality football. He wasn't just a clogger, though he could dish it out and take it. John Fitzpatrick was tigerish in his tackling, and so many wingers took a dive when they came up against him that it wasn't surprising referees were kidded – with the result that United's right back got his name in the book more often than should have been the case.

Sammy McIlroy on John Fitzpatrick, taken from Manchester United: My Team

He used to threaten you before you played the match.

Francis Lee on John McGrath

The only player I wanted to avoid was John McGrath of Newcastle. He was a vicious man. He'd even play in short sleeves in the frost.

Stan Bowles

In one replay, we'd been playing about twelve minutes totally on top in the game, and Mick Bernard goes over the top on Ron Yeats, right on the touchline. Ron Yeats turns round and smacks him. Right hook. Off you go, Mr Yeats. That's it, end of game. We played on and lost, unfortunately, 2–1.

Ray Mathias on Ron Yeats' dismissal against Stoke,
taken from Three Sides of the Mersey: An Oral History of
Everton, Liverpool and Tranmere Rovers

I had some proper run-ins with Chopper over the years. He used to get booked every time we played against each other. I always knew that I'd get a hard time from him.

But funnily enough I never saw him as a dirty type.

Now Johnny Giles from Leeds – he was a bit tasty and sly with it.

He'd wait until the ball had gone and kick you one. Everyone would be following the ball so he usually got away with it.

When Chopper took your legs from under you at least he'd be upfront about it.

I'd seen him after the match and say, '**** me, Chopper, you were a right **** today.'

But there was no hard feelings. It was part and parcel of the game.

Stan Bowles on Ron 'Chopper' Harris

Every time I played against Chopper, I took a right hammering.

But I gave as good as I got. He whacked me really hard one time so I jumped up and down on his chest.

He was coughing up blood according to the papers.

All the other Chelsea players piled in and it was a ******* mass brawl.

But I always stood up for myself. That's how I was brought up. Coming from Holloway, you learn from the pram to nut people who pick on you.

Charlie George on Ron 'Chopper' Harris

The Football League in this is like a sheriff in the Wild West. When he sees a lot of strangers coming into town, to prevent any trouble he takes all their guns away. We have the impression that the League is trying to stop players from taking their weapons (of which gamesmanship is one) on to the field. This means that players and managers are now having to think twice.

There is no doubt these measures are much tougher on defenders. There is also no doubt that a number of clubs are struggling for form because of the new code of conduct. This just proves how much some had previously relied on the physical side of the game. 'Get stuck in', 'Give him stick', and so on are not now as fashionable as they were.

One good thing about the way things are now, is that the attacking forward can go into the best probing positions – within the opponents' 18-yard area – without fearing that when he is taking on the defence he is going to get it from behind. It is distracting to have to keep one eye on the ball and the other on a possible aggressive defender. I always used to worry about dubious tackling from behind. It just crept into the game and got worse and worse as so many people got away with it unchecked.

I notice that now when I manoeuvre to draw people out of position I am better able to do it than used to be the case, simply because defenders have to challenge fairly, and not take me and the ball as they used to like to do. Some of them, that is.

Derek Dougan, taken from The Sash He Never Wore

Roy McFarland was the best I played against. He was very quick, excellent in the air and mean. One player who never gave me a kick was a geezer called John Talbot. He played for West Brom. He wasn't one of the best centre halfs around, but I couldn't make head nor tale of him. I just kept running in to him.

Joe Royle

I was blessed with the traditional Scottish nature, a bit on the fiery side, and Spurs' youth team coach Pat Welton would often warn me that opponents would try it on and attempt to upset me. It was Jack Charlton who taught me to be more professional in my approach when I moved up to the north-east with Middlesbrough. Never one to stand on ceremony as a player, Jack had exactly the same attitude as a manager and his favourite expression to describe an opponent would be, 'He's an effing chicken, man.' He would pick out players competing in my territory and, if it could influence the direction of the game, get me to sort them out. He believed the odd kick or two was quite legitimate within the framework of football.

Only one thing mattered to Jack in football, and that was winning. He was one of the school who knew that there were no prizes for coming second and he was perfectly willing to bend the rules to ensure success. He took me to one side before a game against Luton Town and told me that the only danger to us was through a midfield player named Peter Anderson and that under no circumstances was I to allow him to run the game. I took the point, made early contact and it was us who controlled the middle of the park that day.

Graeme Souness, taken from Graeme Souness: No Half Measures

Bobby Moore marked me on and off for fifteen years, and I couldn't even kick him once to unsettle his equilibrium or agitate him momentarily to swear at me – the only four-letter word to do with Bobby was TIME, he just had all the time in the world. Don't only ask me, either, ask Pele.

Bobby Gould

Although I was enjoying my football at QPR, I also had an occasional reminder that, in a young man's game, I was no longer quite as young as I used to be. We played Chelsea in an FA Cup quarter-final, and they had a strong side, with some good youngsters coming through, like Alan Hudson, Peter Osgood and David Webb. I was marking Hudson, who was then only eighteen. I thought to myself, It's the FA Cup, I'll 'bosh' him early doors.

Unfortunately, when the game started, it turned out that I could not get near enough to bosh him. He never stopped running and passing, had me all over the place and I could not get anywhere near him or the ball. When I finally did arrive in time to challenge him, he was a lot stronger than he looked – it was like hitting a barn door. He gave me 'a right seeing-to' that day.

Terry Venables, taken from Venables: The Autobiography

Left Ex-miner Wilf 'Iron Man' Copping in Arsenal strip, 1936 *(Arsenal Football Club)*

Below The grand old man shows the kid how to do it. Stoke City's Stanley Matthews glides past Ron 'Chopper' Harris as Terry Venables looks on *(Bob Thomas Sports Photography)*

Above Tommy Smith tells the linesman his version, *(Steve Hale)*

Left A bewildered Pele leaves the fray at Goodison Park, 1966 *(Steve Hale)*

Top right Do that again son . . . Dave Mackay in strident mood for Derby County *(Steve Hale)*

Bottom right The notorious Dave Mackay/ Billy Bremner showdown *(Mirror Syndication)*

Above Bryan Robson concentrates on ball control in a World Cup qualifier against Sweden *(Steve Hale)*

Right Peter Reid's words fall on deaf ears as Kevin Moran becomes the first player to be sent off in a Wembley FA Cup Final in 1985 *(Steve Hale)*

Left Norman Hunter (centre) keeps the peace at Wembley *(Mirror Syndication)*

Below Liverpool's captain Tommy Smith and Everton's captain Alan Ball run out on to Goodison Park for their 1969 clash *(Steve Hale)*

Above Frustration for Keegan in Hamburg's European Cup Final game against Nottingham Forest *(Steve Hale)*

Right The pressures of a north London derby tell as George Graham retaliates, 1967 *(Mirror Syndication)*

Above Watford's Wilf
Rostron introduces
himself to Spurs' Steve
Perryman *(Mirror
Syndication)*

Right Hard but fair?
Graeme Souness in
action for Sampdoria
against AC Milan *(Steve
Hale)*

Above Bad tackles, as the aggressor comes off worse *(Action Images)*

Left Paul Gascoigne follows suit on Forest's Gary Charles, and puts himself out of the game for a year *(Action Images)*

The sending-off incident came during a match when Manchester United were playing Bristol City and Gerry Gow and myself tangled. He caught me with his studs, and for a moment I saw red, so I retaliated while we were both still on the ground. When I got to my feet, the referee was holding up the red card, and I trudged sadly off the Ashton Gate pitch.

Sammy McIlroy, taken from Manchester United: My Team

During the late 1960s the First Division became a tougher place. Some clubs looked enviously towards the cruder methods of the lower divisions and then began to import them.

By 1971 the reputation of football was at a desperately low level. The rough play crime-rate spiral found magistrates blaming footballers for practically everything, and football authorities turning round and saying that late tackles and so on were the result of a general decline in morals. Finally the authorities of football took matters into their own hands. By a sort of cloak-and-dagger process, a new code was brought in overnight, so that what had been permitted one season was penalised (and sometimes harshly penalised) in the next. So began a 'clean up the game' campaign.

Derek Dougan, taken from The Sash He Never Wore

Let's face it. A player like me wouldn't last five minutes in the modern game. All the physical contact has gone out of football.

If I was playing now and went into tackles like I used to, I'd be getting sent off every game.

Back in those days, if you'd gone over the top, the referee would have a quiet word in your ear and warn you not to do it again.

These days they flash the red card around like it's going out of bleeding fashion.

Players are different now. They fall over at the slightest touch. Back in the 70s I could wade into Charlie like a juggernaut and he wouldn't complain about it.

He'd wait his chance and give me a kick back.

We all accepted that that's the way it was.

When I had a kick at someone I expected to be kicked back.

When they got me back, I wouldn't go squealing about it either.

Ron 'Chopper' Harris

I was always taught not to show that I was hurt. Someone might tear into me with their studs showing. I'd be in ******* agony but I wouldn't give them the satisfaction of seeing that they'd hurt me.

I mean, they talk about modern players like Shearer and how he can score 30-odd goals a season. Well, that's understandable when he's been playing against defenders who are afraid to tackle.

He wouldn't have scored 30-odd a season in the 70s. He'd have had players like me and Tommy Smith kicking great big ******* lumps out of him and he wouldn't have got a look in.

Ron 'Chopper' Harris

Once you've received a booking during a match, you know that the next offence is liable to bring marching orders, and while I don't think you consciously pull out of a tackle, you have to keep on reminding yourself that you cannot afford any more trouble, so maybe you're not quite as effective after that, because your concentration is divided between the action of the game and the knowledge that you must keep your temper, even when you're coming in for a bit of stick.

Sammy McIlroy, taken from Manchester United: My Team

I'm not sure whether it was an accident or not, but put it this way, if Westie (Gordon West, the Everton keeper) had come out with his hands it wouldn't have happened would it?

**Charlie George on how a clash with Gordon West
fractured his ankle**

Early on David Geddis had elbowed Tommy Smith in the face. Ping! The whole crowd heard it and held its breath to see how Tommy would react. You could see his expression change from disbelief that someone had whacked him to rage and one of the most threatening looks I have ever seen. The referee arrived to stop any trouble, but Tommy looked so angry I expected steam to pour out of his ears. Ten minutes later David Geddis was lying in a crumpled heap. Tommy Smith had gained his revenge.

Terry Butcher, taken from Both Sides of the Border:
An Autobiography

We had a player at Liverpool who was my mate: Ian Callaghan. Ian was never a dirty player, but you would think twice about getting stuck into him. He was so small and compact. He only got booked once in his career, but I can assure you that Cally was just as lethal as myself.

Tommy Smith

With half-time looming, Tony Dunne and Mike Summerbee tangled, and the defender was carried to the touchline with an ankle injury. Dunne took no further part in the game. A couple of things about that match stand out in my mind. There was a confrontation in the tunnel at half-time between Frank O'Farrell (United's Manager) and Mike Summerbee, with United's manager complaining about the injury which put Tony Dunne out of the game for the second half.

Sammy McIlroy, taken from Manchester United: My Team

In those days I was fairly crude in my tackling, with no finesse at all and I admit that I did tend to go over the top in retaliation rather than as an instigator. I was a bit unruly at Middlesbrough and I had left the referee with little alternative when I was sent off at Carlisle. What a waste on that beautiful pitch of theirs. Both Boro and Carlisle were going for promotion that season and it was a close game with little being given away. Stan Ternent and I had already swapped a few verbal punches when we went down on the half-way line in a tangle of legs. We kicked out at each other, he hurt me and I gave him a right hander. This time I had further to walk and longer to reflect on my selfish stupidity. It could have even cost us our promotion.

Graeme Souness, taken from Graeme Souness:
No Half Measures

I was sent off. I don't wish to mention how many times. Occasionally I did react, but over a twenty odd year spell it was rare. Every centre forward will react at some stage, but some seem to be reacting more than others nowadays It took a lot to get me really riled and het up.

Bob Latchford

John Radford was an underrated player. He was a much more intelligent centre forward than Malcolm Macdonald at a time when the tackle from behind was commonplace. He was the first footballer I knew who wore shin-pads down the back of his legs as well as the front. He and Ray Kennedy used to take an enormous amount of physical punishment.

Terry Neill, taken from Revelations of a Football Manager

Jim Holton soon established himself as a firm favourite at Old Trafford. 'Six foot two, eyes of blue, big Jim Holton's after you . . .' So chanted the fans, and car stickers proclaimed the message around Manchester and beyond. Off the field, Jim is a gentle giant; and on it, he's not the wild man some folk would have had you believe. Good in the air, solid as a rock, occasionally he would fall foul of referees because he caught an opponent who was getting past him. But there was never malice aforethought in Jim's tackle . . . just a determination to stop someone scoring a goal against United.

Sammy McIlroy, taken from Manchester United: My Team

It was a sour-tempered, rough match from the start, and never got any better. Tackling was wild and fierce, and that led to our full back Peter Shields being carried off with a broken ankle. All along, the match officials didn't seem to have a proper grip on the game. As Peter was being carried off the park, I lined up to take a throw-in, with Celtic winger Davie Provan providing a bit of badgering. As I say, everybody's blood was hot at the time, and foolishly I had a wee slap at Provan as I released the ball.

I nearly landed down beside him when I saw his reaction. He didn't fall to the ground – he threw himself on it as if he had spotted a tenner. The man's antics were deplorable. He was deliberately getting me sent off.

Then absolute rage overwhelmed me, and I did one of the daftest things I could have done. I made a run towards the linesman. I wasn't going to knee him or butt him. I just wanted to ask him why he was trying to make a name for himself at my expense. That didn't help my case any, and Alex McDonald and Sandy Jardine had to hold me and persuade me to leave the field.

I knew my conscience was clear, but I wonder how Davie Provan can sleep at night.

Willie Johnston, taken from Willie Johnston: On the Wing!

Kenny [Burns] knew people didn't like playing against him and he'd play on that to the extent that he would threaten to volley them out if they ever came in our penalty box. You could see teams would come to our place and Larry would sort one out and Kenny would sort the other out – fairly and squarely for the most part, though with Burnsy there is a very thin line between fair and unfair. But after ten minutes their strikers would be looking over their shoulders and thinking: 'There's nothing for us here.' I believe that first season was Burns' best year. He was made Footballer of the Year by the football writers. Can you believe it? A rogue like Burns alongside gentlemen of the game like Sir Stanley Matthews and Tom Finney. It's unbelievable.'

Ian Bowyer, taken from Viv Anderson

'It was just their sheer physical presence. Frightened is not the right word to use, it was just that other teams didn't look forward to playing against them because of their reputation. You'd be surprised how important a part that plays in the game. Some people thrive on the physical challenge, but 90 per cent don't like to know they are going to be in for a hard time. I mean, if you know every time you hang on to the ball you will get hammered, you get rid of it quicker than you might do with other defenders.'

Viv Anderson on the Kenny Burns/Larry Lloyd partnership,
taken from Viv Anderson

Cloughie was pretty unorthodox. You wouldn't see him all week. Then he'd turn up ten minutes before a game and say, 'Tear into the *****. Don't let those w****** get the better of you.'

That was his team talk. Then he'd go off for a brandy.

He had a funny way of dealing with players. Like he bought Kenny Burns. Now Kenny was the sort of bloke who'd have kicked his own grandmother if you gave him an excuse.

But Cloughie insisted on calling him 'Kenneth'. I could never understand that. It was Kenneth this and Kenneth that.

Well, he was never a Kenneth. He was a ******* animal. But Cloughie spoke to him like he was straight out of Sunday school or something.

Charlie George

Discipline is a touchy subject at Highbury these days. Only Brady and Howard of Arsenal were cautioned.

The various feuds sounded like a boxing bill. Howard v Kidd; Howard v Royle; O'Leary v Donachie; Simpson v Hartford; Nelson v Tuert; Brady v Kidd. The last was a particularly vicious and premeditated assault by Brady for which he should have been sent off. However, there is still the feeling that Arsenal lack fighters in the legitimate sense, in midfield. As a popular new television comedian said afterwards: 'Manchester City were themselves in the second half, but I thought Arsenal were ahead on points in the first.'

Clive White on Manchester City v Arsenal 1977

The injury isn't something I dwell on now. I thought at the time I had broken my leg and perhaps it would have been better if I had. It might have given me a chance that I didn't have with severe ligament damage. I was disappointed that the player concerned didn't apologise but it's all in the past now. These things happen in football and you have to accept them.

Geoff Nulty on the Jimmy Case tackle that ended his career

I had nothing to do with the incident which ended the career of poor Geoff Nulty. It was the result of a tackle by Jimmy Case who was villified for it, yet I was just a few yards away and swear to this day that it was not a foul tackle.

Not that Jim was, or is, any blue-eyed boy. He is the sort of player whom I would always rather play with than against. When he got angry he would turn as white as chalk and the opposition knew that they should watch out. He gave no other indication and would never utter a threat or say a word, he would just do as he had done in a pre-season friendly in Austria when one member of the opposition who had been putting himself about suddenly found himself prostrate on the ground with Jimmy 50 yards away and totally expressionless.

Graeme Souness, taken from Graeme Souness:
No Half Measures

Very definitely a tough customer – the hardest case of the lot in my opinion. Aggression, strength and a natural expertise for saving his own skin are all part of Jimmy's make-up. I accept that since the days Hunter was on the prowl, along with the old 'Anfield Iron', Smithy, things have changed. The clean-up in football, with sterner enforcement of the rules, has sorted out a lot of the old problems. But I have always believed there has to be a physical, competitive edge otherwise it would never be the spectacle it is. I'm not talking about the naughty bits. You can always do without the nasty, over-the-top stuff that actually threatens the livelihood of players. But tough, uncompromising men are always welcome in my idea of football.

You know if you get close to him, too close, you can get hurt. The few times I have dropped into United's midfield I have had a reminder from him that there is going to be no messing about. And I have collected a kick for my troubles. Nothing really vicious, just a reminder that he is there and you are on his patch. Nail him just once and it never leaves your mind that he will get you back. Given time, it's a promise that Casey will have his revenge. But you have to respect him as well. Not only can he look after himself, he can also play. He will destroy you with the ball as well as the boot. You don't collect all the game's top prizes, as he did at Anfield, without having exceptional, skilful qualities. Casey has hurt me a few times, and some of my mates a lot more, but you still have to have a sneaking admiration for the man.

Mark Hughes on Jimmy Case, taken from Sparky, Barcelona, Bayern and Back: The Autobiography of Mark Hughes

I am not that hard. My job is to win the ball and that is what I try to do. The media have built me up a bit and it has got to the stage where other teams try and rile me. I suppose it is something that I have got to live with, although I am determined not to let it stop my enjoyment at playing for Manchester United or my progress in the game.

Remi Moses

I remember Mick Buckley kicking Tommy Smith. Mick was a complete pygmy in comparison, but Smithy was out for the count. When he came round he was wagging his finger, asking, 'Who did that?' I went up to him and said, 'It was me.' He just said, 'Oh, piss off, you!'

**Duncan McKenzie on the Everton v Liverpool
FA Cup semi-final 1977**

We played Everton in the semi-final of the FA Cup and Duncan McKenzie nutmegged me. Joe Fagan said to me after the game, 'Smithy, McKenzie nutmegged you.' I said, 'I know, Joe, I'm a bit embarrassed.' He said, 'It's not going to happen again, is it?' I said, 'No, Joe.' In the reply at Maine Road. After about five minutes Duncan McKenzie went to feed the pigeons. I kicked him up in the air, got booked and little Duncan went and played full back and we won 3–0. After the game Joe Fagan said to me, 'Well done, Smithy, that'll do me kid.'

Tommy Smith

The conditions were perfect for me, we won 2–0 and for 90 minutes I was in heaven. It was one of these days when you know you can do no wrong. Near the end Tommy Smith came flying towards me near the touchline, sliding through the mud and I just slipped the ball through his legs and kept going. I can't recall ever playing better than I did that day.

Stoke's Alan Hudson on Tommy Smith and the Liverpool Team, taken from The Mavericks: English Football When the Flair wore Flares

So many people think of me as a hatchet man because I have always been reported as that kind of player. I want to be remembered for my good years at Liverpool. I did a job for them that they needed at the time and people forget I could play a bit. I want to be remembered for my skills more than my physique. I spent twelve months building myself a reputation for hardness, and the next twelve years trying to get rid of it!

Tommy Smith

Everyone was talking about Ricky (Villa) brushing aside a full challenge from 'Chopper' Ron Harris.

'He went straight through the tackle,' said Chelsea's manager Ken Shellito, incredulously.

Neither Ricky nor I had heard of 'Chopper' Harris but it seemed he was London's senior hard man and not to be treated disdainfully. The incident reinforced Ricky's reputation as a mighty man; in training, no one would contest a 50-50 ball with him, remembering only too vividly his devastating World Cup tackle on Batista of Brazil. I was quietly amused by the way everyone avoided trouble with Ricky; I knew he was a nice guy, not at all violent and that his scything of Batista's thigh was quite unintentional. Immediately after 'Chopper' Harris we ran into Tommy Smith. I'd never heard of Smith either, even though he had captained Liverpool and rejoiced in the nickname 'Anfield Iron'. But I learnt all about him after only a minute of our League Cup-tie at Swansea, who were then in the Third Division. Smith wore Number 4 for them, and their manager, John Toshack had been saying earlier: 'Ardiles and Villa looked good against Chelsea last Saturday but Chelsea didn't have Tommy Smith in their side. His experience and determination will help to make all the difference.' How much experience does it require to commit a nasty late tackle? I'd received a ball in midfield, paused to weigh up the options and then delivered a pass. The next thing I knew was Smith's boot hitting me high on the left thigh. I'm so light and nimble that it's difficult to catch me with a fair tackle, or even with an unfair one if I'm expecting it. I just wasn't ready for a sly trick like Smith's; I was angry with him and with the referee, who didn't even take his name. Treatment with a pain-killing spray kept me going for an hour, then my thigh tightened so much that I had to go off.

Ossie Ardiles, taken from Ossie: My Life in Football

Okay, so I caught him with a tackle in the first minute, but the referee didn't consider it a bookable offence, and Ardiles didn't go off until the 54th minute. I've been playing here and tackling like that for 18 seasons. Why should I change my game just because we got an Argy World Cup star playing here?

Tommy Smith

People think of Smithy as a hard man, which he was, but they didn't realise what a good player Smithy was. He was a good passer of the ball, great tackler, and, every time he played, his sleeves would be up. You needed someone like that in your team, and I think everybody looked to Smithy. If things weren't going well Smithy would get on your back and start shouting. He was vital to the team.

Ian Callaghan on Tommy Smith, taken from Liverpool Greats

Ardiles and others like him have joined the toughest League in the world and will have to take the knocks. How they react is their problem, not mine. I am just making my presence felt as I've done before and as people have done to me. The tackle was a bit late but it was straightforward.

Tommy Smith

Tommy Smith thought he was having a bad game unless he had clattered someone across the knees.

Tommy Docherty

I think Spurs ought to buy a good stock of cotton wool for such poseurs. He can't expect not to be tackled just because Argentina won the World Cup.

Tommy Smith

I once played against Tommy Smith in a charity match and had to ask him to stop kicking me. Tommy said it was his nature; naturally competitive. 'You had the ball, I want you off it.' I told him 'Tommy, this is a charity game. There is no credit in beating seven bags of shit out of a little fat rugby player like me.' Tommy said, 'I was an international player because I'm competitive and I don't have a choice. I didn't do it on purpose. It's my nature. That's what I do, you're on the ball and I want you off it.' And by god he got me off it.

Allan Bessick, GMR radio broadcaster

I think most players in the game are afraid of him. He is in the same class as myself – hard but prepared to work for the cause, that is to win.

Ron 'Chopper' Harris on Tommy Smith

The most difficult opponent I ever played against was Pele. I was 32 at the time. He was 37. I thought, Thank God he's getting on a bit. I couldn't catch him, he was a great player, he could do anything. He played for New York Cosmos and I played for Tampa Bay Rowdies. I can assure you he was something out of this world. They talk about George Best. George was probably the greatest European player I've ever seen but Pele was on a different planet even to Best. I played against Best and after a few shouts in his ear he used to go for a cup of tea. But not Pele, he was scared of nobody, he used to give it and take it. He was a genius.

Tommy Smith on Pele

Pele just could not live with the constant problem of being kicked out of the game. I know it should never happen and a player with his talent is entitled to feel upset and become violent himself when it does. But it is a fact of football life that any dirty trick in the book is used to stop players whom the football gods have gifted with extraordinary ability.

Best was kicked more than any other player in Football League history, and often finished up as the villain of the piece himself, but it never interfered with his dedication to win and come back looking for more.

When the crunching was obviously not going to stop, Pele would limp away. It is a characteristic that doesn't stop him being great – just puts him a shade behind George Best as far as I am concerned. There were psychological aspects about Pele that showed up on the field and constitute the main reason why I put him second behind Best in my all-time greats lists.

George Best was like a wild stallion that everyone admired but no-one could tame. You just couldn't get a rope around his neck.

Johnny Cruyff, like Pele, can be put off by a defender who sticks with him and is not stopped from breaking every rule in the book.

Alan Ball, taken from It's All About a Ball: An Autobiography

I didn't mind people trying to kick me, trying to have a go at me. I accepted that as part of the confrontation. And I was quite capable of looking after myself. One of the nicest things Sir Matt ever said to me was that I was the best tackler at the club. I certainly never regarded myself as a dirty player, however. I broke two players' legs, but in all honesty I never set out to hurt either of them.

One involved Glyn Pardoe of Manchester City, the other Ian Evans of Crystal Palace, and if anyone was at fault I think they were because their challenges were just a fraction late. When we collided I could hear the bones in their legs crack – as soon as we connected I knew their legs were broken. I felt utterly sick. I didn't want to play on. If I could have come off I would have.

George Best

We are very much on the player's side. I can safely say that Fulham will not be taking any disciplinary action. It is like throwing the Christians to the lions. I'm absolutely certain that Best tends to get singled out just because he is George Best. I don't condone bad language, but there is a worse evil – physical violence. And there was plenty of that at Southampton.

Fulham manager, Alec Stock, after George Best was sent off for the fifth time in his career

It wasn't the defenders who caused the real problems. It was the forwards. Players like Chelsea's Peter Osgood, Southampton's Terry Paine, Mike Summerbee of Manchester City and, most especially, Johnny Giles of Leeds. They were hard. But they also had skill which enabled them to get away with subtle fouls that the referee couldn't spot.

When I was playing the fans used to wince at the sliding tackles from the back and they are banned now. But it was never the tackles from the back that damaged you. You might end the game with a few bruises on the back of your legs but it was rare to suffer any worse damage because it's actually very difficult deliberately to break a bone with a tackle. With a back tackle it's almost impossible because your momentum carries you forward, so cushioning the impact.

A tackle from the front is a different matter and the forward players were masters at it.

George Best

I was watching him across the crowded room and I was muttering darkly under my breath. He'd just given me a hard time on the field for the second time and I hadn't taken it too kindly.

He came over to shake hands. He asked me if I had enjoyed the game and I told him: 'Not in the least – you made a monkey out of me twice and I'm still annoyed about it.' He just laughed and said: 'Don't worry – I was lucky. Sometimes things come off for me and sometimes they don't. They don't always.'

I told him firmly that next time we played against each other I'd make sure they didn't happen for him a third time. He laughed again and said: 'We'll wait and see.'

I had already decided that to play Cruyff you must get to him quicker or at least get to the ball quicker if it is a straight man-to-man situation. He gets uneasy if he gets hit by a good hard tackle in the game so it is to your advantage to let him know you're there as soon as possible.

He is so fast over ten and twelve yards that if he gets the ball first and you're any more than six yards from him he'll leave you for dead. He has amazing reflexes and likes to outfox his opposition mentally as well as physically. He'll lie doggo for a spell and you'll think he's not trying. Then suddenly he zooms in when you least expect it and he's scored.

In the later stages of his career in Europe he was getting really uptight about the marking he was getting. Because of his reputation he was the victim of a lot of rough stuff and he was reacting pretty violently to it and having more and more clashes with referees.

Derek Johnstone on Johan Cruyff, taken from Rangers:
My Team

He was a very experienced player with a biting tackle and the sort of indomitable character that we needed at the time. We didn't get it right until Yorath was switched into his best position as the hard man in midfield. He did well for us there, yet I don't think it's necessary for a midfield to be built around a ball-winner. There are better ways of gaining possession than just clattering the opposition with a mighty tackle. Really top-class players can steal the ball and don't need to battle for it. If I had to choose between skill and tackling, I'd sacrifice the tackler.

Ossie Ardiles on Terry Yorath, taken from Ossie:
My Life in Football

About a month after I returned to Ibrox we went into action against Aberdeen in the League Cup, and once again I fell foul of the lawman. During my time in the game I have been dismissed prematurely about fifteen times, a statistic I would prefer to ignore, but it takes an awful lot of ignoring. Included in that infamous bundle of transgressions are quite a few incidents which would have passed almost unheeded had the player involved been anybody else other than yours truly. On the other hand there are a good selection of eminently bad and punishable misdeeds. Without putting too fine a point on it, this incident fell into the second category. I committed a nasty foul on John McMaster, and because of that whatever may have preceded the actionable foul became instantly unimportant. I was justifiably ordered from the field, and I have regretted the episode ever since.

I have often had a go at the cynical brutes who abound in our industry, and have no wish to be remembered as a player who deliberately inflicts damage on another. However, very few players go through such a long career as mine without badly fouling, intentionally or unintentionally, another player. Possibly John McMaster will understand that. I am just glad that it didn't happen too often with me, and that I never put anybody out of the game. Most of the time I went for the early bath it was for shouting my mouth off. Some were for nothing in particular, while others were fully deserved. I have never tried to hide that, and have always accepted my punishment, but I do regret the few occasions when I could have done some damage with a shoddy display of temper or a bad tackle.

Willie Johnston, taken from Willie Johnston: On the Wing!

Here's a player who doesn't mind dishing it out in the tackle and also verbally. I clashed with 'Jimbo' during our heavy defeat at Southampton last season; losing 4–1 was not very pleasant for us and I was guilty of a clumsy tackle on young Ray Wallace. 'Jimbo' came steaming over to me snarling, 'Leave him alone, he's only a kid.' I stormed back, 'Never mind he's only a kid, he's just scored against us, he's no kid to us.' In fact, Rod Wallace had made a goal as well as scoring one. Just like Norman Whiteside, who played in the World Cup Finals at the age of seventeen, there's an old football saying, 'If you're good enough, your old enough.' I don't regret having a 'dig' at Wallace; he was running us ragged. He didn't do too much more after my tackle, but by then he had helped inflict one of our heaviest defeats for some time. At the end of the day, he had the last laugh.

Steve McMahon on Jimmy Case, taken from Macca Can!
The Steve McMahon Story

There has always been this idea that we (black players) can't take stick. Don't you believe it. The black player can dish out just as much heavy stuff as the white man.

Vince Hilaire

I learned something about self-discipline that day. Some people think that because you are black it is an excuse to have a go. I accept it now as part of football today and have taught myself to walk away and just get on with the game.

Bob Hazell on being sent off against Arsenal in a 1978 FA Cup-tie. (There were allegations that Graham Rix subjected Hazell to racist abuse.)

We were playing San Jose Thunders, who boasted my former World Cup captain Bruce Rioch amongst their stars. Rioch started giving me stick right from the off in a deliberate attempt to needle me into losing my head. He taunted me and fouled me until it was almost beyond endurance. But I endured. Oh, how I endured! The score was level at full-time, so we went into the penalty shoot-out. With the scores still level I was last to have a go, so I dribbled up and skelped the ball past their keeper. We had won with the last kick of the ball.

As soon as it hit the net I turned to Rioch, the big bad man, and bared my backside to him to show him what he was – a big bum!

Willie Johnston, taken from Willie Johnston: On the Wing!

Willie Johnston of Rangers and Scotland had tremendous ability, he was skilful and quick but so easily riled when things weren't going too well. Then he became an animal. He would make wild lunges at you not caring whether he caught you or the ball, and his elbows would be everywhere. Willie was also a great one for the verbals – particularly when he had beaten an opponent – and would wind them up until they could take no more and punches were exchanged. More often than not, though, it would be Willie who would find himself either in the referee's book or on the lonely walk back to the tunnel. Because if ever a man had a reputation as one of football's bad boys, it was him and the referees were always on the look-out for trouble.

Phil Neal, taken from Life at the Top

The only thing I remember about my debut for Manchester United at Goodison Park against Everton was a kick on the head from Mick Lyons. We won 6–2, but all I remember from the game is the kick on the head.

Andy Ritchie

He was, by now, getting towards the veteran stage but he was brilliant that day. The manager had told me to get in against him and be aggressive. I seldom needed encouragement to do that, but it was to no avail as the great little man, past his best or not, taught me a lesson in football that day. Every time I had tried to do something against him he must have sensed that I was still very naive, and exposed me with a single touch as I rushed in. He had time on the ball because I could never get close enough, teaching me a lesson that I will never forget.

Steve Bruce on Alan Ball, taken from Steve Bruce: Heading for Victory

Let me say categorically that I have never deliberately set out with the intention of injuring another player. They are all the same to me – it's their living too, and they are entitled to respect as fellow pros. Mind you, I HAVE got stuck in and I may have mistimed a few tackles in my time and fouled people, but even the skilful stars at top international level do this. Every player mistimes a tackle on occasions.

I tackle hard. I go into a tackle hard and I admit I have tried to soften a suspect opponent (suspect for courage that is) by letting him know early on in the game that I am a hard man.

Ron 'Chopper' Harris

The whole England team has autographed my leg.

West Germany's Gunter Netzer on playing against England, 1972

Nicknamed 'The Dog', Harry Cripps was an enormously popular star at Millwall in the 1960s and 1970s. Millwall fans applauded the terrier-like enthusiasm with which Cripps committed himself to reckless tackles on opposing players and regarded him as a symbol of the toughness for which the Lions had such a reputation. His various achievements with the club included breaking more legs than any other player in the history of the League.

David Pickering

I've got a little black book in which I keep the names of all the players I've got to get before I pack up playing. If I get half a chance they will finish up over the touchline.

Jack Charlton

I had Manchester United's last match in the First Division, prior to them being relegated in 1973/74.

Early in the game, Manchester United's young left back Stewart Houston was injured in a tackle with Stoke's outside right Jimmy Robertson, and had to be carried off. The tackle incensed the United players, but in my opinion it had been a complete accident.

As I stepped out of the dressing room to take the field for the second half, I caught a glimpse of Robertson turning away from United's manager Tommy Docherty in the corridor – and Docherty wiping what looked to be tea from his face and shirt. He was furious. 'Did you see that?' he asked. I insisted I hadn't seen anything. Robertson, too, was angry. 'No one calls me that,' he was muttering but, again, I said I didn't want to know, as I hadn't actually seen the incident.

During the early part of the second half, I was convinced that United's players were out to 'do' Robertson, and in fact I advised him: 'Keep as far away from them as you can!' Towards the end, I told him: 'Stand by me at the final whistle so I can accompany you up the tunnel, and keep your trap shut!'

Gordon Hill, taken from Give a Little Whistle:
The Recollections of a Remarkable Referee

In the Leeds-Everton match I refereed last season, Everton's centre forward Bobby Latchford was on the receiving end of at least three or four clouts from Norman, and afterwards I asked Latchford for his reaction to this. Latchford replied: 'Gordon, I expect to be hit hard by this man – that's his job. But I know jolly well that a tackle by Hunter will always be an honest tackle.'

Gordon Hill, taken from Give a Little Whistle:
The Recollections of a Remarkable Referee

Nowadays if somebody commits a foul and it's seen on television you get the whole country against him. A player can be meek and mild but if he once steps out of line and punches somebody and is seen on TV then he is inclined to be stamped as a villain for the rest of his career.

Francis Lee, taken from Soccer Round the World:
A Football Star's Story from Manchester to Mexico

Yesterday against Villa, we were 1–0 down from pretty early on, and things were looking rocky. They were very physical.

Now Benny (Fenton) does not kick. It is a strong principle of his. But he said Villa are like bullies in the playground. If you do not stand up and fight back, they will really demolish you. You cannot turn the other cheek in football, particularly in the Second Division. You have got to fight fire with fire. He said that it was no good taking a pride in not kicking people up in the air if people are kicking you up in the air. The only answer was to go out and kick them back. He did not spell it out as clearly as that, but that is what it amounted to.

We mixed it physically, and we came out on top in the second half.

Coming off the pitch, I said to Trevor Hockey, who had been their main hatchet man. 'How does it feel to be a navvy among artists?'

He just walked on, sneering, 'How many caps have you got, then?'

'Twenty five.'

The crowd were really baying for blood as we came off. There was a really violent, almost evil, atmosphere around the place. Vic Crowe, the Villa manager, was shepherding his players off. When he saw me, he said, 'What a terrible place. You deserve £100 a week playing in front of this lot.' I've never believed that terrace violence has anything to do with what happens on the field, but the way Villa played you could see why the fans felt like they did.

Eamon Dunphy on playing for Millwall against Aston Villa in the 1970s, taken from Only a Game: The Diary of a Professional Footballer

I could never get on with Bremner. It was like a red rag to a bull.

Referee Clive Thomas

Norman Hunter was a hard man, but he was a fair man. If he wanted to kick someone he'd do it and not hide it. He didn't do it slyly.

Clive Thomas

Really serious offences should not be given the name 'foul', but should be seen as what they are: criminal assaults. This happens when the tackler has no interest in the ball but only in digging his studs into the other man's shin.

You can go into a tackle with most English professionals confident of playing with gentlemen, but there are a few of whom you have to be careful. They don't go for the ball. I don't know how they can look another player in the eye.

Ossie Ardiles, taken from Ossie: My Life in Football

Over-the-top tackles were part and parcel of the game during my time as a player. And when you live by the sword you had to be prepared to die by it.

You could say it was the law of the jungle in my day. But then you looked at Bobby Charlton and you knew there was no excuse.

I needed somebody to sit me down and tell me it would not be tolerated. And as a manager now, that's what I do.

Bruce Rioch

At Grimsby the visitors' dressing room is between the tunnel to the pitch and the home dressing room. The Grimsby players used to have a tendency to bang on the away teams' dressing room wall as they came down the tunnel. You'd be sitting there listening. When you went out on the pitch and beat them you'd think, 'Bang on the way back up if you want lads.'

Leighton James

Any person deliberately or recklessly causing any harm or injury ... to any person concerned with, before, during or after any sporting activity shall be guilty of an offence.

Edward Grayson, London barrister who advocated a Safety of Sports Persons Act in the 1970s

A violent assault which is outside the rules of the game is also outside the rules of the law, and therefore amenable to its jurisdiction and punishment.

Professor Colin Tatz agreeing with Edward Grayson

Legal intervention in sport has become the hobby-horse of many publicity-seekers. Justice on the field is undeniably rough justice, but it is accepted in sport and is something on which sport relies totally.

the Secretary of the FA replying to Professor Tatz

When Steve Waddington makes it obvious from the kick-off that he has been detailed to mark me tight for 90 minutes, I feel completely cheesed off.

The guy whacked me six times in the opening ten minutes. On the seventh – lucky for some but not for him – my fist laid him out. I'd taken all I was prepared to take.

The referee, quite rightly, sent me off. I was in the wrong and had to go. But he also showed everyone that he knew the cause by booking Waddington. And if he knew the bloody cause, why did he not clamp down on Waddington after the second or third foul? Had he acted at the right time I would not have lost my temper, Waddington would not have been floored and the fans would have seen a proper game instead of the inferior 10 v 11 scrap that usually results when a team loses a man early on.

I am not very proud of my behaviour that day, but I am convinced it could all have been avoided if the official had seen from the beginning that a 'stop him from playing' instruction had clearly been issued to Waddington. But until referees become more aware of such obvious potential flashpoints, they will continue to tarnish the game.

Liam Brady playing for Arsenal against Stoke,
taken from So Far So Good

Thinking he was in it, Ossie [Peter Osgood] wound him up about his little black book after a testimonial match at Brighton. Jack had talked about it on TV and it was supposed to contain the name of a player he intended to sort out, so to speak. 'It's not for you,' Jack told Ossie, 'It's for that twat next to you.' I was that twat.

Ian Hutchinson, taken from The Mavericks:
English Football When the Flair wore Flares

Jack Charlton had only two names in his black book. Terry Paine of Southampton and Johnny Morrissey of Everton.

Norman Hunter

The only reason that Jack Charlton kept a black book was because he couldn't remember names. I could remember names and I could remember people and very rarely did it happen twice that I got kicked.

Tommy Smith

I suppose it was natural to think that Billy and I were at each other's throats after what happened, but I did not feel any animosity towards him and I know he did not feel any towards me.

**Kevin Keegan on his sending off with Billy Bremner in the
Charity Shield, 1974**

Oakes and Smith dovetail very well together. They are both the type of player who set their own high standards. They have a rotten season if they have three bad games out of sixty. They are completely dependable whatever the occasion, and are the life blood of the game.

Liverpool's Smith is another Dave Mackay. If you had Smith and Oakes battling for you then you would have a fantastic start to any team.

Francis Lee on Alan Oakes of Manchester City and Tommy Smith of Liverpool, taken from Soccer Round the World: A Football Star's Story from Manchester to Mexico

If everyone who swore during games was sent off, there wouldn't be too many players left.

Terry Venables

In the Premiership now the comparison to be made with the last five to ten years is that every game is televised. It's not one camera, it's half a dozen and they are looking for every little incident and the referees are under the microscope. They have to be assessed. They are reminded regularly by the authorities; if it's not from the FA it is from FIFA and UEFA and if they spotlight a certain offence such as the tackle from behind they have to come down hard on it because they want to keep their job. What you look for is that little bit of common sense, humour and the ability to make good firm decisions and the ability to take the bit of flack that will come.

Lawrie McMenemy on referees

Violent conduct is not acceptable.

It has been my duty to ensure that all my players perform within the rules of the game.

Bruce Rioch

There was never any love lost between him and me, and it all spilled over when he left Aston Villa for Wolves.

He's always been an outspoken so-and-so, and he had a right old pop at me.

I was incensed and had a right go back, but I could never

have imagined what would have happened when we played Wolves after he had gone there.

We both went for a ball in midfield and he came in studs up. There is still no question in my mind that he would have snapped my leg in half if he had made contact.

Dennis Mortimer, recalling playing against Andy Gray

This is the fifth time I've been sent off . . . and it's the only time I haven't deserved it. This one was ridiculous. I didn't swear at this referee. I didn't even argue against the booking. I accept I was out of order for retaliating against Hector, but I had to tell the referee that the reason I'd done something stupid was because he hadn't taken stronger action for a foul against me in the first minute. I might have been a bit heated but I wasn't malicious or foul mouthed.

We don't know where we are with these refs. If I'd said that to Gordon Hill, he'd have told me in no uncertain terms to snap out of it, then laughed at me and told me to get on with the game.

Alan Ball after being sent off playing for Arsenal against Derby, taken from It's All About a Ball: An Autobiography

I believe that officials should make a bigger effort to know the players and the different aspects of the pro game. Following the laws and waving plastic, coloured cards around is all very well. But if more referees got inside the game and really understood the little tricks and ploys of the players, the whole situation would change. They would earn a damn sight more respect for a start.

Too many so-called experts pontificate about the behaviour of players and the problems referees have keeping control of the games.

What I feel obliged to point out to these people is the very important fact that football is our living – it pays our bills. But it is not the living of the man with the power to stop me from earning mine!

Liam Brady, taken from So Far So Good

Ever since the time Burnley's chairman Bob Lord described Manchester United's players as 'Teddy Boys', matches between these two clubs have invariably been difficult to handle. This particular match certainly was.

The game soon got very, very nasty and mid-way through the first half a Burnley player hacked Bobby Charlton down. My reaction was one of disgust. When Charlton is hit to the dirt somebody's got to take notice because people don't normally hit Charlton in this way.

Gordon Hill, taken from Give a Little Whistle:
The Recollections of a Remarkable Referee

I have no hesitation in naming Southampton's Terry Paine as the greatest player I've ever played with. But having said that, he was an aggressive character who could be a right Paine in the neck. I've played with some greats like Bobby Moore, Alan Ball and Kevin Keegan. And I've faced Franz Beckenbauer and Johann Cruyff and George Best. But Terry Paine comes out on top of the heap for me.

Painey, however, was hated by nearly everyone in the game at one stage or another. He had a great knack of getting up everyone's nose. He had a terrible reputation for going over the top in the tackle and kicking people. But, I tell you what, he could play. Having that rotten streak in him made him the player and competitor he was. He would kick his own mother and could be really nasty. He wasn't the bravest of players, he wouldn't go up face to face and kick you. But he would take every advantage. Not many people took liberties with him and everybody wanted to kick him. He wasn't much different from Johnny Giles and probably liked about as much. Loads of people thought bad thoughts of Gilesy and wanted to top him. Players like that normally build up a long list of people wanting to go on revenge missions, but Painey was too shrewd to get done.

Mick Channon, taken from Man on the Run

There are times when you have to stamp on Lee, because he's quite capable of causing a great deal of unpleasantness in some situations. Unfortunately, I wasn't doing enough to stamp on him in this particular game, and the Plymouth players were really uptight about it, Sullivan in particular.

Mid-way through the second half, I booked Sullivan for a very bad tackle from behind on Lee, which caused Lee to be carried off. It was so bad I had a real job on my hands to prevent Mike Summerbee from hitting Sullivan.

Gordon Hill on Francis Lee, League Cup semi-final Manchester City v Plymouth, 1974, taken from Give a Little Whistle: The Recollections of a Remarkable Referee

In this particular match, Coventry were really showing Derby how to play and Gibson, in particular, was having a tremendous game. Just before half-time, he jinked up toward Carlin in the middle of the field, and impudently nutmegged him, pushed the ball between Carlin's legs. Not only that, as he ran around Carlin, he gave a really loud, evil laugh. Carlin's face just changed colour.

As Gibson went off towards the right-hand corner flag, Carlin went chasing after him. 'This is going to be interesting,' I thought, and I set off as well. Within seconds, I realized I'd no chance of getting there in time, so I blew my whistle to stop the game. I ran up to Carlin, who'd not managed to catch Gibson, spun him round, put my finger in front of him and said: 'You were going to do him weren't you, Willie?' And he replied: 'I'd have f******* killed him!' I restarted the game with a dropped ball.

Had I not stopped the game, I am convinced Carlin would have kicked Gibson off the park. I suppose correct refereeing would have been to wait for it to happen, and then send him off the field. But that would have ruined a game of football.

Gordon Hill, taken from Give a Little Whistle: The Recollections of a Remarkable Referee

It was a hard game – it always was a hard game with Southampton – but I thought I was handling it well. However, everything changed mid-way through the first half when Southampton's Hughie Fisher fractured his leg in a collision with Arsenal's goalkeeper Bob Wilson.

To me, it was a complete accident, but what I didn't realize at the time was that Wilson had a reputation in the game for being perhaps too physical in these types of situations. Obviously, he didn't set out to break anyone's leg or anything like that, but when he came out for a ball he really didn't care who was in his way.

So on reflection, I think the reaction of Southampton's players was quite probably based on that.

Certainly, from that moment, the game became very ugly. I believe Southampton provoked their own retaliation and, due to my inability to handle the situation, it became almost a kind of gladiatorial spectacle.

Gordon Hill, taken from Give a Little Whistle:
The Recollections of a Remarkable Referee

I was marking John O'Rourke, then of Ipswich Town. We had been niggling away at each other all the game, an elbow going in here and there. At one stage we almost ended up in a stand-up fight.

Hill stopped the play and walked over to us, and I thought: 'We've done it now, he's going to send us off!' The least I expected was a booking. Instead, he said to us: 'You two can piss off up the tunnel if you want to fight, but don't interfere with the football going on here.'

Colin Waldron on Gordon Hill, taken from Give a Little Whistle:
The Recollections of a Remarkable Referee

In the early days my temper was very quick. Now it takes a lot to get me riled. It was sheer impetuosity that got me booked in my first Football League game at the age of 16. Recently against Everton someone had stopped me breaking through by really hanging onto my shirt. Two or three years earlier I might have turned round and clocked him one. But now I contented myself with a quiet word to him before placing the ball for a free kick.

I can understand players who do fly off the handle when they beat opponents but are continually hacked down. And as a striker who gets a lot of attention I suffer as much as most, but I'm glad to say that I do not let things get out of proportion. Probably this is because there are other things in my life.

Francis Lee, taken from Soccer Round the World:
A Football Star's Story from Manchester to Mexico

133

All the frustration that has been building up trying to win acceptance at Hamburg erupts in one moment of wild anger. I throw a left-right combination that stretched defender Erhaud Preuss out on the pitch after he whacked me for the third time in as many minutes. I walked off with a glance at the referee.

Kevin Keegan after he was sent off playing for Hamburg in a friendly against Lubeck. He received a two-month ban

6 Big Bucks Big Kicks

The 1980s

Only once did I deliberately set out to try and hurt someone and that was years later in a charity game for a little amateur club in Belfast. The manager told me: 'There's a lad playing on the other side who says he's going to kick you.'

I replied: 'If he wants to kick me he will.'

It didn't worry me. I'd spent my professional career playing against players like Smith, Harris, Reaney, and Dave Mackay of Spurs, who was unquestionably the hardest man I ever played against and certainly the bravest. This time it was just a cocky kid with ideas above his station. He was as good as his word, however. He followed me everywhere. He kicked me and he kicked me again. I told him: 'This is ridiculous, this is an exhibition game. It should be fun.'

He kept on kicking and he started insulting me. All the usual stuff like, 'You're past it, you're a has-been, you won't finish the game.'

I said, 'If you kick me again, *you* won't finish the game.' He did. So about ten minutes later I deliberately knocked the ball a little too far forward, or so he would think, knowing he was going to come for it. And when he did I turned him and hit him above the knee. As they carried him off, he was crying like a kid. While he was lying on the ground the captain of our team went over to him and said, 'Kittens don't fuck cats.'

I felt very upset about it afterwards. I went to see him after the game to apologise. His manager said, 'Don't worry, George, it's taught him a lesson – don't fuck with a truck.'

George Best, taken from The Good, the Bad and the Bubbly

What dampened our challenge most of all, however, was the shocking injury to John McMaster. John was starting out on one of his beautifully smooth runs, beating one man then another as he cut diagonally across the field. It looked like the start of something promising. Then in came Ray Kennedy and felled him with a knee-high tackle which not only put him out of the game for a year but raised some doubts that he would ever walk properly again, let alone play football. I am not saying Kennedy went out to crack him but if you use that kind of tackle, there is a fair chance that you will do your opponent some nasty harm. Personally I would discourage such tackles in the strongest possible way. Justice would be best done by banning the tackler for the same length of time as the injured man is out of the game, although that would no doubt be regarded as impracticable. The incredible point about that particular tackle was that Kennedy didn't even get a booking. It was the last we saw of John McMaster for a long time and if you had seen the injury you could have understood why. With ligaments severed, his leg from the knee down was hanging away in the wrong direction. You wouldn't have believed it. I'll tell you it made us all stop and think about how easily your career could be ended in just one tackle.

Gordon Strachan on the European Cup tie v Liverpool,
taken from An Autobiography

As a striker you take a great deal of stick in every match you play. It is something that you accept as part of the job, but it is not something that any striker relishes. Ribs, back, ankles and legs are all target areas for the defender who wants to slow you down . . . and believe me there are quite a few of them about in Scottish football.

Derek Johnstone, taken from Rangers: My Team

The ones I don't worry about are the ones who tell you what they are going to do to you. A classic example was when Martin O'Neill, who likes to think of himself as a busy player, got himself into a situation he couldn't handle and had to leave the field for treatment. He couldn't play on but he came out with us in his civvies in the second half and he started to tell me what he was going to do to me. I was listening to him and laughing when Notts County's last man, Ian McCulloch, turned round and glared. Naturally I thought it was directed at me but then I heard the Scot say, 'He wants to do it on the pitch instead of off it.'

I was, however, guilty of a similar, but worse, outburst myself after a game against of all teams, Everton. We had played well and deserved to win but Andy King, so often a thorn in Liverpool's side, knocked in a late goal to snatch a draw. I was even more annoyed than usual because we had been direct opposition that afternoon. We were going at each other hammer and tongs when he threatened to sort me out after the game. It was the sort of thing which is often said in the heat of the moment but this time I would not let it pass and when I saw him standing with his wife at the bar in the players' lounge I went up to him and told him I was ready. I was red in the face and boiling inside and I snapped, 'I don't want to embarrass you in front of your wife – are you coming out on to the pitch or not?' Andy saw I was in earnest and sensibly would not budge and I went home seething but gradually feeling more and more foolish. When I think of it I feel embarrassed.

Graeme Souness, taken from Graeme Souness:
No Half Measures

Liverpool always used to have some right battles with Ipswich when they were going well under Bobby Robson and they sometimes got a little teethy. But I didn't always get my own way and in one particular game Paul Mariner went over the top, through my stocking, through my pads and through my skin. Ronnie Moran came running on and told me to lie back and not to look but I did and I didn't let it upset me. It wouldn't have done to show Paul and his Ipswich colleagues that he had hurt me and I didn't even bother to have the half-dozen stitches inserted until after the game.

Graeme Souness, taken from Graeme Souness:
No Half Measures

Every time I played against Graeme Souness I wanted to kick him. He always ran the show against us, whether he was playing for Scotland or his old club Liverpool, and his arrogance and the way he strutted around the pitch as though he owned it made players want to bring him down a peg or two.

Terry Butcher, taken from Both Sides of the Border:
An Autobiography

At Sunderland when their big centre half Shaun Elliott, who I had had problems with while at Middlesbrough, was kicking Ian Rush and David Hodgson black and blue. My chance to put him in his place came when he challenged for a ball near the tunnel, I turned into him and caught him in the chest with my shoulder, almost sending him into Alan Durban's lap. That, I admit, was deliberate; I wanted him to know I was there and that I also knew what he was up to.

Graeme Souness, taken from Graeme Souness:
No Half Measures

I can put my hand on my heart and swear that I have never tried to put someone out of football and when the Argentinian Ricky Villa was off for a long while after we had clashed I felt far from proud. I was upset even though there had been no malevolent intent in the challenge.

Graeme Souness, taken from Graeme Souness:
No Half Measures

He was hard but fair. During our tussles he'd not complain when he was on the receiving end of a tackle, and I wouldn't complain when I felt the full force of one of Graeme's tackles. We shared the same sort of hard man's motto, if you like; if someone whacks you, you accept it, get up and get on with the game, and wait for your chance to whack them back.

Steve McMahon on Graeme Souness, taken from Macca Can!
The Steve McMahon Story

He was as tough as he was gifted. In an FA Cup-tie against Liverpool at Anfield, the home side's midfield had not only taken control but were taking a few liberties. Souness, however, illustrated that nobody took the piss out of him. At one stage he pinned Liverpool hard man Jimmy Case to the turf by the throat and, with clenched fist, indicated that the midfielder's afternoon might end there and then. He was a bruiser but, when it came to pure skill, he had the touch of a maestro.

Craig Johnston, taken from Walk Alone: The Craig Johnston Story

I was in a tussle with Souness and, as I kicked the ball away, he kicked me in the shin with his studs showing. I squared up to him and was sent off. If anyone should have gone off, it should have been Souness. He went over the top, it was as plain as anything – I've got the stud marks on my shin to prove it.

Steve McMahon, taken from Macca Can! The Steve McMahon Story

I once saw him in action against a mate of mine, Peter Nicholas – another guy who could handle himself – when we took on Scotland in a World Cup qualifying game. I can tell you it wasn't very pretty.

As I saw it, Peter went in to make a challenge on Souness. He obviously didn't like it because, while Nicko was still on the deck, Graeme just backheeled him straight in the face. A bit out of order, really.

My reading of it was that he probably recognised Nicholas as the tough guy of the Welsh team and made sure he sorted him out early. He clearly aimed to get the pecking order laid down before any of the real nonsense blew up. It was like the law of the jungle – a bit too callous for me. But I think all great players have that vital mean streak on the field. And Souness certainly had it. He was the minder of the Liverpool team for years. Let anybody step out of line in the opposition ranks and Anfield didn't have to whistle up Graeme. He was there already.

Mark Hughes, taken from Sparky, Barcelona, Bayern and Back:
The Autobiography of Mark Hughes

Peter Nicholas has been around and has done his fair bit of kicking. He can be vicious when he wants to be, but he met his match in Graeme Souness. Nicholas tried to 'do' Souness in a tackle and it hurt our Liverpool skipper, but he waited patiently for his opportunity the next time their path crossed on the football field. In the first ten minutes Nicholas was off with a gashed shin, courtesy of Souness. Souness was not a player to

139

be crossed on the field – he was the master at picking the time for retribution.

Steve McMahon, taken from Macca Can! The Steve McMahon Story

I recall seeking a little vengeance on Ray's behalf in a Milk Cup duel with Arsenal after Peter Nicholas got our big fellow sent off. With the tie going to a replay it was all a bit tense and I went after him with such obvious intent that Peter turned to Ian Rush and asked him why I didn't like him! The Welsh international eventually had to go off after a rather high tackle in the first half of the second game from Graeme Souness but that was a case of live by the sword – die by the sword and I felt little remorse at the time.

Graeme Souness, taken from Graeme Souness:
No Half Measures

In the League Cup-tie at Highbury, Peter Nicholas kept catching Ray with flying tackles. Ray Kennedy snapped and took a swing at Nicholas under the ref's nose. In the second leg at Anfield Nicholas over ran the ball just as Graeme Souness connected with a tackle. Nicholas was carried off, but didn't complain.

Later in the Wales–Scotland match another violent clash took place between them. Graeme had still not forgiven him for getting Roy sent off.

Mark Lawrenson, taken from Mark Lawrenson: The Autobiography

I seldom bear a grudge and it has never entered my head to keep a little book of names as my former manager Jack Charlton was reputed to do – but I dare say that my name might be in a few other players' books. I don't just mean opponents I have tangled with but youngsters who are seeking a reputation. Because of my notoriety built up through publicity, I know I would be a fair old scalp for someone, probably the most desirable, for an instant reputation. There have already been a few who have tried and one or two waiting for their chance. I know who some of them are but I wouldn't give them the satisfaction of naming them. I have no doubt that one or two managers give their instructions just as Jack Charlton used to with me and I swear one or two of them would like a go themselves judging by some of the torrents of abuse I have heard coming from the touchlines.

Graeme Souness, taken from Graeme Souness:
No Half Measures

I did detect a weakness. He does not like the sight of blood, especially when it is his own! Once we were playing one of our usual fierce, five-a-side games and Graeme was driving players on and challenging for 50-50 balls as if it were the FA Cup semi-final. Suddenly I found myself in one of those situations where I could not have backed out even if I had wanted to with the ball falling between Graeme Souness and Kenny Dalglish who, as usual, were on the same side, and me. You will win no prizes for guessing who came out of the challenge with the ball but as I was sandwiched between the two Scots I was nudged off-balance by Dalglish and caught Souness on the bridge of his nose with my elbow.

He went down but appeared to be all right until he noticed the blood dripping off the end of his Roman nose. His legs gave way and he had to go off for a while. When he came back he looked at me and said quietly: 'I hope you did not do that on purpose, Bruce.' 'If I had,' I replied, 'you would still be lying there.' He believed me, or at least I assume he did, for I never got kicked back.

Bruce Grobbelaar, taken from Bruce Grobbelaar:
More than Somewhat

Have you got a licence to go about kicking people in training?

David Johnson to Graeme Souness during a training session

I can't argue with the fact that there are people in the game and a lot on the terraces who think of me as a hatchet man. But I am not an arch villain and I take grave offence at the suggestion that I am. That I am a good player and a sound passer of the ball and not just a hatchet man.

Graeme Souness, taken from Graeme Souness:
No Half Measures

I've never been more depressed. I remember seeing the red card and looking up, there was 30,000 people jeering and I could see my Dad in the front row of the directors' box. I can still feel the shame now. I know it sounds like Hollywood but I've never felt so alone. I'd let my Dad down, humiliated him in his own street. That was my lowest moment in football.

Graeme Souness after being sent off against Hibernian

The Welsh method is based mostly on the physical side of the game. We haven't the same amount of skill as the rest of the top teams, so we go out to smother and stifle rivals with our application, workrate and aggression. Leading us into battle is Nicholas. I'll never forget the European Championship qualifier against Denmark with Nicko. They still show it on the box and the short-run TV clip is very good knockabout entertainment! There Peter the Great is, going hell for leather to win possession, with at least five Danes sprawled in a heap at his feet. It was just like something out of a skittle alley. And he is still looking at his victims as if to say, if they want more they can have it.

Mark Hughes on Peter Nicholas, taken from Sparky, Barcelona, Bayern and Back: The Autobiography of Mark Hughes

It was a Premier League game up at Pittodrie and in the first few seconds or so Neale Cooper, an old mate of mine from the Scotland Under-18 Youth International team, let me know he was playing. Big Neale flattened me with a crunching tackle before I was out of the centre circle. When you're suddenly kicked just after you take the kick-off in a game, you say to yourself, 'What's going on here?' It happened in another game, and whenever we played Aberdeen I'd find myself man-marked by Neale Cooper. I was convinced then that Fergie had sent the big fellow out to hammer me. My old man couldn't believe that Neale would do that to me. Neale and I had been in the youth team together, and we had got on all right off the park. My Dad wasn't able to come to terms with the fact that the big lad could whack me the way that he did. But I didn't bear any grudges towards him. Life is too short in football terms to go through your career harbouring bad feelings against another professional who is trying to do his job.

Charlie Nicholas, take from Charlie: An Autobiography

That last season I played in the Scottish Premier League we played against Celtic SEVEN times, and the atmosphere surrounding these games was becoming really nasty. By the end of it all we were like the hillies and the billies – just feuding and fighting our way through the game. The whole scene became poisonous. You would be going off the field after a game and a player would be saying to you, 'just you wait, I'll get you next time.' That happens in England too, but the next time is months away and everything is forgotten. In the Premier League the 'next time' could be three weeks off, maybe even less, so you had these troubles lying in wait for you at just about every game. And when you are my size you can do without all of that!

Believe me, I was not enjoying my football any more. I couldn't. I was waiting for someone to hammer me every time I went out on to the field. There was a nasty feeling about the games and an intensity in those clashes which I simply did not enjoy. I doubt if any player could say with any honesty that he did enjoy these matches. I just wanted to be away from all the bad feeling.

Gordon Strachan, taken from Strachan Style: A Life in Football

It's a man's game and men make tackles and I hope men accept tackles without bleating too much.

Steve Coppell

I remember being bitterly disappointed in my first Old Firm game at Ibrox when we lost 3–0. I was taken off because Derek Johnstone marked me out of the game. Beforehand I had reckoned that I could take him because he was overweight and has slowed down a lot, but he had a lot of experience behind him and during the game he'd be grabbing my jersey or giving me a little nudge or hitting me from behind. But there was nothing really nasty about it. What happened in that game was what happened week after week in other games in the Premier

League, the kind of thing you expect and accept.

Charlie Nicholas, taken from Charlie: An Autobiography

I was in Argentina when Brian Clough, the Nottingham Forest manager, was asked on a live television show if he would be interested in signing me. He said I was too 'fly' for him because I wanted to play centre half despite having scored all these goals. I can only interpret Clough's 'fly' remark as meaning I think I can 'skive' in defence and have an easier time.

All I can say is I'll show Mr Clough or anyone the scars and bruises I get on my legs playing centre half. I'm sure Clough, as a player, gave defenders as good as he got and kept them on the hop.

Derek Johnstone, taken from Rangers: My Team

I remember playing against Andy Gray and you knew you were going to get cuts and bruises. It's part and parcel of the game.

Terry Butcher

I must admit that I don't normally go around minding other people though, on one or two occasions, I have taken offence at the treatment meted out to my own room-mate Kenny Dalglish. Where he and Ian Rush rule is the hardest place to survive, that is, where you get really kicked just trying to do your job. They play where it gets positively naughty and the truly great strikers often have a quality the fans don't see – a large heart that keeps them going even when they are carrying injuries.

Playing against Pompey at Fratton Park in another of those so-called friendlies, a young Scot was trying to make a name for himself by kicking Kenny and anyone else who came within range. When the chance came I gave him a little nip only to be severely reprimanded by Bob Paisley for not letting people sort out their own battles. There are plenty of defenders around the world who would testify to Kenny being quite capable of doing that.

Graeme Souness, taken from Graeme Souness:
No Half Measures

Week in, week out, his consistently high level of skill is remarkable. From a referee's point of view, though, Kenny can be a difficult player to control. He will put his arm out and his rear anywhere in an effort to get the ball and I know that at times, he is guilty of backing into his defender and then, when he finishes on the ground, appealing for a free kick, when in fact he is the one who perpetrated the foul. But I also think that there are times when he is genuinely flattened by a defender and he does not receive the necessary protection. Referees sometimes do not read him properly.

Keith Hackett on Kenny Dalglish, taken from Hackett's Law: A Referee's Notebook

When he had his left cheekbone shattered in a clash with Kevin Moran of Manchester United, I was one of the first on the scene and was horrified by what I saw. The injury was so bad that it made me feel physically sick yet there he was, up on one knee and trying to push Moran away once more.

When frustration or anger overtake him he tries, now and again, to kick people but usually ends up getting hurt himself simply because it's not his game. Don't worry, Kenny can also look after himself out there when the boots are flying. He has to because otherwise he would not survive. He is cute, he uses his whole body, legs, arms and elbows and often sails on the borderline of foul play himself. He is exceptionally brave and physically a lot tougher than the critics give him credit for. He is kicked all the game long but I have never once seen him accept it and admit that he was beaten.

Graeme Souness on Kenny Dalglish, taken from Graeme Souness: No Half Measures

Kenny Burns didn't give a toss about anybody or anything. He wandered about the dressing room in exactly the same cocksure frame of mind, whether we were playing Liverpool or Lincoln. I still have a vivid picture of Burnsy, in one match with Liverpool, angrily turning on Kenny Dalglish and pointing a finger at him. That's all he did – pointed a finger. It was reminiscent of Dave Mackay. I think Dalglish finished up on the Kop because we didn't see him again.

Brian Clough, taken from Clough: The Autobiography

It felt as if they were lying in wait for me at Pittodrie. I'd take a look at the match programme in the dressing room before the game. Sure as fate, there would be a piece stressing how dangerous I could be. It would be written by Willie Miller or Alex Ferguson or someone else – but the message which hit me was always the same. I was going to be hammered!

Charlie Nicholas on playing Aberdeen, taken from Charlie: An Autobiography

He is a hard tackler and sometimes, his keenness to win the ball becomes too vigorous and over-physical, perhaps even cynical. It would be a tragedy if Williams' character prevented him becoming an established England international, because the man has skill in abundance. He must learn to win the ball with his hard tackles, but legitimately, and keep his mouth shut.

Keith Hackett on Steve Williams of Southampton and Arsenal, taken from Hackett's Law: A Referee's Notebook

I was crocked early on by a big raw lad called Forbes. A little later, another Motherwell player 'kneed' me in the back. The crowd was howling that I was faking it but I was injured all right, so much so that I didn't appear after the interval.

Gordon Strachan, taken from An Autobiography

I'm not a dirty player and I wouldn't even say that I am a hard player, but I do play to win. Defending is not always meant to be a pretty game. When I am tackling I always go for the ball and if a man gets in the way then that's too bad. I'll make no excuses for the fact that I've kicked a few people in my time and I've been kicked by a few people as well, but that's the way of football. When I'm marking a player I have to think that it's either him or me. I know it's a mercenary attitude, but the centre forward will take money out of your pocket if he scores. Obviously you don't kick him to bits but it's important to beat him.

Terry Butcher, taken from Both Sides of the Border: An Autobiography

This particular Graham is another fierce, uncompromising character and I have had a few run-ins with him. I suppose when he meets a player like myself it's inevitable it turns into a head-to-head personal contest. He loves a scrap, that's for sure. He will kick you without batting an eyelid, but whack him back and there is not a murmur. He is not a screamer.

Mark Hughes on Graham Roberts, taken from Sparky, Barcelona, Bayern and Back: The Autobiography of Mark Hughes

He kicked people in England and now I suppose he'll go up and kick people in Scotland.

Spurs manager David Pleat after transferring Graham Roberts to Rangers

Bull may not have the skill of some, but he's very strong and keeps nudging into you, putting you off balance. We exchanged a few comments during the game but I couldn't understand a word he was saying. That's some accent he's got.

Craig Short on Steve Bull, taken from The Umbro Book of Football Quotations

Graeme Souness is my idea of a hard man, so too is Graham Roberts, but not the likes of Vinny Jones.

Steve McMahon, taken from Macca Can! The Steve McMahon Story

For some reason Cyrille doesn't punch his weight on the pitch. I wish I could make him push, dig and challenge a bit harder. He would be a much better player for it. These are not just my thoughts, a lot of people have told me the same things. We are still looking to stoke up the fire.

Bobby Robson on Cyrille Regis

Gentle giant. I've heard it once, twice, a hundred times. Man, who do they think I am? I could change my image tomorrow. I could announce to the media that I am going to start frightening players by knocking them all over the pitch. My greatest asset as a player is my explosive pace and strength. It is not kicking lumps out of defenders. If I am doing badly in a game I hold my hands up and say, 'Look, I'm trying like hell, but it isn't working.' Belting someone isn't going to make it any better.

Cyrille Regis

I just won't tolerate markers taking liberties with me or my team-mates for that matter. And I am firmly convinced that defenders get the best part of the bargain as far as match officials are concerned. It seems to me that they are allowed two or three whacks at an opposing forward before the ref steps in and maybe dishes out a well deserved booking. Let a front man take a swing with a stray boot and there's no second chance. No reprieve. It's a case of 'What's your name, son?' and you are in the black book in no time.

With me I suspect there is an added handicap. Rival players realise I have powerful legs and am probably physically stronger than a lot of forwards. So they consider they have a licence to lean on me even more heavily than the rest. Because of this they tend to whack me harder and when I don't crumble, go down and start squealing they tend to get away with it. Yet the fact that I am capable of taking the punishment better than others doesn't make it any less of a foul. It hurts me just as much. But I grit my teeth and try not to show it. You can't allow the so-and-so's to think for a split-second that they might be winning.

Mark Hughes, taken from Sparky, Barcelona, Bayern and Back: The Autobiography of Mark Hughes

I'm used to the game being physical, especially in Scotland. The defenders were allowed to get away with much more than in England when I first came to Arsenal.

Charlie Nicholas, taken from Charlie: An Autobiography

Ron Harris was in the Brentford team that day. I'd obviously heard about his reputation, and although he wasn't marking me there were times when he came close to giving me a good kicking. Luckily my speed kept me out of trouble and we came away with a 1–1 draw.

Peter Beardsley playing for Carlisle against Brentford,
taken from Beardsley: An Autobiography

The season was only two minutes old before I was on the receiving end of my first foul, a kick from David O'Leary. That was harmless. The next, a couple of minutes later, was much nastier. A ball was cleared from our penalty area and, as I chested it down, Steve Williams put his studs down my leg. I felt Steve had gone to get me deliberately. People were crowding around as I lay on the floor and that shows they felt it was a bad tackle. I got another knock in the same place later on and had to limp off before the end.

Peter Beardsley on his debut for Liverpool against Arsenal,
taken from Beardsley: An Autobiography

Beardsley looked a great player, an absolutely brilliant player. I caught him with a couple of good early tackles early on – they were good tackles, too – and he just got up, forgot about them and got on with the job. He looked great.

Peter Reid on Peter Beardsley,
taken from Everton Winter Mexican Summer: A Football Diary

I went to have a look at him playing for Wealdstone on a stinking night at Yeovil. After eight minutes he put in a thundering tackle and the Yeovil winger landed in my wife's lap. I said to her: 'That's it. I've seen enough. We're going home.'

Bobby Gould on Stuart Pearce,
taken from The Umbro Book of Football Quotations

Players like Barry Horne and Peter Nicholas have always knocked opponents down, but now they have learned the old Norman Hunter trick of shaking hands and helping them up. In the old days, we'd knock them down and then want to fight them. In fairness I was probably the leader of the pack.

Terry Yorath

I don't really mean to kick anybody, but I do like to get involved. I certainly don't like to be considered a kicker, or a destroyer. When I first got out, my ideals were to be a creative midfield player, capable of stopping goals by defensive work and scoring them by attacking – really a bit of everything, an all-rounder.

Steve McMahon, taken from Macca Can! The Steve McMahon Story

The game in Scotland is much faster than English football.

Consequently the game is more physical and you have to be on your guard against high flying elbows. It can be very naughty at times. There aren't really any madmen about, but the game is physical and players are aggressive and want to square up to you all the time.

Terry Butcher, taken from Both Sides of the Border: An Autobiography

He has all the subtlety of a rhino, but see how he keeps winning the ball. And if a team isn't in possession of the ball, then it can do nothing – except, possibly, back-track, hoping for the best. Bryan wins the ball, then he uses it well. He is no tanner-ba' player. He is a formidable competitor. He might be approaching the stature of Dave Mackay. He would be in my team any time.

Jim Baxter on Bryan Robson, taken from Baxter: The Party's Over

Forget all the talk about Vinny Jones being the player to frighten the life out of you – they don't come any harder than Bryan Robson.

Glenn Roeder

I don't expect we shall see the Wimbledon of three or four years ago again.

They were a motley crew, with players like Vinny Jones, and they used to try to frighten you as a matter of course, very often succeeding as well – and I only sit on the bench! In the FA Cup Final when they shocked the football world by beating Liverpool I'm told there was an incredible atmosphere of intimidation in the tunnel as the players waited to come out at Wembley. I believe more than a few Liverpool players were shaking in their socks. Stories abound in the football world of how they tried to foster this physical presence, of how their manager at the time, Bobby Gould, used to encourage bust-ups among the players in training to get their pent-up aggression bubbling. It's a form of tribalism with rituals and you cannot knock it altogether – it has got them where they are today, up among the big boys.

Alex Ferguson, taken from Alex Ferguson: Six Years at United

If someone went through and I could catch him by bringing him down, I'd bring him down. If I didn't, I'd feel I'd let my team mates and my fans down.

Bryan Robson

If someone is through and likely to score, then I will definitely up-end him. That's part and parcel of the game. I'd do that without thinking. I'd commit a professional foul, if need be, if it was the right thing at the right time. The alternative is him going round me, putting the ball in the net and us losing 1–0. If it means me getting sent off and it's probably right that I should be – and the team getting something from the game, that is better than us getting nothing. Nine times out of ten I think I can get the ball in a tackle anyway, but the tenth time, by hook or by crook, I've got try and stop him. Probably my views are wrong, but I'm a professional and I can't let somebody just run through and put the ball in the net without me trying to do something about it.

You would probably say that I was a cheat, but I'd just say I'm a professional trying to win a game on Saturday afternoon. Whether that means handballing accidentally-on-purpose to score, or upending someone, I'd do it and it's up to the referee to spot it and penalize it.'

Viv Anderson, taken from Viv Anderson

All hell was let loose. Players were pulling each other about and it was one of those things you could do without. Viv was lying on the floor unconscious. Later, after an FA inquiry, Graham Kelly, the chief executive designate, in a *Guardian* report said that the Commission was satisfied Fashanu had hit Anderson, but that our man had 'directed insulting and improper comments' at the Wimbledon player. Fashanu was banned for three matches and fined £2,000. Viv was suspended for one game and fined £750. The sad part is that John has a bubbling personality and projects himself well on television. He does a lot of charity work which is tremendously worthy but there is another side to him. Football is a game of emotion and for some reason it appears he decided to take his feelings out on Viv Anderson that night.

I asked Viv to press charges with the police because I don't think that kind of situation should be tolerated.

If it had been the old handbags at dawn that we experienced with Arsenal the following season then you would have simply said behave yourself and let it go at that. This was totally different. I had never seen anything like it in football before, which is why I called the police.

Alex Ferguson, taken from Alex Ferguson: Six Years at United

There is no better exponent of the hard, but scrupulously fair tackle in the modern game than England and Manchester United skipper, Bryan Robson. He goes into the tackles, winning a ball he has no right, sometimes, even to consider winning. And he will come out of the challenge with the ball. But that's why he gets so many injuries, he is often too brave for his own good. While Bryan has suffered so many nasty injuries, he has never wilfully gone out to cripple an opponent. He is the perfect example of a highly motivated professional committed 100 per cent to win the ball, and nine times out of ten he will win it.

Steve McMahon, taken from Macca Can! The Steve McMahon Story

I watched them play Newcastle, who didn't make a single tackle! If they beat us 4–1 I can guarantee several of them would be on the treatment table on Monday morning.

Kevin Ratcliffe after watching Liverpool beat Newcastle 4–1

The turning point of the game, I think, was the ordering off of Kevin Moran for an innocuous tackle. He should never have gone. It was a bad decision by the referee. Kevin had made a tackle on Peter Reid, the Everton midfield player, and Peter had gone down. Suddenly the referee was ordering poor Kevin off. It was the ref's last game – I mean, his last ever game before retiring – and the FA had given him the final as a long-service award. He decided to make the headlines, and it could have ruined the game but instead the match caught fire because all of us were so upset at what had happened.

Viv Anderson, taken from Viv Anderson

You are trying to establish a physical dominance over an opponent, particularly as a full back. I didn't think about it so much earlier in my career because I did not need to, but now I'm a bit older and people start taking liberties, so I think: 'Well, I'm not standing for this, I think I'll get one in first.' Just so that he knows it's not going to be an easy afternoon for him and that anything he gets he is going to have to work for. It might be cynical, but that's football.

I like to get a strong tackle in early in the game, just to leave my mark. But, after that, giving away stupid fouls in stupid areas can cost you goals. The best place is either side of the halfway line because if it's a free-kick they're not going to score from there, are they? Fouling is part of the game because football is a physical game, but my disciplinary record is pretty good considering how long I've played.

Viv Anderson, taken from Viv Anderson

He was uncanny. You'd just think you'd got past him and this long leg would come out and the ball was gone. With his legs and his elbows, which were lethal, you had a helluva job trying to get past him in one piece. If the opposition had a particularly fast and tricky winger, Anderson would say: 'Yes, but he can't play without legs.' It was only half a joke, no joke at all if you happened to be on the receiving end of one of Anderson's early tackles, which he refers to with a grin as 'just saying hello'.

Tony Woodcock on Viv Anderson, taken from Viv Anderson

When you are young and somebody kicks you, you just accept it and get on with it, but when you get older it hurts more.

Viv Anderson, taken from Viv Anderson

Tottenham Hotspur. Graham Roberts used to be their hard man, but now I would have to nominate only one man at Spurs, Pat van den Hauwe. Their skipper, Gary Mabbut, is not afraid to go where it hurts, but Pat is a one-off. Actually, he's not a bad lad off the pitch when you get to know him. But on the pitch something can just snap. He can get wound up, particularly if he is annoyed. As a former Evertonian, I will best remember Pat van den Hauwe for one of his derby match tackles on Craig Johnston. It was enough to dissuade our Aussie colleague from taking any liberties during the rest of the match!

Steve McMahon, taken from Macca Can! The Steve McMahon Story

7 Elbows and Litigations

The modern game

Playing for Carlisle in the Third Division although the game was more physical than I'd been used to, I escaped without getting too much of a kicking. I was lucky to have a big fellow like Paul Bannon playing up front who took most of the knocks. The big, hard defenders normally marked him and I was given a bit more freedom. But I was on the receiving end of one or two fierce tackles that season. The worst was the first. Ironically it was the work of Steve Bruce, who I knew from our days in schoolboy football in Newcastle and who was by now playing for Gillingham. He caught me with a high tackle and with such force that for one moment as I lay on the ground in agony, I thought I would never walk again. The memory of that incident still makes me wince.

Peter Beardsley, taken from Beardsley: An Autobiography

Never would I describe myself as a hard man, because I cannot stand the way some players try to make up for a lack of ability by kicking everybody in sight. When I was young my enthusiasm sometimes ran away with me, but even then my most serious crime was nothing more than excessive enthusiasm. Nowadays, my colleague at Manchester United, Paul Parker, says he remembers me having a bit of a reputation when he was playing for Fulham and I was with Gillingham. That was as a result of what happened in my first season. I was suspended by the end of September and finished the season with a record number of 46 disciplinary points. If I had come up before the disciplinary commission any more times I think they might have shot me! I like to think that I have learned from those early days, even if I was the first man to be sent off when they brought in the ruling about professional fouls. I am proud of neither record and would rather be remembered as a decent footballer than as a hard man.

Steve Bruce, taken from Steve Bruce: Heading for Victory

John Fashanu had written what was described as an 'exclusive' newspaper article about coming back to his old club where he was going to frighten the life out of me. I was interviewed before the game by the local radio station in Norwich and said that however much John Fashanu and Wimbledon ranted and raved and tried to enhance their tough, 'Crazy Gang' image, there was nobody who could frighten me on a football pitch.

I was at home having something to eat on the Friday evening when the telephone rang. Janet answered it, and the caller asked for me. When she asked who it was, the caller said, 'Just tell him it's Fash.' A very clear and articulate voice greeted me, 'Brucey, it's Fash. What's all this I've heard on the radio while we were travelling up here? Is that right what you were spouting about not being frightened of me?' I discussed the matter, saying that he should not have put his name to the newspaper articles like he had as they were not good for the image of the game. After listening to what I had to say he just said, 'Well Steve, I can't wait to meet you by the far post tomorrow where we will mince heads,' and put the phone down. I could not finish my meal.

During the game there was an incident when the Wimbledon goalkeeper, Dave Beasant, punted the ball upfield and it bounced horribly between Fash and me. It was one of those where I had to shut my eyes, stick my head in and hope for the best against a man who weighed twelve stone of muscle. The two of us were flattened by the impact before getting up and exchanging meaningful glances. For the rest of the game his big mate, Vinny Jones, was going all over the pitch saying comforting things to me like, 'You're going to die; he'll kill you!'

Steve Bruce, taken from Steve Bruce: Heading for Victory

A lot of people are afraid to ask me about being sent off in that match. What they forget about is that it never really bothered me being sent off because we won the game. If we had lost the game I think that even now I'd feel a bit sick about it.

Kevin Moran on becoming the first player to be sent off in an
FA Cup Final

In the quarter-finals of the 1983 Scottish Cup that year we were
drawn against Kilmarnock. This player was taking things in
hand out there and he was going to 'do' me after the match and
he was going to 'do' the boss as well. When I reached the club
tea room, where families and guests congregate after the match,
I found Lesley, my wife, near to tears. The Kilmarnock players
had been sitting near her and this one had been vowing he was
going to break my ******* leg. A woman accompanying the
Kilmarnock party apparently joined in the abuse and my wife
was in quite a state. The player had no right to be behaving like
that in the tea room and when I arrived I picked up the gist of
his threat. Apparently if nobody else broke my leg before next
season he would do it. I chipped in with the remark that he
would be too slow to catch me and finally big Doug Rougvie
had to step in and tell him to shut his face. The big fellow is
handy in situations like that.

Gordon Strachan, taken from An Autobiography

During one game I was slumped down in the dressing room at
half-time with my head in my hands. 'Hey, what's the matter
with you?' Brian Clough demanded. 'It's the opposition, they
keep calling me a black bastard.' 'So what?' Clough said. 'Go
out there and call them white bastards.'

Viv Anderson

Years ago, I remember, somebody mentioned another aggressive
player, Mike Summerbee, who earned his corn across the road
at Manchester City. Apparently, so I'm told, Mike's basic phil-
osophy was to kick the defender first because he was always
going to kick you at some stage. I'm not quite like that, but I do
believe I have a right to some sort of protection from the
intimidators and kick-first merchants. In other words, I can
look after myself when it gets nasty. I'm lucky because I have
got the physical capability to do it. At one stage I was the

original 9–stone weakling and only about 5ft 6in into the bargain. These days I feel I can handle myself with the toughest customer.

Mark Hughes, taken from Sparky, Barcelona, Bayern and Back:
The Autobiography of Mark Hughes

Inchy (Adrian Heath) went in on McCall, and Cooper and Terry Butcher had a bit of a go at him. So I said to him, 'If you're going to do it, do it properly.' Not to be malicious, but little things like that can get people wound up and something might just break for you out of it. Butch reacted and had a right go at me. '. . . you dirty little ****' and I said, 'Shurrup, and get on with the game, you big, stupid ****,' and we were effing and blinding at one another, all 5ft 6in of me and 6ft 1in of him, and then slowly we both started smiling. Butch is a great fellow, and we had a joke in the bar afterwards. He had had to have stitches in a cut over his eye and I said to him, 'See, that's what you get for messing with me.'

Peter Reid, taken from Everton Winter Mexican Summer:
A Football Diary

I prefer to be marked by a big, gangly centre half, who commits himself to a tackle and gives a little fellow like me the chance to nip past him.

I've been lucky in that I've never been marked by out-and-out thugs. There are a few in the League, more so in the lower divisions. There are some who try to intimidate opponents by muttering things like, 'I'm going to snap your legs,' and similar threats. I have a moan from time to time if I think things are getting out of hand but I'm lucky to have the temperament which means I don't react. I'm not unsettled by tough talk and I think that once your opponent resorts to that then you know you've got him worried.

Peter Beardsley, taken from Beardsley: An Autobiography

He can be intimidating at times, and his tackling can be best described as 'ruthless'. I can understand it when Bobby Robson said, 'Who would want to play against him?' But it does annoy me that our Swedish international defender Glen Hysen was sent off for two 'nothing' challenges without any malice, when there are occasions that Pearce gets away with a diabolical tackle without any punishment. I have seen him get away with it.

I clashed with him in the League match at Anfield – there were a few words exchanged! When we are together with England, we're the best of mates, but that all changes when the Cup and the Championship are at stake.

Steve McMahon on Stuart Pearce, taken from Macca Can!
The Steve McMahon Story

Jimmy Case hit him with a shocking tackle (Adrian Heath) there was no way Case could have played the ball. It was a stupid tackle, Inchy went down and I went flying over there and ran into Wallace, who caught me in the face. I usually keep my head, but this time I lost it and struck out at him, which of course you should never do. It just goes to show that even at my age you can make mistakes.

The referee called us over and he said I ought to know what he (Case) was like, and to count myself lucky that he wasn't sending me off. Case's tackle was ridiculous and that started everything, but I could easily have gone.

Peter Reid on Everton v Southampton, taken from Everton
Winter Mexican Summer: A Football Diary

Do that once more pal, and I'll rip your ear off and spit in the hole.

**Vinny Jones to Kenny Dalglish after being on the receiving
end of a hard tackle from the Scot**

Vinny Jones has a more intimidating mouth than tackle. When he was at Wimbledon he was the king of the verbals.

Vinny Jones has been given a lot of credit for nullifying my impact in the FA Cup Final, but the truth is that Liverpool as a team didn't play well and I take my fair share of the blame for that. It has nothing to do with the fact that Vinny Jones made a neck-high tackle on me in the first five minutes of the Final. I got up and got on with the game; that tackle didn't worry me in the least. It is perfectly true that Wimbledon made it difficult for us, but it annoys me intensely that it has been suggested that Vinny Jones had more than six kicks in the entire Wembley Final! And two of them sent the ball into the stands. That was his only contribution.

Steve McMahon, taken from Macca Can! The Steve McMahon Story

Vinny is tough, there is no question about that, and he has this 'couldn't care less' attitude. He is the kind of player that nothing scares or worries. The first time I played against him he almost pulled my ear off when we were all battling in their area for a corner. I didn't say anything about it and then did it back to him a few minutes later. He thought it was a great joke and we had a good laugh about it for the rest of the game. I wouldn't call Vinny dirty – I wouldn't describe Wimbledon as over-physical – but he has got to learn to walk away from certain situations.

John Aldridge, taken from Inside Anfield

It had been in the papers about Gazza leaving Newcastle and how he was worth £2 million and, during the warm up, photographers were running all around him and I thought, 'What a fat so and so! Who does he think he is?' He was bubbly and looked like he was a bit of a character and a laugh. He didn't know who I was, or anyone on the Wimbledon side, but he didn't seem too bothered. He thought the whole day was about him and nobody else. There were 90 minutes to be played and he was prancing around like he was man of the match already. So I thought I would give him a rude awakening.

I stuck to Gazza right from the first whistle and I was so close he started taking the mickey. 'Is that all you can do, follow people around?' he said. I said, 'Well, that's what I'm getting paid for today, son, so you'll have to put up with it.'

Then I say, 'If you're so good, and are meant to be the business, why are you so fat?' And he said, 'I pay more in tax than you get wages.' It was just banter. When I went to take a throw-in and said, 'Don't go away, Fat Boy, I'll be back,' he shook his head as if he thought I had a screw loose.

Then Newcastle got a free kick near the half way line. I was marking Gascoigne on the edge of the box and got in front of him. As the kick was about to be taken, he whispered something. I can't remember what, but it was probably something cheeky. I just grabbed out behind me and got hold of his nuts. I just squeezed to teach him a lesson for being so mouthy. It wasn't planned – it was just a split-second reaction. He yelled in pain and I let go and carried on playing.

I had been told to mark him tightly and I went about it in such a way that he never touched the ball, but I touched his balls! Gazza was giving as good as he was getting with the verbals, and I honestly don't think I went over the top.

He came out for the second half a different person. He had shut up and wasn't giving me any lip anymore. He went so quiet I really didn't have to stop him getting the ball – he didn't want it. That was it then – I knew I had done the job.

Vinny Jones, taken from Gazza! A Biography

If you're going over the top on me you've got to put me out of the game because I'll be coming back for you, whether it's in the next five minutes or next season.

Vinny Jones

A first-class prat and an embarrassment to football

Shaun Teale on Vinny Jones

The idea that they were a bunch of thugs isn't true. They've attracted a bad reputation and people say they kick and intimidate opponents but I don't agree with that. They have never caused me any trouble, and players like Andy Thorn and Eric Young, who were marking me, were both fair. I don't remember getting kicked in any of our three meetings over the season. The Wimbledon team were shouting things in the tunnel (before the FA Cup Final), a few of their players were making comments in midfield but we're experienced enough to cope with that and laugh it off.

Peter Beardsley, taken from Beardsley: An Autobiography

We have to remain the British Bulldog SAS club. We have to sustain ourselves by sheer power and the attitude that we will kick ass. Before we go down, we'll have a stream of blood from here to Timbuktoo.

Wimbledon Chairman Sam Hammam, taken from The Umbro Book of Football Quotations

This team is nothing like the one I had at Wimbledon. That team would have been alright against Frazier and Tyson.

Former Wimbledon manager Dave Bassett, taken from The Umbro Book of Football Quotations

In the past we've heard so much about southern softies, but we have the character and desire of any northern team. It's one of the qualities of being successful.

Former Arsenal manager George Graham, taken from The Umbro Book of Football Quotations

They were all shouting at each other (the Arsenal team). It was 'f' this and 'f' that. I stepped in to calm things down, otherwise I'm sure punches would have been thrown.

Dion Dubin, taken from The Umbro Book of Football Quotations

Gascoigne's running style is provocative. With his arms flailing, his elbows flapping and his hands grasping, he resembles a late commuter attempting in desperation to board a train which is leaving the platform. Anyone in his way risks having the contours of their upper body instantly and painfully rearranged. To guard against such damage opponents tend instinctively to fend off the blows. Gascoigne and Birch, his marker, were like a pair of rudderless rowing boats, their oars constantly clashing. Olney was flattened by another of Gascoigne's inadvertent swipes and had to receive treatment for a facial wound. At one stage Birch was in danger of more serious injury. Gascoigne, after a free kick had already been awarded in his favour, turned his shirt into a tourniquet and threatened briefly to strangle him.

Stuart Jones on Spurs v Aston Villa, 1990

When you are defending against a player of that quality there are bound to be one or two fouls.

Jozet Vengles, Villa manager

I'd get angry with some of the things that were going on. He was pulled back nearly every time he went past someone. That is frustrating for him and for supporters. They want to see what happens when he has gone past someone.

Terry Venables on Gascoigne's treatment by Villa

When the ball is there to be won in the midfield Paul Gascoigne will go in, probably with his arms, to try and get his body in the way of players. Players do take bangs on the face. Paul is never going to intentionally elbow somebody in the face. It's not part of his make up. He just wants to play football.

Terry Butcher

Paul Gascoigne just gets carried away from time to time.

Gary Lineker

If I had to single out one defender who had made life difficult for me it would be Tony Adams. The Arsenal skipper is a hard man. When he tackles you from behind you feel it. As well as being strong on the ground, he is good in the air, organises his fellow defenders and refuses to accept defeat. My idea of the perfect defender would combine the best attributes of Adams, Des Walker and Neil Ruddock. If you added Tony's tackling, grit and determination Des's pace and marking ability and Neil's power and passing ability, you would have a real Frankenstein's monster – a striker's nightmare.

Alan Shearer, taken from Alan Shearer's Diary of a Season

I personally have been battered on a number of occasions. The only difference from when I played and current-day football are two things: one, the no tackling from behind rule, which came into force in 1971. This has actually made the game a bit easier. It has slowed it down, but made it easier for forwards. They used to be able to tackle you from behind at any height, whatever height they wanted.

Two, there wasn't, when we played, as much detailed camera work. If you saw a game when we played television had one camera, which was at the back of the stand and nobody ever saw what went on on the pitch. Now you can get inside players minds virtually with the camera.

Jimmy Greaves

When I played with Fash, if he was on his game, flying and winning all the headers, roaring about, he would give the rest of us such a big lift. But if he wasn't at it, all the other boys used to say to me: 'Hey, Vinny, set your mate going. Get him livened up.' Because we were looking for him to spark it all off for us. I used to shout at him, but sometimes Fash wasn't at it. He'd have five good games and one bad one. Sometimes you'd know before the game that Fash wasn't at it. On the coach going to the game he'd say, 'Who've we got today. Who plays at the back for them?' The manager didn't know it but I did. If I'd have been picking the team I'd have said leave him out today.

Vinny Jones on John Fashanu

At Southampton he was a bit of a tearaway, although you could have said that about me in my early days, too. But I calmed down a hell of a lot, and that was what he had to do too.

He always wanted to make it to the top, but he had a bit too short a fuse at that time.

Neil needed to calm down a bit, but without losing his aggression. He can certainly play a bit and he is good on the ball, but that aggression is his big strength.

His ability was all there, but his temper was one of the only things that could stifle it.

Most people's fuses go off once in a while, but Neil's would go off several times in the one game. He would run 15 or 20 yards to an incident that had nothing to do with him.

I said to him that you've got to look after number one. If you've got a reputation, there could be fifteen fists flying but if you step in, it's you who will get sent off while the other fifteen stay on the pitch.

Jimmy Case on Neil Ruddock

I am clear through with only David James ahead of me. I am tackled by John Scales and Neil Ruddock. When I'm down on the floor Neil tramples all over me. He could have avoided me. I am so angry that I stand up and grab him around the throat. He tries to push me away. The referee Roger Dilkes is quickly on the scene. The ref insists he could send us both off for raising our hands to each other but settles for a yellow card apiece. But I was so angry at being trodden on, it was just an instinctive reaction. I go up to the player's lounge afterwards but don't see Neil. Nor do I want to. I have a very sleepless night tossing and turning and playing the events of the match over and over again in my mind.

Neil rings me up later. I ask him, 'Are you ringing up to apologise?' He replies, 'No, I am not.' He laughs and says he thought he was going to get sent off for the tackle, so he decided he would go off in style by walking all over me. I'm not sure whether he's being serious but we agree it's an incident best forgotten.

Alan Shearer, taken from Alan Shearer's Diary of a Season

He'll come towards you aggressively, with his face twisted in rage, giving out a load of verbals.

**Referee Brian Hill on the Alan Shearer method
of contesting decisions**

Kelly's remarks that he would watch four games a week and see 200 such tackles was the most ludicrous statement I have ever heard. It is almost an encouragement to players to behave recklessly.

Kelly has given the impression that football is the equivalent of a bar-room brawl. But clubs like ours spend an enormous amount of time, effort and money trying to attract the general public. Kelly has brought the game into disrepute.

Mike Bateson, Chairman of Torquay after Graham Kelly, FA Chief Executive told the Crown Court that Gary Blissett of Brentford had been involved in an 'ordinary aerial challenge' with Torquay's John Uzzell; Blissett was acquitted of causing grievous bodily harm to a fellow professional

I am absolutely gutted, not only for John Uzzell but for football. Kelly had an ideal opportunity to help rid professional football in this country of one of the biggest ills in the game today – the elbow in the face. He did not take it.

As a result of all this, referees will have lost the credibility they deserve. Having heard the verdict and Kelly's evidence, players will think that it's quite legal to go and challenge for the ball in the way Blissett did. It is surprising, because in 1987, when I was president of the Football League Referees and Linesmen's Association, the theme of my speech to our conference was 'The Arm and the Law'. Graham Kelly spoke on the subject and condemned the illegal use of the elbow.

Lester Shapter, former leading referee, on the Uzzell–Blissett case

I would refer everybody to the fact that the FA did find that, under the laws of the game, the player concerned did commit an offence because, after its own enquiry, the FA subsequently suspended him for three games.

Peter Willis, a spokesman for the Referees' Association

I have no regrets and have had no second thoughts about my role in the court case. It would have been simple for me to take the easy way out and not become involved but I did not do that. I believe I did the right thing and I feel very sorry for Gary Blissett that this had to come to court.

I could have said that because of my position with the FA this was too delicate an issue to become involved with, and that it was not a good idea for me to be put on the spot and possibly take the opposite stance from a referee in court. But I did not because I believed that I should do the right thing.

Graham Kelly's response to the criticism

Never mind the fact that he has exquisite touch and incredible vision, Cantona is simply something else – sort of mystical in a way. And I've felt the hairs on the back of my neck stand up just watching him training.

When I first came to Old Trafford, I couldn't wait to check out whether all the talk was true about Cantona or if it was media hype.

Well, I'm here to tell you Eric's been undersold. He's better than the headlines make him. Not only has he the skill, he has the spirit, he has the brain power, the magic.

Also, he has the brawn and the brute strength. I have been amazed at just how powerful he is, how determined to keep the ball he is, under the most brutal pressure.

Even at training, the lads don't mess with him. They know he won't stand for being shoved around. It's because he generates an amazing aura of respect.

Andy Cole

Players like myself, Roy Keane and Eric Cantona can dish it out but it's just our natural aggression.

But the real hard men are people like Steve Bruce and Mark Hughes. They get battered and bruised every game but they just get on with it.

Paul Ince

When I get on to the field I've always found that I can express myself better that I can off it. I am very combative on the pitch – but I will say one thing: no-one ever gets seriously hurt playing against me. I just need to be very physically involved in a game.

Mark Hughes

As soon as I'd done it I knew it was wrong. I'm not stupid. It was just two seconds of madness and I'm sorry for what happened.

I've let a lot of people down. People from the club, the fans, my family and obviously myself. It happened at a really bad time following the death of the fan the previous weekend.

I'm just so sorry it happened. It was something on the spur of the moment which I now regret. Everything happened so quickly. As soon as it happened things were okay with Gareth Southgate and me. We knew the score. He probably knew it was a late tackle and I overreacted. Simple as that.

But it didn't help when all the other players ran in – that made it worse. When I ran off after the red card I knew I had done wrong.

The timing of the incident was really bad and that's an under-statement. It's been a bad season for football with a lot of trouble. I don't really know what went through my mind.

There was no doubt though that I had to be sent off. But it's the first time I have been. I have been booked a few times but I've never gone out to hurt anyone. Ever. I have often been done myself but I've never gone out to do another player. To be honest, I didn't put any weight on Southgate. But that doesn't matter, I should not have done it.

I've seen it on TV and in pictures since and it was just madness.

Roy Keane after being sent off for stamping on Gareth Southgate

Aggression is fine in football, provided it is channelled in the right direction.

He thinks he is a little hard man, but he isn't in the same class as some of the real hard men of football. There is no doubting his ability, and he gives everything he has got. But he should forget this idea that he is a hard man. He struts around as though he owns the place, and he seems to have this personal vendetta against anyone who tackles him and takes the ball off him.

He gets the red mist in front of his eyes and goes looking for them, and it was obvious that he was looking for someone when he tangled with Gareth Southgate.

Ferguson's excuse is that he has a passion for the game. So did I, so did Tommy Smith, Graeme Souness and others – but we knew when to draw the line.

Larry Lloyd on Roy Keane

Maybe I have got a reputation as a hard player, perhaps a little fiery at times, but I consider myself a fair player. Hard but fair. Midfield is perhaps the most competitive of areas. I've played at right back and it's different. Midfield is more intense; more confrontational.

Roy Keane

Manchester United's Roy Keane is a strong aggressive player, and also a very good footballer, but Newcastle are top of the league with people like Robert Lee and Beardsley, they play football, they haven't got an enforcer. Liverpool are the same. There's not that many enforcers around nowadays. We certainly haven't got any at West Ham. Our midfield players are footballers. Julian Dicks has deserved all he's got, but he's a good footballer, with a magnificent left foot. He can really play, he's international class when he plays, but his problems have come with his disciplinary record.

Harry Rednapp

Until last year I have never had a discipline problem . . . I think that I am unfortunate in the players I have got together to form a winning team.

I mean that we have players who burn the fuse. They need to win. When they lose, they go way, way down. You can see it, feel it, smell it. That's the quality you're looking for. But when they get together you don't always know what's going to happen. There will be explosions at times. But that is part of the character of winners. And people don't like Manchester United to win. We're not the most popular side, because we are the biggest. So we'll always be attacked. As manager, you have to go inside yourself, be single-minded and get on with the job, and not let yourself be affected by all this bloody nonsense.

Alex Ferguson

Paul Ince may do a lot of yapping, which upsets referees, but he is not a violent man.

Alex Ferguson

He's as hard as nails and doesn't give you a moment's peace. Fantastic stamina, very strong in the tackle and a real threat going forward.

Gary Speed on Roy Keane

United have the ultimate dogs of war in Paul Ince and Roy Keane.
When I used that phrase for my players I was taken out of context. I didn't mean it in a derogatory way.
Paul Ince is the most complete midfield player in the country. The only chink is possibly his temperament, but you know he will be there for you on the ice and mud as well as the good pitches. He is the ultimate dog of war.

Joe Royle

He's a disgrace. I'd have cut him in half had I played against him.

Brian Clough on Paul Ince

It's my opinion that Saunders has jumped towards the ball with the intention of missing the ball and causing harm to Paul Elliott.

Terry Butcher to the High Court during the case brought by Paul Elliott against Dean Saunders, 1994

This incident could have been avoided by Mr Saunders taking evasive action. He could have jumped out of the way.

Tony Ward, former Football League referee, who saw the incident on Match of the Day

I think Dean Saunders was more interested in Paul Elliott than he was in the ball.

Don Howe

You can't let him get away with that. It was over the top.

Ronnie Whelan, Saunders' team mate, who was the nearest Liverpool player to the incident, to Malcolm Allison, retained by Liverpool as an expert witness

After I spoke to Ronnie Whelan I was in great doubt. Players know better than anyone else.

Malcolm Allison

If you are off the ground, the tackling player hits you and you tend not to get hurt so much. Had he (Saunders) kept his feet on the ground he could have been seriously hurt.

Larry Lloyd

It was a damage limitation exercise by the Liverpool player. When a defender comes in as low as Paul (Elliott) you are not really going to win the ball, all you can do is remain on the field. You keep the ball between your studs and your opponent's studs.

Geoff Hurst

Only one person in this room knows if Saunders intended to go over the top and that is Saunders. Players are going to get hurt. I believe there is enough money in the game to compensate in these circumstances.

Vinny Jones

My strong impression was that he was telling the truth when he said his intent was only on going for the ball and it was instinct which at the last minute, made him take both feet off the ground in an attempt to avoid possible serious injury to himself.

Mr Justice Drake after finding Dean Saunders not guilty of a deliberate foul tackle that ended Paul Elliott's career. Elliott was seeking £1 million compensation from Saunders, but was left with a £500,000 legal bill to pay

The judgement means that the floodgates are now unlikely to open on similar actions by other professionals. However, it is likely to force the football authorities finally to set up their own form of compensation court for players whose careers are ended by injury.

Richard Duce

All I can say is that we should never have been here in the first place.

Dean Saunders on hearing the verdict

People say it's a physical sport – and it does demand your aggression. You've got to have that aggression to do well in it. But I would never go out to injure an opponent or deliberately try to put them out of the game. I'll go in for a tackle. I'm not renowned as a ball-winning player, but I'll go in for tackles and I'll be aggressive in the way I play the game. I'll try not to react if I'm getting fouled or bad treatment. Fans say that they've noticed that.

I do react now and again. It's a very emotional game. You're at 90 miles an hour out there. Things happen and your temper can get the better of you sometimes.

I think sometimes that if you say you're a Christian people think that you're supposed to be holy and perfect, but as Christians what we're saying is we're not perfect. You're still going to swear now and again. You're trying not to and you don't swear as much as you used to, but sometimes your temper will get the better of you. Sometimes you will worry about things that you know you shouldn't do – heat of the moment stuff. It is something that I will obviously work on and probably will always be working on. We'll never be perfect but God's definitely helped me there.

Gavin Peacock, taken from Never Walk Alone

Some wives shout at the games, jump up and down and get really into it. But I sit very quiet, the only time I get worried is when he goes down with an injury. Sometimes those tackles can be the end of your career. You hear of players swallowing their tongues and that's my worst nightmare. I can imagine myself running down the gangway to try and reach him.

Amanda Peacock, wife of Gavin, taken from Never Walk Alone

I tend not to fear opponents, I try to make them fear me more than anything. I try to lay down the law in the first ten minutes and let them do the chasing.

Jason McAteer

There's a great spirit in the Nottingham Forest team. You know everybody's going to be fighting for each other. You know you're not going to get shat on by your mate who's going to think, 'I'll get out of a tackle' or whatever. If someone goes past you, there's going to be another lad there.

Steve Stone

There was an incident between Incey and Stuart Pearce. Ince went down. Pearce claimed that he dived, which he doesn't do, and they had an exchange of views. Nothing unusual in that, except that Pearce made some racist remarks, and Ince, understandably, reacted angrily. Match of the Day was very selective. They didn't show the Pearce–Ince incident; they hardly showed any of the bookings. And they never showed the incident when Brucey was elbowed. His teeth went right through the gum. I couldn't see, and the linesman didn't flag, but the players said Stone hit him with the elbow. A good wee player Stone, but he can be really difficult. He's had three broken legs himself. A tough wee bugger, but difficult as well.

Alex Ferguson on Manchester United v Nottingham Forest,
taken from A Year in the Life: The Manager's Diary

You seem to pick up bookings for nothing this season. I was substituted against Newcastle because I'd already been booked, which is ridiculous.

Joe Parkinson

I would have loved to have played in Colin Harvey's era. The manliness seems to have gone out of football since then, that kick and be kicked mentality.

Neville Southall

At times I think Vinny Jones gets carried away with the reputation that has been built up for him. I've played against the guy on lots of occasions, and I'd have to say that on occasions he shows a lot of ability. But too often he seems to get involved in everything that is wrong about football.

Gary Stevens

I don't know how you define the word 'hard man'. Certainly there's skilful players and there's tough players who give 100 per cent. It's the media that gives you the label. My definition of myself would be a tough all-rounder.

Who would people want in their side. A 100 per center, or a 'Mr Nice Guy' like Gary Lineker?

Managers want players who are going to put their life on the line for him. If you were at the bottom of the League struggling, would you call on Gary Lineker?

Vinny Jones

I don't think you can knock Vinny Jones's enthusiasm. As a footballer? Quite frankly 25 years ago he wouldn't have got a game. I honestly don't think his football ability is of a great standard, but his enthusiasm is unbounding. I think the difference between being hard and dirty is that you go out to actually assault people. Being just hard you go out to play the game. It might be in some people's books that having a word with one or two players, like I did, is not the right thing to do. But if that is going to assure you that you are going to have an easier game, well, that is the way it was then. This is not having a go at Vinny Jones because he is making a living out of it and good luck to the lad. I don't think he is respected by his fellow professionals though, the way that say Norman Hunter was.

He was the first player to get a Players' Player of the Year Award. Doesn't that say something for Norman when all the players voted for him? That's how good a player he was. I never voted for him by the way! I think the difference is that the likes of Vinny Jones has not been mentioned for this type of award. If I was looking to pick a team, Vinny would never get in it.

Tommy Smith

The game is rapidly becoming a non-contact sport. Against Holland, they leaned on us, they held us, they'd just push you off balance a little bit. They're strong, but they're not gonna put a foot in and give you a free kick.

You've got to do what the Dutch do, lean on the opposition, don't go diving into tackles giving away free kicks. The Europeans have recognised this in English football. We are behind them, miles behind.

Jack Charlton

I'd have been sent off every game nowadays for ungentlemanly conduct, some of the things that I got up to.

There's no laughter on the park nowadays. The spectators are not laughing, the players are not laughing, it's too serious.

Jim Baxter

People think you can't tackle from behind, but you can as long as you play the ball. But if you mistime it or the ball should bobble up and there is contact with the player instead then it is a cautionable offence.

It's very difficult. But with the advent of the mandatory instruction after the World Cup last season there are no ifs and buts.

If, for example, a player has played the ball from behind and the player he's tackled goes over, there is no problem at all because we have completed the law.

Referee Pat Partridge

In the current climate with referees, challenging from behind, unless you get it absolutely 200 per cent perfect – no chance.

Ron Atkinson

I notice on Teletext that David Batty and Tim Sherwood could be charged by the Football Association for challenges they made during the West Ham game. As far as David's tackle was concerned, it was late and he probably deserved to get booked but it was no worse than the one on Chris Sutton which earned

Julian Dicks a caution. Tim caught Don Hutchinson with a flying elbow but, again, I do not believe there was anything malicious involved. It was a game with so much at stake that you were bound to get total commitment and a few bumps and bruises. West Ham's Hutchinson and Jeroen Boere finished up with broken noses, Colin Hendry with a gashed eye and me with a swollen mouth but no-one from either side complained. That's the way it should be and I am surprised that the FA has got involved.

Alan Shearer on the West Ham v Blackburn game,
taken from Alan Shearer's Diary of a Season

I've watched him on TV a few times and he's running around like a lunatic. He appears to have gone back to the bad old days when he first injured himself at Spurs and I can't understand it. He's totally lost it and has no discipline. I can't believe England are picking him, and more worryingly, relying on him.

Jimmy Greaves on Paul Gascoigne

So Paul Gascoigne thinks he's being victimised in Scotland. He should have been around when Graeme Souness joined Rangers.

Souness was the first superstar to hit the Scottish game in years and really was a target for opponents. The Ibrox player-manager was sent off for retaliation before half-time on his debut.

I've seen him play eleven times for Rangers and I'm unaware of any vendetta against him by opponents. Referees have been more than lenient in their dealings with him. In fact, some have been too soft. For me, the bottom line is that most of Gazza's troubles are in his own head. He gets far too wound up trying to impress. He should relax more and allow his natural ability to shine through.

But he must accept opponents are entitled to challenge him for the ball, and he simply must keep his arms to himself. Unless he learns this quickly, his time in Scotland will end in tears.

Bill McFarlane

It's about time Paul Gascoigne was given a bit of protection from Scotland's referees.

Many of them appear overawed by him, and wary of his reputation. They go into games with a preconceived notion that Gazza will be out to con them from the kick-off. As a result, when opponents actually get at Gascoigne in an effort to unsettle him, they very often get away with it.

Eventually Paul, who's not renowned for being tolerant, reaches breaking point and ends up getting in bother with the ref himself. He's now been booked five times in just thirteen games for Rangers, a record no-one would be proud of.

Ian St John

I remember an interesting game between Spurs and Leeds when David Batty was given the job of marking Gascoigne. The strange thing was that Leeds were on top, but Gascoigne was in control of his shadow. It was no reflection on Batty who in fact had a good game, but it still didn't stop Gascoigne teasing Leeds and producing his full bag of tricks. Of course he overdid it, which is his weakness.

Alex Ferguson, taken from Alex Ferguson: Six Years at United

After the World Cup they cut out the tackling from behind because there is no way you can fairly and squarely win a tackle from behind. There is no way you can do that legitimately without catching the player.

Now it's creeping in again. So-called 'quality defenders' with a lot of experience are whacking forwards from behind and getting away with it. They make rules, then after about four weeks it goes out the window.

Tommy Docherty

I remember playing Middlesbrough at Ayresome Park.

The dressing room atmosphere that day was a bit too light-hearted for my liking. So I thought I would liven things up a little, and Vinny was just the man to get the whole mood changed.

I went out of the dressing room for a couple of minutes and

then came back in and told Vinny that I had heard two of their midfield players bad-mouthing him.

Well, he started kicking tables and doors and punching the walls and suddenly we were up for the game and there was no way that the fellow Putney – the player he was marking – was going to be allowed to play. In fact he didn't kick a ball. Vinny made sure of that. Then, with about ten minutes to go, when we were winning 2–0 and I was congratulating myself on the way it had all worked out, the whole thing almost rebounded on me. Vinny suddenly slapped the other lad, Brennan, on the head and turned to me and asked: 'What was he saying about me before the game, wee man?' The Middlesbrough lad just stood there looking totally bewildered by all of this. I mumbled something and moved off in another direction before the story had to be explained.

Gordon Strachan, taken from Strachan Style: A Life in Football

He's Jekyll and Hyde. It's not that he loses his temper but that he wants to win so badly he goes for tackles he shouldn't. Often, on the side, I'd be saying to myself, 'Don't go for it, you can't get it,' and he'd go diving in. The referees know it's him and so do the crowds. It's not the ref's fault. Vinny has earned that reputation. It's exuberance.

Don Howe on Vinny Jones

He joined Leeds in the close season, a few months after I had signed. I did wonder at the time if he was going to be able to fit into the strict disciplinary code which the Boss laid down.

When we played in a pre-season match in Belgium against their champions, Anderlecht, I thought all my worst fears were going to be realised. For the first twenty minutes nothing much happened and Vinny hadn't even kicked the ball yet. Then from behind me I heard this thud and Vinny trotted by me grinning all over his face. 'Well that's the first one of the season,' he said. I looked round and there was this Belgian lad with his nose all over his face and blood everywhere. It was suddenly and painfully obvious to me what had happened. Vinny had just done him. I couldn't believe it. I thought to myself this is not what we need at this club. This is really not what we need at all.

What had happened was there had been a throw-in and the ball had been cleared upfield. Vinny had whacked the opposition player in the face and the ball had not even reached him. No-one saw it and Vinny escaped scot-free.

Gordon Strachan, taken from Strachan Style: A Life in Football

I remember once getting involved in a 50–50 tackle with Vinny a few years ago. We both went in for the ball at 100 mph and were determined to win it.

I ended up with stud marks from my ankle to my groin while Vinny was left with eight stitches in his shin. But we both tried to pretend we were not hurt.

We had a row in the bar afterwards about who actually won the tackle. To this day I still believe it was me, Vinny!

Neil Ruddock

Vinny Jones speaks his mind and four hours later is on a charge. David Ginola says Jones does not deserve to be considered a footballer. What happens? Sweet FA.

Ian Wright brands refs as 'Little Hitlers'. What happens? Next to sweet FA.

Bryan Robson says: 'You talk rubbish – you can't play football, Vinny.' What happens? Sweet FA.

The FA rulebook has been rewritten. Rule 1 now reads: 'You can shoot your mouth off as long as your name's not Vinny Jones.'

The *Daily Mirror*

He did growl at some of the opposition. Sometimes they froze and some of the rest of us were given room to play. He is a frightening looking guy but he is a funny man too, and he can laugh at himself. I don't mind playing against him now because while I'm sure he will attempt to intimidate me, I know that he would not go out of his way to deliberately hurt me. Anyhow, I have heard all the threats before, and they don't worry me when I'm out on the field. Besides, I know Vinny's secret – he can really be a big softie.

Gordon Strachan, taken from Strachan Style: A Life in Football

The game has lost a bit of edge now because there is just not so much blood and thunder.

I remember before the Spurs game earlier this season when Jurgen Klinsmann came over to say hello and I asked him if he was enjoying English football. I said to him that he'd come just at the right time because there isn't any tackling any more.

Some defenders try to use their skill to play the ball out from the back . . . just as Alan Hansen used to be so good at. And there are those who try to beat you with sheer physical power. I find those easier to play against because that is my type of game.

When the skilful ones steal the ball of me I find that very intimidating and unnerving.

Mark Hughes

I have to learn to keep my temper in check, I know that. Sometimes it boils over through frustration – mainly when things aren't going for us, but what annoys me is that the papers make more of it. It was claimed that my sending off this season was for elbowing when it was actually for kicking and tripping up. But I am trying to cork it and I think I'm getting better.

Paul Devlin

He does go in for the intimidation side of the game – and I know I'm always going to get ruddy hell – but there are never any hard feelings between us when we leave the field. We've had a few cuts and bruises over the years.

Mark Hughes on Neil Ruddock

No player wants to be remembered for being dirty and I don't know of any player in the game who goes out to try to injure an opponent.

We all genuinely go for the ball – it's just that sometimes we can miss it by quite a distance and unfortunately the tackle looks worse than it really was.

But there is a difference between a hard player – and therefore an aggressive tackler – and someone who just tries to be hard for the sake of his image.

Neil Ruddock

Now and again things gets a bit frustrating and people get carried away, but this was not me losing my temper.

When I went for the ball it was just unfortunate the Portuguese player's leg was under my foot when it was.

Alan Thompson after being sent off playing for England Under-21 team against Portugal

I haven't played against a team like them for a long time.

They showed a total disregard for the laws of the game. There was loads going on. And it was all down to them.

If the referee isn't going to give you any help, what chance have you got?

Oldham's Andy Richie after playing against Millwall, 1995

We all just wish that referees would understand what players will tolerate during a match.

Tackling is part of the game, but I can see a situation developing where the game will go more like it is in Italy, with teams defending deeper and trying to intercept rather than win the ball.

Barry Horne

The referees haven't played the game at the top level, and I feel sometimes they don't know what to look for. I'm constantly having a go at referees, in a nice way, just to let them know that sometimes they have got to keep their eye on a player after a pass has been made. They tend to follow the ball when sometimes they should watch what happens. I know certain players who are going to be late in a tackle and if I was a referee I would know that there are certain players, who after the ball is gone, will carry on with the tackle. They get away with it because the referee has turned his head and followed the ball. It is very difficult, because players know what to look for because they are doing it half the time. Players know how to look for it because they have got to try and avoid injury from the players who are doing these things.

Matthew Le Tissier

They are a very physical side, Everton, and if you don't stand up to them they'll jump on you.

Stuart Pearson on Joe Royle's Everton

Earlier in my career, strikers used to try and wind me up, but that doesn't happen as frequently now.

I have calmed down a lot and don't let them get to me. The crackdown on tackles from behind has improved me, I used to dive in, take a chance and end up sliding on my backside. Now I try to judge my tackles to perfection. It calls for a different level of concentration.

Neil Ruddock

Defenders are having to think a lot more before diving in.

I saw Jack Charlton interviewed last week, when he said that the game had changed so much you could hardly tackle any more. It's certainly a big concern.

When I was sent off this season against Manchester United it was for two fouls in quick succession. The second was a pretty irrational challenge and, in that respect, I made the referee's mind up for him.

It's something defenders everywhere are having to keep in their minds during matches, especially when you've already been booked.

It might encourage attacking players to run at defences, but it's hell for defenders!

David Unsworth

I have been in the professional game for fifteen years and the first thing I was taught as a defender was to let the centre forward know that you're around.

You had to make sure that he knew he wasn't going to have it easy when the ball came to him. But when the tackle from behind was totally eradicated, you couldn't even touch someone without getting a yellow card. I found that very difficult to come to terms with. I'd be in the middle of a game and questioning whether I should commit myself to a tackle or not. Overnight, the game became much easier for the striker. It took me about six months to get used to it.

Steve Bruce

Playing against Tony Adams, the first tackle from him was always straight through you BANG! This happened every time. He's a good player, but the fact that you can't get away with that now has taken something from his game.

John Aldridge

As a player he was hardly whiter than white himself – yet he does a thing like this to me.

As far as I am concerned he instigated all this. He's the man who put me up in front of the FA. Spencer accepted my explanation that it was not intentional. He tried to help me and I'll be ringing to thank him for that. But Andy Gray? I've no intention of speaking to him and I will certainly never shake his hand.

I accept he's got a job to do and know that football is a game of opinions. But he should keep opinions like that to himself.

Julian Dicks on Sky TV pundit Andy Gray's criticism of his tackle on Chelsea's John Spencer that led to a three-match ban

Julian Dicks is a good player. I always thought he lacked a little bit of discipline after the ball was won, or he'd fouled somebody. He kept going on about it. He would do something after the ball was away. The big problem he has got these days is the fact that there are so many cameras knocking around the grounds. He's going to get copped. I disagree with Andy Gray having a go at him. Andy Gray is entitled to his opinion, but to say that Dicks should be banned, or sent out of the game is a bit over the top. If the cameras followed every player on the pitch I think they can always pick out one or two things that happen. They then go on and on, and on about it. At the end of the day the football is lost. It is a man's game and it is a physical game.

Tommy Smith.

I was with him at Birmingham and remember thinking that this was a kid who had got absolutely everything.

It's very sad that there's this other side to him, because he's got all the ability in the world. I like to believe that these outbreaks are nothing more than blind enthusiasm.

He would die for West Ham.

Dennis Mortimer on Julian Dicks

Unfortunately, this kind of thing seems to follow Dicks around. There was no need for it, particularly in a testimonial game. Dicks has kicked me before in games but then again he has kicked most players. I don't know why he does it and it's a shame because he is such a good player.

Woking's Clive Walker after being on the receiving end of the Julian Dicks treatment in a pre-season friendly

I thought there were far too many men booked – it's got to the point where you can't touch people.

QPR manager Ray Wilkins after seven of his team were booked and one sent off against Manchester City

Glyn Hodges and Charlie Hartfield came up to me before the FA Cup replay and apologised. They said, 'Sorry Wrighty, that was bang out of order, you didn't do anything.'

That made me feel better, but it didn't stop 100 or so United fans trying to get at me when our coach parked outside Bramall Lane. I had to be pushed into the dressing room, protected by a dozen security men and policemen, just to stop the fans getting to me.

Perhaps Nilsen was trying to psych me out for the replay. If so, he did a good job because I played rubbish.

Ian Wright after allegations that he spat at Sheffield United's Nilsen proved unfounded

I do regret what happened, there was an aggressive verbal confrontation between three people that ended in handshakes after the game. Kevin was very good about it afterwards. He wished us well and there were handshakes all round.

There was no physical contact made during the incident. But there was out on the pitch. And that was much more damaging.

I was concerned for Lee Dixon. He could have been lying in hospital now with a fractured jaw, fractured cheekbone and injured eye.

I'm disappointed about the situation I got in. But I've lived in America and seen two entire teams of baseball players slug it out on the diamond. I've seen head coaches and referees go face to face on the touchline.

You can sit down afterwards and think: Christ, I wish that hadn't happened.

Bruce Rioch on his touchline bust-up with Kevin Keegan and Terry McDermott after David Ginola was sent off for elbowing Lee Dixon

I went to watch Liverpool v Leeds on Saturday – or at least I thought I did.

It certainly wasn't like the Liverpool–Leeds matches I remembered from the sixties and seventies. There was no blood and thunder and Leeds were very disappointing.

I sat and watched the match with Norman Hunter. I took £5 off him when Leeds came to Goodison Park recently, and I knew Leeds weren't going to be up to much when Norman refused to take double or quits with me!

Tommy Smith, 1996

Almost as disappointing as the 1–1 result was the Everton fans' reaction to Dutch master Ruud Gullit.

A performance oozing class and composure was almost terminated early when Craig Short clattered him with a tackle that was late, high and ugly.

Gullit was able to limp painfully on after a couple of minutes' treatment – only to have his every subsequent touch booed! Whatever happened to Evertonians' appreciation for elegant football?

David Prentice

At the moment there is an atmosphere of hysteria surrounding the game which is fanned by some newspapers, radio stations

185

and television channels. The premise is that everybody has to win. Losing is a disgrace to one's manhood.

Howard Wilkinson after several of his Leeds players were threatened physically and verbally by Birmingham supporters, 1996

McDonald was called to the referee's room at the interval and cautioned for crossing himself going off the park. It's normal practice for him, you can ask any player at the club – he does that every time he steps on or off a pitch.

But I'd never seen anyone in Italy getting cautioned for it.

The ref said he was inciting the crowd. You know which city you're in then, don't you?

Partick Thistle manager Murdo McLeod after Roddy McDonald was sent off against Rangers for two yellow cards; one of them for crossing himself

There is so much pressure on players for results these days, so much money is invested in making teams successful that it takes a terrible toll on the players' minds. The fear and pressure is getting through to players. That leads to reactions like that incident with Le Saux and Batty, and these are being high-lighted.

We need now in the modern game to pay far more attention to psychology and making sure players' heads are right for dealing with the incredible pressures they're under.

Gordon Taylor

Duncan Ferguson for me has got the lot. I see something of myself in him, I really do. But he's a bloody fool the way he carries on. He's gotta take the knocks, every centre forward gets a boot up the backside now and then, but he's gotta take it and come back for more. He's potentially a great, great player. He can either end up a millionaire, or end up in the gutter. It's up to him.

Tommy Lawton

I was as shocked as the next man when the big Scot was sent

down for something that happened on a football field. Where will it all end?

I've seen cricketers bowling bouncers at an opponent's head. It's the sole reason why batsmen wear helmets these days. Will we see a top bowler jailed in the future because he has intimidated an opponent to the point of hitting him with a ball?

Or will a boxer who uses his head on purpose find himself disqualified and sent to prison for assault?

This is a real can of worms. People have said I would have been a prime candidate for the nick because I went in where it hurt.

I certainly didn't hold back, but I was never sent off for serious foul play. The only time one of my tackles put an opponent in an ambulance was when I slid in with Frank Clarke for a loose ball when he was at Newcastle. Frank broke his leg, but it was a complete accident.

My dismissals were for having a little chat with referees, not least Clive Thomas. The Ferguson verdict means that we might even find ourselves up in court for that! What if you call a ref a name in the heat of battle and he decides you have slandered him.

I'm glad I'm watching my football from the press box these days, otherwise I would be in more trouble than it's worth.

Tommy Smith on the jailing of Duncan Ferguson

I've noticed I've been coming off the pitch black and blue while Duncan's been out.

If you play as the main target man you get knocked about a lot more than you do if you are playing off someone. I find Duncan easy to play off – like Peter Withe in my early days at Aston Villa. And I find it easier to score when he's around.

Paul Rideout on the return of Duncan Ferguson

I don't think in any way that Duncan [Ferguson] should be inside a prison. It's a disgrace. First and foremost his offence was committed on a football pitch. I thought it was only mild violence. I've seen a lot worse things on the pitch. If he's going to be punished at all it should be by a football committee. To go to prison for what I think was a very minor offence on a football pitch is I think totally out of order and I can see no sense in that.

Roy Evans

I don't condone Ferguson's actions. But Big Dunc didn't do anything on the afternoon of 16 April 1994 that hasn't been done before on a football pitch.

The long arm of the law decided to intervene, Ferguson's previous criminal record was taken into account and he's now doing porridge.

During my playing career, I was sent off more than once for retaliation. If a defender went over the top in a tackle, your automatic reaction was to whack him back. If the referee saw it, you were heading for an early bath. You felt hard done by, but it was part and parcel of professional football, and you accepted the consequences.

Football's own brand of justice has been seen to be done and there was never, ever any suggestion of the police becoming involved.

Ian St John

Think of professional footballers today. Neville Southall? Me, I'm eccentric. Roy Keane? He's short tempered. How about Vinny Jones? He's just a barmpot.

The truth is, off the football field none of us are as we have been portrayed. But such is the power of the media, people in authority believe those misconceptions. Particularly referees – or in Duncan's case members of the legal establishment in Scotland.

I watched Vinny Jones' sending-off on Monday against Nottingham Forest and thought it was ridiculously harsh.

It was interesting to see that the referee who sent him off was the same man who red-carded Barry Horne at Bolton recently. After that match the paper talk was all about how Paul Alcock was wrong to dismiss Barry.

Do you think it would have been the same state of affairs if

Duncan Ferguson had challenged Keith Branagan? What do you think?

Neville Southall

It was major surgery, but even though the bone was pushed backwards and smashed it hadn't got into my brain. And that's where I was lucky.

I was all swollen up, disfigured, no hair where I had been shaved, and black and blue around my eyes. It's something that happened. I was unlucky to get caught on a tender place.

I've had it before. Steve Ogrizovic of Coventry punched me instead of the ball when attempting to clear, and fractured my skull.

And I've done it to other players. Never deliberately of course.

It is sometimes inevitable when you jump for the ball. Most times your arms go up for leverage.

Trevor Morley on how an elbow from a Portsmouth player left him needing neuro-surgery

The use of the elbow is the worst crime in soccer. People talk of over-the-top tackles but at least you've got a chance, albeit a small one, to save yourself as the boot comes in. The elbow is a heinous crime, used only by the lowest of the low. It's virtually impossible to protect yourself against it. Anyone who uses the trick deserves everything thrown at him. Players don't know when it is going to happen. As a defender, your eyes are on the ball so there is no way to avoid it. I was just eighteen when I first suffered the elbow. It was for Preston against Grimsby and I lost three teeth. We've had players with fractured cheek bones and court action and still the FA don't learn. An elbow is a dangerous weapon – it must be outlawed.

Mark Lawrenson

8   Spitting and Kicking

The foreign experience

There was that time in Italy when the crowd was at me. 'Kay, Bastardo, Bastardo.' They were behind this wire grille. I banged the ball at their faces. So what happens when we come off at the end? I'm there, with our team in the dressing room, and I'm standing at the tunnel thanking everyone, and I go up to this Italian trainer, who's only about 7 feet tall, I hold my hand out, and what does he do? He's only got both me arms pinned behind me back. And all the Italian team's giving me one as they go off the field.

Tony Kay, taken from The Football Man:
People and Passions in Soccer

These games must go on until we learn to accept each other's ways.

Sir Matt Busby on playing foreign opposition

They call me 'Chopper' Harris but, believe me, when I see some of the tactics used by players on the Continent I reckon I'm almost a soccer angel. They're the choppers of football, not the British players.

There is a world of difference in our attitudes to the game. That is why I believe there will always be trouble when we meet.

Ron 'Chopper' Harris, taken from Soccer the Hard Way

Ronnie Rooke often recalls an incident in a match in Rio. In a goalmouth skirmish, he suddenly found himself being throttled by the opposing goalkeeper, whom he had been charging heavily.

Ronnie, losing his breath rapidly, felt the only thing he could do was to put his hands behind him and try to hurt his assailant so much that he would release his grip.

Ronnie did this and squeezed hard. He was conscious of someone sinking to his knees under his fierce grip but, unhappily, he swiftly realised that he had caught hold of the wrong individual. The grip round his own neck had not relaxed, and did not until a colleague came to his rescue. But the Brazilian player whom Ronnie was manhandling could not see the funny side of this.

Bob Wall on the 1950s Arsenal tour of Brazil, taken from
Arsenal From the Heart

You in England are playing now in the style we Continentals used so many years ago, with much physical strength but no method, no technique.

**Barcelona coach Helenio Herrera after their 5–2 win against
Wolves in the 1950s**

The atmosphere was intimidating, but we had some strong characters in our side, such as Wilbur Cush, who was known as the 'Iron Man'. Wilbur was a fierce tackler and didn't like cheats. He clobbered one of the Greeks and the stretcher was called for to remove the injured man. When the Greeks scored as the stretcher party was making its way to the dressing room, the 'victim' rolled off the stretcher and jumped up and down in celebration. 'I'll be waiting for him when we play in Belfast,' said Wilbur.

Ireland were defeated 2–1.

Ten days later came the return game against the Greeks and, as he promised, Wilbur Cush duly sorted out the Greek player who had upset his sense of fair play in the first match.

Terry Neill on Greece v Northern Ireland, taken from Revelations
of a Football Manager

I didn't even have the satisfaction of hitting anybody. Spurs were playing OFK of Yugoslavia in the first leg in Belgrade.

They were ultra defensive and nasty with it. There were a lot of boots flying around and they were giving us plenty of stick. So Dave Mackay and Smithy started to even things out a bit and I cannot think of two blokes I would rather have on my side in a rough house.

It was to what I merely call Smithy's enthusiasm that I got my marching orders for the one and only time in my life. Going for a ball, his elbow caught their centre half in the stomach. It really took the wind out of the bloke and he went down on his knees. I stood looking on quite innocently when suddenly this fellah jumps up and comes at me like a bull. He wasn't a bad judge picking on me rather than Smithy, was he? Anyway, he threw a punch and missed and I immediately threw one back – and missed. I never was any good at counter-punching.

The Hungarian ref, I shall always be convinced, saw the whole incident. Certainly the British football writers didn't. Without exception they all wrote they were mystified that I was sent off.

At first I thought the ref had made a mistake and didn't walk right away until I realised he was waving at me. He was quoted as saying I wasn't gentlemanly and tried to kick somebody. I hope he was misquoted because, word of honour, I never raised a foot. It was then I'd wished my retaliation punch had landed, though it would more than likely have broken my hand. But it's a bit hard being expected to take a wallop without instinctively countering.

Jimmy Greaves, taken from Let's Be Honest

There remained some ruthless and cruel tackling which brought the flint sparks that we had first seen in Belgrade. It was not altogether a healthy thing, this feeling on these nights. Victory, at times, would seem to cost too much a price in dignity.

It is human, I suppose, and understandable, but at moments animal instincts seemed to creep in.

The Times **on Spurs v OFK Belgrade, European Cup Winners' Cup**

Like all of us Smithy was choked about playing badly and losing in Bratislavia. As we came off the pitch he made some sort of 'I'll have you at home' gesture to the centre half who had been giving him a bit of a rough time. Then he showed a clenched fist to the Slovan keeper, only a little bloke, and was muttering something about 'Londres' which was the nearest he could get to being understood in Slav. Anyway, they must have got the message. I've never seen two blokes go white so quickly. They knew what was coming.

Smithy didn't disappoint them. He charged the goalkeeper into the back of the net in the opening minutes and the poor bloke lost all his appetite for the game. We knocked six past him because he was always too busy for Smithy coming at him to worry about the ball.

Jimmy Greaves on Spurs v Slovan Bratislavia in the European Cup Winners' Cup, taken from Let's Be Honest

They were up to all the cynical stuff. Pulling your hair, spitting, treading on your toes. Altafini was one of the worst.

Andy Nelson on Ipswich v Milan

That was a real fight, literally! The match over there ended in a big punch-up. I still smile when I think of little Alex Young running round with his fists up like John L. Sullivan!

Everton's Jimmy Gabriel on playing against Real Zaragoza

Above all things in Continental football you expect to get protection for the goalkeeper. The referee never protected Lawrence in this case and Peiro kicked him on the arm to get possession of the ball. The goal was a disgrace. That referee haunts me to this day.

Bill Shankly, after Peiro kicked the ball from Tommy Lawrence's hands and scored Inter Milan's second goal

That referee (Senor Mendilbil) is on my hit list. I've never come across him since but I'll admit that as we came off the pitch in Milan I actually kicked him. I just booted him and he never changed his step, or even registered that I kicked him. He just kept on walking and I thought, 'Yeah, you have been fiddled.' Because at the end of the day he actually should have sent me off, or done something about it. If somebody kicked me I'd give them a clip back.

Tommy Smith

The slightest bodily challenge or contact in going for possession of the ball brought a free kick for Inter. Inter were awarded 20 free kicks for fouls to Liverpool's three. It was ludicrous, but infinitely damaging to the hopes of Liverpool whose players were frightened to make a tackle in case the referee pulled them up.

Michael Charters on Inter Milan v Liverpool,
European Cup semi-final

George Best was set upon by two defenders whose orders must have been to maim him. But he took them on like a matador, weaving away out of distance of their savage tackles. No-one I ever played with or saw could ride a tackle better than George Best. He was, quite simply, the greatest player of my time.

Terry Neill on Northern Ireland v Uruguay,
taken from Revelations of a Football Manager

Unlike some skilful forwards, George could look after himself when the going got tough.

Although he lost his temper on occasions I never saw him go over the top on an opponent – despite the number of times he suffered that kind of treatment. One night, playing against Bulgaria in Sofia, he took some terrible stick. It seemed the only Bulgarian tactic was to kick George at every opportunity, and they were virtually lining up to have a go at him. Finally, it was too much even for George to take and he had a kick at a defender and was sent off. What's more Bulgaria were awarded a penalty and converted it. The biggest tribute I can pay to George is that not a single Irish player blamed him afterwards.

Pat Jennings on George Best, taken from An Autobiography

The South Americans and the Italians made an art out of dirty play, with every game a succession of professional fouls.

When you were about to jump for a corner they would stand on your foot and by the time you had kicked their foot away the ball was gone. Or they would stand really close to you and punch you in the kidneys just as the ball was coming over. The very least that did was take your mind off the game for a moment. But you got to know their tricks and how to deal with them. You learnt that if you stood still they would clobber you so you learnt to keep moving. When you did that the shirt pulling would start, but at least that way you were likely to get the free kick awarded in your favour instead of having it awarded against you for trying to push them away as they were about to punch you in the back. If you did make any contact with them they would instantly fall to the ground. By the time they stopped rolling they would be 20 yards away from where the incident took place.

George Best, taken from The Good, the Bad and the Bubbly

Bertoni's frustration at his team's ineffectiveness gradually increased until he could take no more and, after Cherry had again denied him space, he turned round and punched him in the mouth. No acting was needed in this instance as Cherry was lying on the ground with blood streaming from his mouth; one tooth knocked out and another split clean in half. The South American referee consulted his South American linesman and, quite correctly, sent Bertoni off the field for violent conduct. Then, to everyone's absolute astonishment, he also showed the red card to the blameless Cherry who went off to a barrage of coins and other missiles. It was explained to us later that the referee had made this outrageous decision to ensure that no riot broke out in the infamous Bon-Bon Stadium. It seems that this was quite normal and that if a home player was sent off a member of the opposition team had to go as well.

Steve Coppell on the sending off of Trevor Cherry and Bertoni, Argentina v England 1977, taken from Touch and Go

Betini was an artist at fouling a man without getting caught. Whenever he came close he managed to dig me in the ribs, or put his fist in my stomach, or to kick me in the shins during a tackle . . .
Betini was an artist, I must admit.

Pele on Italian International Betini

Nobby Stiles is a dangerous marker, tenacious and sometimes brutal. He takes recourse to anything to contain his man. Very badly intentioned. A bad sportsman.

Otto Gloria, Benfica's coach

Chelsea were playing a pre-season tour match in Stuttgart and Tommy Docherty introduced the idea for that game of me, as skipper, wearing an armband so that I could be the accepted person to query any decisions or for the referee to recognise. It was a local referee and, when he gave the Germans a disputed goal, I am afraid that some of us 'took the mickey'. We went across to him and sarcastically applauded his decision to allow the goal. The referee spoke some English and he said to me: 'Once more you are off.' Well, the next foul was down to me and I took the long walk to the dressing rooms.

Ron 'Chopper' Harris, taken from Soccer the Hard Way

When you were playing foreign opposition, even looking to avoid incidents didn't stop them developing. In a match at Old Trafford against the Yugoslavian side Sarajevo I fell over in the penalty area trying to go for a cross. The ball ran out of play and their keeper came across to help me back onto my feet – or so I thought. But as he started to lift me he started digging his nails into my back. I swung out with the back of my hand, which may have looked as if I was being ungracious but was really no more than irritation combined with self-protection.

That was the start of it. For the rest of the match, whenever I went near the keeper he would wag his finger at me and say in broken English. 'You, after the game.' I told Paddy Crerand that the keeper was going to get hold of me the moment the final whistle blew. Paddy told me I was being stupid. I wasn't. When the game was finished and we were walking down the players' tunnel the goalkeeper moved to get hold of me. Paddy stepped in and tried to get hold of him.

The next moment everyone was involved. Fists and boots were flying, everyone was shouting, people were wrestling with each other. The fight carried on right up the tunnel, almost into the dressing rooms.

We were told afterwards that poor old Sir Matt had caught a stray blow.

George Best, taken from The Good, the Bad and the Bubbly

Competing in Europe has also taught us, and I suppose this applies to me in particular, self-control against opponents who will try anything on the field to irritate and anger rivals. Since starting our Fairs Cup campaign many people have told me that I am a more restrained player these days, that I am not quite so prone to retaliate at provocation as I was.

It has taken many pep talks from our manager, Don Revie, and personal experience for me to realise that it is pointless bringing one's ability down to gutter level and thus handing the initiative to the opposition.

Calmness in such situations comes with experience and I think I am just a little more experienced these days!

Mind you, I thought I might really blow my top in that clash against Valencia of Spain, a team who put on the worst show of hacking, shirt tugging and body checking I have ever seen at any level of competition.

Centre half Jackie Charlton, of course, came in for the biggest hammering of all. It is understandable that he hit out and I would have done the same. Human endurance has to snap at some time!

Billy Bremner, taken from You Get Nowt for Being Second

Omar Sivori got away with murder during a game against Leeds United. The victim was Mike O'Grady. In Naples he was the 'fall guy'. I suddenly realised that the huge crowd were treating us to one vast wolf-whistle, for some reason which I could not fathom. I looked round, and spotted Mike walking along in a sort of daze, with blood streaming down his face. On the ground lay Sivori, for all the world as if he were dead, except that he was laughing. I asked Mike: 'For crying out loud, what's been going on?' Mike was too bemused to answer, and I won't repeat everything he said. But the sum total was: 'The so-and-so butted me in the face – and he just lay down!'

Up came the referee. He virtually ignored Sivori, who was

having treatment for his so-called injury from a corps of attendants, and took out his notebook to enter Mike's name in it. Mike had been having a great game up to then; but that booking put him right off. The butting didn't help any, either. If ever a guy was 'conned', that guy was poor Mike O'Grady. Especially when Sivori finally rose to his feet, laughed in Mike's face, then sauntered upfield.

Billy Bremner, taken from You Get Nowt for Being Second

The date was 2 February 1966. And that tie against Valencia really erupted into violence – with me right in the thick of things. Looking back, I blame myself for having allowed my temper to flare as it did; and I know I have never allowed myself to get into quite the same state since. At the time, as now, I could plead only the direst provocation. They said I went beserk ... and I can scarcely argue with that term.

Fifteen minutes to go, and I raced upfield to add my weight to one of our attacks. As I challenged an opponent in the Valencia penalty area, I was kicked. This angered me, of course – but before I knew where I was I found myself having to take much more ... for one of my opponents slung a punch which would have done credit to Cassius Clay.

Right there and then my anger boiled over ... I chased around that penalty area, intent upon only one thing – getting my own back. I had completely lost control of myself, after these diabolical fouls upon me, and neither the Spaniards nor the restraining hands of my team mates could prevent my pursuit for vengeance. Suddenly players seemed to be pushing and jostling each other everywhere. Police appeared on the field to stop this game of football from degenerating into a running battle. And Dutch referee Leo Horn walked off with his linesmen, signalling to club officials of both teams to get their players off, too.

I was still breathing fire when I reached the dressing room – then I got the word that I need not go back. For a moment I thought the referee had called off the match ... then it sank home that it was only Jackie Charlton's presence which was not required any longer. For eleven minutes the teams remained off the field, to allow tempers on both sides to cool down. By that time, I was beginning to feel sorry for myself, and not a little ashamed of the way I had lost my self-control. The only consolation I had was that a Valencia man – left back Garcia Bidagany – had been told he need not return to the fray, either. So it was ten against ten.

But that wasn't the end of the excitement, though. With only seven minutes left for play there was more trouble when Valencia inside forward Sanchez–Lage kicked Jim Storrie . . . and was sent off for this misdemeanour. However, both teams realised that this must be the end of the feuding, and the game was finally finished, with the score still standing at 1–1.

Jack Charlton on Leeds v Valencia,
taken from For Leeds and England

I have always regarded Charlton as a fine man. He was the cleanest player on the field, until he lost all control. I saw a Spanish defender kick him, and if Charlton had given a reprisal kick I could have understood and let it pass, because it happens so often. As captain of Leeds, and an international, he should have been the first player to exercise complete self-control.

Money has made them too eager. After sixteen years of international refereeing, I believe money causes all the trouble, all the nervousness and desperate play. It is no use clubs expecting referees to impose discipline, the referee is there to control a match. Players must be taught to control themselves.

Referee Leo Horn after sending off Jack Charlton against Valencia in the Fairs Cup

Most Continental players are excitable by nature and tend to flare up very easily. They are also masters at the art of antagonising opponents behind the referee's back and getting the match officials on their side.

A classic example of this was Leeds' clash against Naples in the 1967–8 Fairs Cup which we won on the toss of a coin. In the second leg one of the Naples' players butted Mike O'Grady in the face with the ball yards away.

The Italian then fell to the ground with both hands over his face and writhing in mock agony. He should have been on the stage with an act like that! He was smiling as he received 'treatment' from the Naples trainer, but the referee was completely taken in by the ruse, and issued a stern lecture to O'Grady!

Johnny Giles, taken from Forward with Leeds

There was one occasion, and one occasion only, when I played a game of football with murder in my heart. It was the time I saw the greatest little player in my days at Leeds United chopped down ruthlessly. As he lay there, with his thigh bone broken, I was so upset that I found myself weeping, and I honestly believe that there and then, had the chance come my way, I could have 'done' the player who had so crippled one of my team mates.

The game was in Italy, against Torino. It was an Inter-Cities Fairs Cup-tie. And the victim of the incident was a fellow Scot, wee Bobby Collins.

That foul was just about the worst I have ever seen. When I realised what had happened, I lost my head completely, and I snarled at the opponent who had felled Bobby: 'I'll kill you!' Believe me, right there and then, I meant it. Tears were spilling from my eyes; tears of hot anger and rebellious resentment. I don't imagine that the player knew what I had said, or that he even understood one word; but there was no doubt that he got the message, for he never came within a mile of me during the remainder of the game. Perhaps it was as well – for me, as for him.

That was a long time ago now, and since then I hope I have learned something. Certainly I have never gone on the field with such an attitude of mind before or since that match. But at that moment of blazing anger and white hot passion, when a red mist completely obscured my better judgement, I could not have been fully responsible for my actions, had we tangled in a fight for possession of the ball. For Bobby Collins was 10 yards from the ball when he was literally jumped on.

Billy Bremner on Leeds v Torino,
taken from You Get Nowt for Being Second

In a European Cup-tie Tommy Smith was being given the run around by the Polish player he was supposed to be marking. One of the lads shouted across to Tommy: 'Smithy, hit him for Christ's sake!' The 'iron man' grimaced, his shirt steaming in the bitterly cold night air: 'Hit him? I couldn't get f****** near enough!'

Ian Hargraves

The Spaniards are better intimidators than the Mafia. Somewhere along the line the Spanish FA must have legalised spitting, because the Bilbao players seemed to be European Champions at it. They could hit a goalie between the eyes from the halfway line. If you felt a dampness on the back of your neck there was a 50–50 chance it wasn't sweat. Unfortunately, again I lost my rag and was shown the tunnel for retaliating.

Willie Johnston on Rangers v Bilbao, taken from Willie Johnston: On the Wing!

When Celtic played their ferocious series of International Cup matches against Racing Club of Buenos Aires, Jimmy Johnstone, at half time in the play-off in Montevideo, had to wash the spittle out of his hair.

Brian Glanville, taken from Champions of Europe: The History, Romance and Intrigue of the European Cup

One man in particular was to be remembered from our opening World Cup match. The name was Mihai Mocanu. Occupation: marksman.

He made his mark on Keith Newton, Tommy Wright, and yours truly. For days afterwards I still had the scars on my legs to prove it. He put Newton out of the match with a desperate tackle that the Everton full back described: 'I thought my leg had snapped. My eyes watered like they've never done before. The pain was the worst ever.' As Mocanu hit him Newton had already parted with the ball. The story was the same with Wright, and then I pushed the ball past him and was starting to think about the next man and he felled me.

I think he must have created a new tackle. For the general impression was that he started kicking at knee level, and worked up to the throat. He kicked me on the left knee and his boot ricochetted onto the right, leaving identical imprints from the pattern on his boot on each knee.

Looking back it was incredible that he was not sent off.

Pele had nearly everything. Maradona has everything. He works harder, does more and is more skilful. Trouble is that he'll be remembered for another reason. He bends the rules to suit himself.

Morais, of Portugal, had a field day fouling me, and eventually putting me out of the game. He tripped me and when I was stumbling to the ground he leaped at me, feet first, and cut me down completely. It wasn't until I actually saw the films of the game that I realised what a terribly vicious double-foul it was. The stands came to their feet screaming at the foul, but the English referee, George McCabe, allowed Morais to remain on the field, although again, even in the most inexperienced league in the world, he would have been thrown out for either of the two fouls, let alone both. Dr Gosling and Mario Americo came to help me from the field, and Brazil went on to play with ten men, and ended up eliminated from the tournament.

I had been the target of merciless attacks from Zhechev of Bulgaria throughout the entire game. I have heard it said since, and I firmly believe it, that Sir Stanley Rouse, the British president of FIFA at the time and the man who selected the referees at Liverpool where the game was played, had instructed those referees to go easy on the 'virile' game played by the European teams against the South Americans, with the result that Zhechev did everything he could to physically cripple me, and the referee, Jim Finney gave neither me nor any of the others on our team the protection we had a right to expect from an official in a game.

Jock Stein had asked me to do a man-for-man marking job on him. Jock said to me 'Have you even done a marking job?' and some of the Scottish boys shouted out, 'Well he's done a few marking jobs on people!' Jock said 'No, I'm not talking about him marking them.' I said 'I'll do it.' Pele was in his pomp in 1966. He was absolutely magnificent. He was backing into me, just before he was receiving the ball. As he's backing in, he gives me a little nudge and then he's off. I got two or three good tackles in on him and I was getting all the dirty looks from him. I thought 'At least you know I'm about.'

In the second half a ball was knocked into the box and the ball was just above me and I'm looking up at Pele, who is looking down at me low and behold he gives me one with his elbow. Whack! right in the cheekbone.

Straight away my eye started to swell up and started to close. John Clark came across and he was threatening Pele 'I'll kill yer, I'll do this to yer.' I'm lying there semi-conscious. Then when we came in at time-up Willie Bell of Leeds United, who was a right religious type of guy, was really downhearted. He comes up to me, he's nearly crying. He says to me, 'Pele, I'll never, ever, have any respect for that Pele.' I said 'Why?' He said, 'Doing that dastardly deed to you. Elbowing you in the face. Who would think Pele would ever do a thing like that?' I said, 'Willie, I kicked ten bells of you know what out of him out there, he's entitled to sort me out whenever he gets the opportunity.' Willie must have been living in a dream world!

Billy Bremner on Pele

I was completely disgusted with what happened in 1966 and today, more than ten years later, I still am.

Besides, who needed to face the type of refereeing we faced in England that year? And when I say 'we' I mean not just Brazil but all the South American teams. The play of Zhechev in the game between Brazil and Bulgaria led one French journalist to say he was sure that, being the target I was and with the refereeing that was in evidence, I wouldn't last through the tournament – and he was right. Another journalist wrote that the play of Morais in the game between Brazil and Portugal was '. . . the most scandalous of World Cup play'. But the referees, under orders in my opinion, managed to overlook every infraction, and I was left with a leg that could well have meant the end of my football career.

Pele, taken from My Life and the Beautiful Game: The
Autobiography of Pele

I have come to accept that the life of a front-runner is a hard one, that he will suffer more injuries than most men and that many of those injuries will not be accidental.

Pele

For all his fantastic skills and reputation, Pele was playing on his past and would go down for a free kick if anybody went near him.

Francis Lee on Pele, World Cup 1970

I was disappointed with the way he performed against Northern Ireland during a World Cup-tie in Amsterdam. That day, Neeskens' mission in life seemed to be to make sure that George Best received as much stick as possible during the whole of the 90 minutes, and I felt that a player of the Dutch star's reputation and skill really shouldn't have needed to go in like that, even though he might have been instructed to make sure he kept on breathing down George's neck.

Sammy McIlroy, taken from Manchester United: My Team

The Dutch detailed Neeskens to mark George in that match. Neeskens was some player, but George made a monkey out of him and 'nut-megged' the Dutch star so often that he finished by offering Neeskens a tie-up from his socks to tie his legs together.

Pat Jennings, taken from An Autobiography

The first time was in an Under-21 match at Casale in Italy when I was a 17 year old.

At one stage in the game the ball bounced between myself and a Casale player. In my attempt to get it, I caught him on the chest with my boot, splitting his shirt. It was a clumsy foul and there was blood everywhere from where my boot landed. The incident provoked a nasty scene.

There was a free-for-all on the touchline and Tommy Docherty was involved in a skirmish with some players. Bottles were thrown and I needed a police escort to the dressing room. Tommy Docherty and I sat out the rest of the match there, with the police in attendance.

Ron 'Chopper' Harris on his first sending-off,
taken from Soccer the Hard Way

The Italians, like the Spaniards, are Grand Masters at spitting, but their favourite ploy is nipping. Nipping bottoms, faces, arms and any other bits they can tweak between two fingers. Inevitably one of the Italians was ordered off for dangerous play, but as often happens against the Latins, the poor intimidated referee feels obliged to even up the situation, especially when the stadium is full of Sicilian waiters with bulging jackets. Eventually a Rangers player had to go off as well – me!

I had been doing nothing wrong, except running about like a Blackpool donkey at the Glasgow Fair trying to avoid the hatchet legs of their defenders. At least one of them chopped me, and in exasperation I resorted to the native dialect.

'Eff off, you big Italian b–,' I roared.

The referee took his opportunity like a ferret takes a one-legged rabbit. 'No Italian b–s here,' he yelled, pointing furiously towards the tunnel. I was raging, because of the decision and because I forgot the referee could speak English. I was somewhat reluctant to obey his rantings, so the next thing this big New York policeman comes across to the touchline and 'escorts' me off at gunpoint!

Wille Johnston on playing for Rangers v Florentina in America, taken from Willie Johnston: On the Wing!

One of their Italian internationalists was doing a marking job on me, and I'm not exaggerating when I say that during the game I found myself being spat upon and my shirt being tugged. Even when you tried to avoid him, you would find a kick being aimed at you. The business started in the first minute of the match. The ball was cleared up the park, and I was about to turn and see if I could get possession when I felt an elbow gouging into one of my eyes.

The atmosphere was horrific, with the Italian fans screaming their heads off, and what went on off the ball was incredible. Stuart Pearson, Steve Coppell, myself – just about every United player came in for the treatment at one stage or another, and you felt as if you were taking your life in your hands whenever you ventured near the ball. Certainly I wouldn't like to come up against opposition like that week in, week out.

Sammy McIlroy on Manchester United v Juventus,
taken from Manchester United: My Team

I was one of the linesmen when Jim refereed a match between Hertha Berlin and Vitoria Setubal at the Olympic Stadium in Berlin in 1970.

The game began to get rather tough towards the end of the first half and one Setubal player, in particular, was giving Jim a hell of a lot of trouble. At half-time, Jim said: 'I'll have him in the second half, even if he bloody sniffs.'

Just after half-time, that player committed a foul and then tried the old trick of hiding behind some of his team mates, hoping to hide himself. And in this stadium full of Germans – Jim, myself and the other linesmen were quite probably the only English people there – he shouted down the field: 'Come here you bastard.'

I felt proud to be British on that occasion!

Gordon Hill on referee Jim Finney, taken from Give a Little
Whistle: The Recollections of a Remarkable Referee

Throughout the tournament, in which we knew that straight-forward tackling would be condemned, we earned a reputation for showing restraint under extreme provocation. This was something we had to do because we knew that everybody was gunning for us, and waiting to pounce on the slightest slip.

The lads stood up to everything magnificently in this way, but it was worth reflecting when we got back home that the respect we earned for turning the other cheek was back again. We had always been termed good losers before we met with any world success. Now we had lost the title, and we were getting the same write-ups again. For my money that is the kind of tag I do not want on an England team. I would rather come home hated by everybody in the world, and winners.'

Francis Lee on the 1970 World Cup, taken from Soccer Round the World: A Football Star's Story from Manchester to Mexico

I'd remembered reading in the Press that they'd had to lock the dressing rooms after the first leg at Molineux to make sure the two teams didn't confront one another. I didn't notice an air of unpleasantness when we took the field in Rome, but there must have been because Wolves' striker Hugh Curran was assaulted in the very first minute.

From the kick-off, the ball was immediately pushed into Wolves' half, I followed it down, and it went dead. I turned and Curran was unconscious in the centre circle. Nobody saw it – the linesmen didn't see it. I didn't see it, because we'd all turned to follow play. Wolves' trainer Sammy Chung told me that as soon as I'd blown the whistle to start the game, and the ball had gone away, a Lazio player had walked up to Hugh Curran and hit him, just blatantly knocked him out.

The game suddenly erupted when Lazio's goalkeeper came rushing out of the penalty area and flattened Wolves' substitute Bernie Lutton. When I approached the goalkeeper, I tried to tell him in Italian that I was sending him off, and asked his name. He replied: 'Michael Angelo . . . ,' and I told him: '**** off.' You know, I thought he was taking the mickey. I later learned that his first two Christian names were Michael Angelo and he hadn't quite finished telling me his full name!

Gordon Hill, taken from Give a Little Whistle: The Recollections of a Remarkable Referee

We had two key players booked well before half-time, Roy McFarland and Archie Gemmill. As far as I can remember their only crime was to stand somewhere adjacent to an opponent who flung himself on the floor. Now wasn't that a coincidence? McFarland and Gemmill – two players who just happened to have been booked in previous games – would now, automatically, be ruled out of the second leg. It stank to high heaven.

207

I'd heard lurid tales of bribery, corruption, the bending of match officials in Italy, call it what you will, but I had never before seen what struck me as clear evidence. I went barmy.

Our anger afterwards saw Taylor arrested – for something minor like a murder threat to the referee, apparently! Meanwhile I was ranting on to the Press about 'cheating, f**king Italian bastards,' and I meant every single word of it. We had been done.

Brian Clough after Derby County's European Cup semi-final against Juventus, taken from Clough: The Autobiography

We were being spat on.

We were being punched when the ball was maybe 50 yards away.

We were victims of vicious forearm smashes across the face when the referee and linesmen were not looking.

We were having our hair pulled by them when they came to help us up after savagely hacking us down in a tackle.

We were being punched in the back when we waited for a throw in to be taken.

You would see a shadow or sense that someone was coming up behind you and then – WHACK! You braced yourself for the punch and you then counted to ten to keep your temper. Nothing was going to stop it. Nothing but the final whistle would end the madness.

Gordon Strachan on Scotland's World Cup game against Uruguay, taken from Strachan Style: A Life in Football

In global terms we British are non-starters when it comes to the seamier side of the game. We are mere novices compared with, say, the notorious Spaniards or the volatile South Americans and when we do foul it tends to be blatantly obvious to anyone with the slightest knowledge of the game.

In only my second international game I played against Spain and finished head to toe with an opponent. Tiny he may have been but harmless he was not, since he kicked me straight in the windpipe before I could move and it was 15 minutes until I could get my breath. I thought that I was going to choke to death. Our fouling tends to be straightforward but on the

Continent it includes body checking, shirt pulling, spitting, fingers in the eye, hair pulling and other nasty little habits. Like the one Steve Coppell tells about in an international against Italy when he suddenly found himself completely immobilised by a hand firmly gripping his testicles. Steve, more than anyone, knows about that side of the game having had his outstanding career ended in its prime as a direct result of an over-the-top tackle by a Hungarian at Wembley... and they call Graeme Souness dirty? They have got to be joking.

Graeme Souness, taken from Graeme Souness:
No Half Measures

Our manager Tommy Docherty warned us beforehand of what the style of play would be like. He told us that they would go through every trick they knew in the game plus a few recent ones of their own invention.

In common with most British players, I find the spitting and hair pulling abhorrent but, incredibly, Juventus managed to surpass themselves in the return leg with something new and even more sinister. I can take it only as a compliment that, having been followed around Old Trafford by Tardelli, I was assigned to the care of Claudio Gentile in the second leg when despite our first leg pressure, we were defending a lead of a single goal only. It was a wet night far removed from the sort of weather that holidaymakers usually enjoy on the Adriatic coast. The greasy pitch was tailor-made for the typical British sliding tackle and as I went skidding in alongside Gentile, he belied his name by firmly grasping my testicles! I completely froze, more from shock at the deed rather than from any pain involved. Ever since that tackle I have physically winced every time I have seen Gentile on television.

Steve Coppell on playing against Juventus, 1977,
taken from Touch and Go

It was Friday, 30 September 1983 when the specialist, Jonathan Noble, confirmed my worst fears and told me that, at the age of 28, my playing career was over, wrecked by the continued deterioration of my left knee. It had been finished by a foul tackle committed some eighteen months earlier! The tackle had been so unnecessary and futile. The date was Wednesday, 18 November 1981 and the occasion a World Cup qualifying game between England and Hungary at Wembley.

I vaguely remember picking up the ball in the inside right position and running towards the full back. His name was Josef Toth, a raw-boned 30-year-old and not unlike Norman Hunter in looks. I had played against him once before, in 1978 when we beat them 4–1, and he was the sort of defender I felt comfortable playing against – big, strong and square rather than the nimble, nippy type who could match me for pace.

I saw Toth diving in, almost as if in slow motion. I had time to think that I would knock the ball down the line and go past him before kicking it into the middle. The only other coherent thought I had in the next moments was of my knee exploding as if someone had let off a firework inside it.

Steve Coppell on the tackle that ended his career,
taken from Touch and Go

Scotland were playing Czechoslovakia in Prague in the opening qualifying match for the 1978 World Cup Finals.

I was being marked by a giant of a centre half by the name of Anton Ondrus, who like so many of his team mates played with a stern, unfriendly look on his face. He was a hard player all right, and from the start his tackles and challenges in the air carried the force of a sledgehammer. Suddenly when the ball was not even near me, I felt a sudden sharp blow as Ondrus rammed his elbow into my face. We were jogging side by side at the time with ball having been played behind us and Ondrus followed up by pushing me to the ground. He ran off, but without thinking, I jumped up and chased after him. I grabbed hold of Ondrus, spun him round, and delivered a powerful right hook to his face which even old Henry Cooper would have been proud of. Ondrus collapsed to the ground with his face buried in his hands and began to roll over. The punch may have stung him, but this was Ondrus the actor at work as he writhed in make-believe pain.

The referee sent both Ondrus and myself off. As I made my way off the crowd jeered and whistled, and inside I was blazing with anger for being so stupid. We'd been warned to keep out of trouble before the game, as sides like Czechoslovakia were masters at baiting players. Like a fool I had fallen for their trick and retaliated. It was one of the few moments when I've lost my head on a football field and perhaps it was the Glasgow boy inside me that had risen to the trouble.

Andy Gray, taken from Shades of Gray

They know that when they spit on you they are doing something to you that you hate. Their view from then on is to keep doing it because it will affect the opposition during the game. If you're angry then you won't be as effective as a player. All of it is calculated. I don't know how they can look themselves in the mirror if they have spent 90 minutes spitting at opponents, but it does not faze them one little bit. As long as their manager is happy and they are getting some success then anything goes.

Gordon Strachan on Uruguay, taken from Strachan Style:
A Life in Football

Spitting is part and parcel of the game now.

George Graham

I will never forget the guy who marked me in the game – and I mean marked me! He was called Sunda; he was a great big, rough fellow, a proper villain, about ten years older than me. He kept pulling my hair and poking me in the eye. I was just eighteen and this was the first time I'd come up against anything as vicious and as blatant as this. Looking to the Greek referee for protection was a waste of time. Everything went the Romanians' way from the moment Danny McGrain won the toss. He chose the way he wanted to play and was allowed to do so. You didn't have to be very intelligent to realize that things were going to be stacked against you after an opening like that!

In the opening quarter of an hour the referee made it totally clear that we were in trouble. He booked three of our players – Tom McAdam, Peter Latchford and Murdo MacLeod. A few minutes later he sent off Roddy McDonald along with one of the Romanian players. The game was a disaster for us and a personal low point for me because that was the first time I'd known the despair of losing in a European tie. I took it very badly. I still remember weeping in the hotel after the game, reacting to the combination of all that had happened to us – the biased refereeing, the personal abuse I'd had handed out to me and the fact that Timisoara were a bad team. Honestly they were rubbish.

Charlie Nicholas on Celtic v Timisoara,
taken from Charlie: An Autobiography

In one first round game the Greek side Aris Salonika had three booked and one sent off. Eric Gates finished the game with his legs covered in bruises. When we went there about 3,000 hostile Salonika fans turned out to spit, jeer and hurl stones at us while we trained. The hospitality didn't improve much for the game. The officials seemed to be turning a blind eye to some of the Greek challenges and we were continuously kicked, punched and elbowed. Eric Gates once again had taken the brunt of the Greek violence. Eric never wore shinguards and in the treatment room his legs looked like a woodcutter's block.

Terry Butcher on Ipswich v Aris Salonika UEFA Cup-tie,
taken from Both Sides of the Border: An Autobiography

I was sent off during the UEFA Cup second-round tie in 1978 when Arsenal met Hadjuk Split of Yugoslavia. And this time I was the most astonished person in the stadium.

They detailed a hard man to follow me wherever I went, and he took his job seriously. He pulled my shirt, kicked the backs of my legs and spat at me now and again just to make sure I knew I was playing in Europe.

But things were made worse because I could sense that the referee was growing tired of the whole situation. He gave me three or four free kicks in as many minutes, but I could tell he was losing his patience.

Things came to a head when I tried to escape the clutches of my marker for the umpteenth time and pushed him away with a sweep of my arm. It was not even a foul that I could see, just a case of trying to wrestle myself out of his grasp.

When the referee came over and reached into his pocket I remember feeling relieved because I believed that if he booked the man then I would get a bit of peace for a while. So imagine how I felt when he showed us both the red card.

He honestly interpreted my movement with my arm to be a strike at an opponent. And why he sent off the Yugoslav on that occasion is really beyond me because he had done nothing except get pushed to one side!

The referee wanted us off the pitch. He did not want to send off one so he solved his problem by getting us out of his way for the rest of the night.

Liam Brady, taken from So Far So Good

I was still only nineteen and was marked that night by Claudio Gentile, one of the most feared defenders in the world. He had a formidable reputation and I knew that I mustn't allow myself to be dominated. As it turned out, Gentile was the hardest player I have ever played against in my life. He would do anything to upset me. He nipped me, he pulled my hair, he held my jersey – all the annoying, niggly things that referees don't always pick up on; even the fans can't see what's going on. But they are enough to distract you or hold you back or simply keep you on edge wondering what the hell he's going to do next. Who would imagine that a defender would nip your backside during a game? That was the way he carried on. Gentile had it down to a fine art – he'd catch you when you least expected it. He was able to stop you in your tracks when you were ready to make a run by grabbing you. He was seldom caught at it because he was so clever. I managed to hold my own against him but it was a hard match. I've never come up against anyone else who has the dirty tricks off to such perfection.

Charlie Nicholas on Celtic v Juventus, European Cup,
taken from Charlie: An Autobiography

On the day of the match, there was an attempted coup, with the son of the former king trying to make a come back with a landing on the beach. Bullets were flying about and the landing party was later reported to have been shot.

During the game we were thinking twice about putting in a real tackle in case somebody might think about getting trigger-happy with us. There was a 20,000 crowd in the Qemal Stafa Stadium and the Albanians proved to be very pleasant hosts. One of the players, Gega, kept coming up to shake my hand and wanting to pose for pictures – before kicking me halfway round the park and getting himself booked for his trouble.

Gordon Strachan on Dinamo Tirana v Aberdeen,
taken from An Autobiography

At the beginning of the 1978–79 season Arsenal went on a pre-season European tour.

We played a Bundesliga team, Fortuna Dusseldorf, in a so-called friendly that turned out to be a dummy-run for World War III.

We were in danger of missing the whole season the way the Germans were tackling.

One minute later I gave the ball to Alan Sunderland . . . and the next thing I knew, Alan was sprawled on the ground, his legs chopped from under him. The referee, standing only a few yards away, waved play on.

I was in the unfortunate position of being the Arsenal player nearest to the situation. I honestly believe that in the heat of that battle any one of the lads would have done the same thing. When the next German came within range, I tackled him the way I'd attempt to stop a Panzer tank.

Out came the red card. He saw that tackle, of course, and satisfied the baying fans by sending me off.

Liam Brady, taken from So Far So Good

We took control and the Paraguayans resorted to some rough stuff. One of their defenders elbowed Gary Lineker in the throat. Gary went down in obvious pain and they were claiming that he was pretending to be hurt. Paraguay turned up the rough stuff. One of their defenders punched me in the throat at a corner, his fist landing directly on my Adams Apple. At the end I refused to swap shirts with any of the Paraguayan players. Bobby Robson and Don Howe tried to change my mind. They said: 'Come on, the game is over. You've got to be a sportsman and swap shirts.' But I am a sportsman that's the whole point.

My England shirt means more to me than a Paraguan. So I kept mine.

Terry Butcher, taken from Both Sides of the Border:
An Autobiography

Just once in my life I've been running scared on a football field. It happened in Brescia, Northern Italy. And let me remind you that this particular contest was supposed to have been arranged as a prestige friendly. The Italians were simply warming up for the European Championship Finals in West Germany a week later. We – that's the Wales team – were heading nowhere. They came gunning for me from the start. Bergomi and Ferri, the hatchet man on my tail, knew exactly what they were doing. It was absolutely crazy.

First of all I was nailed by one of this lovely pair as I went to collect a ball on an angled run. It was vicious and brutal. Both my socks were completely shredded down the back from the knee-joint to ankle. I might have had both my legs snapped in half with a tackle of that kind. How the hell that didn't happen I still haven't a clue.

I still shudder to think that my career could have gone for a burton in a split second. I just felt sick. Next I was chasing a long pass down the middle of the park with goal chances very much in mind when the world suddenly went dark. Two elbows came jutting out like a couple of boomerangs and dear old Sparky was almost sparkout.

As I staggered off the park I had a right shiner to show for my pains. In that one split-second I discovered the chilling truth about Italian defenders – they definitely like to hunt in pairs. Worse was to follow. Jumping for a high ball I was suddenly stunned by one hell of a whack on the back of my head.

Added to that there were the usual stunts of shirt-tugging, elbow smashes, and Latin spitting campaign which really gets to the British professional. I've never come across anything so vicious and it's the one and only time in my career when I couldn't get off a pitch quick enough.

Mark Hughes, taken from Sparky, Barcelona, Bayern and Back:
The Autobiography of Mark Hughes

We've just lost to the hatchet men of Panathinaikos in the first leg of our UEFA Cup-tie. To say it was rough would be like saying that Everest is a pretty big hill! It was murder, the tactics of the Greek defenders made those back home in Italy seem like choirboys.

The game had been going for just two minutes when I was kicked, quite deliberately and cold-bloodedly, on my injured ankle. I felt the defender should have been booked straight away. But he was let off scot-free. I was kicked five times altogether on that same ankle.

Ian Rush on Juventus v Panathinaikos, taken from Ian Rush: My Italian Diary

A classic case was a monster of a man called Guido Buchwald. He's built like a brick outhouse and I bumped into him for the first time when I played for Bayern Munich. Guido is a West German international and obviously very proud of the fact. Any time he wants I can certainly give him a written testimonial to his physical strength. Maybe even a medical certificate to go with it – mine!

Mark Hughes, taken from Sparky, Barcelona, Bayern and Back: The Autobiography of Mark Hughes

The sweat was pouring off me within minutes of the kick-off. And it wasn't only the heat which was making my temperature rise. The first time I went to make a run I was halted by a defender pulling my shirt. And that set the tempo for the game. I had to struggle to keep my temper as defenders obstructed me in every way they could.

And what was making it all worse was that the referee just accepted it all. He didn't even pull the offenders up, when he should have stamped on it from the start by booking the first culprit. A yellow card in the first five minutes might have had the desired effect of preventing the others indulging in their petty fouls.

If my shirt wasn't being pulled, there'd be a defender's arms wrapped around me or a body in the way preventing me from making any kind of run. It was sickening. I had to fight to control my temper, to make sure I didn't commit the cardinal sin of retaliating.

Ian Rush on Juventus v Empoli, taken from Ian Rush: My Italian Diary

I was sent off in my first match at the San Siro. It was against Brescia in another friendly and it was my first real taste of what goes on in Italian football. Forwards are always under threat – or they were back when I started to play for Milan. Defenders were sent out to stop you and referees seemed to think I was big enough to look after myself. So while I was turned into Brescia's target for the day, the referee didn't afford me too much protection. Eventually I turned to remonstrate with one of the worst offenders and he just went down in a heap. I was sent off.

The fans didn't mind. I think most of them enjoyed it even, but I knew I'd made a bloomer. I hadn't touched the lad but he made it looks as if I had butted him. It was in the very last minute of the game so I didn't leave the team short for half a match or anything, but the next day I was hauled in front of Gianni Rivera, a one-time Milan player who was now one of the directors. He told me that I would have to adjust to the Italian game, that defenders went out of their way to provoke you. He was talking from a lot of experience so I listened.

Mark Hateley, taken from Top Mark! An Autobiography

We had our chances. One came late in the game when Charlie Nicholas was going through on goal and was hacked down by their midfield player, Claus Berggren. It was a shocking professional foul and the Danish player was later to admit that to the world's Press. He said quite cynically. 'I am a professional and I had to stop the Scotland player, Nicholas, from scoring. I would do the same again.' He was booked but Charlie limped off with around ten minutes to go, and was also missing from our next match against West Germany. In fact he only made it as a substitute against the Uruguayans, and was not 100 per cent fit for that appearance.

Ironically, if FIFA had tightened up their disciplinary code then the Danish player Berggren would have been automatically carded. Today, under the new code, there is no doubt that he would have been off. That might just have given us the breakthrough we needed to get a result.

Gordon Strachan on Scotland's 1–0 World Cup defeat against Denmark, taken from Strachan Style: A Life in Football

Borussia had adopted their own tactical strategy over the two games based on kicking and body checking. It was deliberate provocation. European teams seem to think that Scottish teams will lose their heads and they laid into us.

Ted McMinn received some of the worst treatment and his legs were a mass of cuts and bruises after the game, but the referee gave us no protection. The villain as far as I'm concerned was the referee, Mr Alex Ponnet, of Belgium. Inevitably frustration began to set in. Stuart Munro was sent off for retaliation. He'd been hacked down and as he lay on the ground the man who had fouled him continued to kick him. Stuart flicked out a boot in self-protection. Compared to the tackle there was certainly no malice but the referee sent him off. The game exploded. David Cooper went next. He'd had enough and told the referee what he thought.

I don't know how I stayed on the pitch. I was so angry. It's a good job Mr Ponnet hasn't got a good grasp of English swear words. Games like that leave a bad taste in the mouth. With a stronger official we would have got a result. We were the better side over the two legs but still went out.

Terry Butcher on Rangers v Borussia Moenchengladback, UEFA Cup, taken from Both Sides of the Border: An Autobiography

Les Ferdinand was quiet and shy. He had problems coming to terms with being in the first team. Then we took on a Dutch side in the pre-season and I warned Les they might try and wind him up by spitting at him. So I told him to ignore it and smile back instead. But instead he smacked the geezer in the face and got himself sent off!

Jim Smith

We were to play Bastia on the island of Corsica.

I was reliably told by my colleagues that this was a game to be avoided. No professional in France relished the prospect of playing at this tiny ground. Mafia influences on the island were second only to those on Sicily, and bribery and corruption were rumoured to be rife. Referees on occasions were known to turn a blind eye or give outrageous decisions for the home team. I listened, but thought it to be a typical footballers' tale, slightly exaggerated and embellished.

After ten minutes of the game, I had comprehensively changed my mind. I had been spat at, elbowed, punched and finally tackled so late and high I needed several stitches in a gashed shin. All these incidents had happened under the nose of the referee, but for some strange reason he had failed to see any of them.

Lee Chapman, taken from More Than a Match

We were left counting our bruises. It's not what you expect in what is basically a friendly.

Roberto Mancini on Sampdoria v Arsenal, Makita Tournament

To cap it all, Paul Ince got sent off for dissent. He knows it was wrong. In Europe you cannot argue with the referee. Paul was lucky he wasn't sent off in Barcelona for a display of dissent. Now he might miss two or three games. The PFA have a tariff of permitted fines, and being booked for dissent is ten per cent of your salary. But I had a meeting at the start of the season in which I said I wasn't accepting that in Europe.

Alex Ferguson on Gothenberg v Manchester United, November 1994, taken from A Year in the Life: The Manager's Diary

He is as fast and aggressive as Alan McInally was in Villa colours and like greased lightning in front of goal.

David Platt on Jurgen Klinsmann

I just want to ask you fellas is there any diving schools in London?

Jurgen Klinsmann to the Press on his arrival at Spurs

I've got this scar where Klinsmann tried one of his famous volleys on my chin, it happened during the game in Dusseldorf. I don't remember much about it except for the five stitches I had inserted in the wound.

He's very elusive, a real thinking man's footballer. He makes playing the game look so easy, but marking him can be a defender's nightmare.

Kit Symons

Gascoigne makes some crazy tackles and these have cost him in the past. It is a mental problem and it is obviously still there. I know because I can be very aggressive myself at times. But in the long run this will not be good for Gazza – and may cause him problems.

He fouled me and I told him that wasn't necessary. Then he started swearing at me. My English is good but I didn't understand some of the things he said.

It was only a friendly game and there was no need for that.

But I don't think Gascoigne knows the difference between a friendly and serious game.

Brondby Captain Vilfort on their pre-season friendly v Rangers

Gascoigne elbowed my player in the face and left him with a broken nose.

I can't say whether it was an accident or not but we certainly didn't like what we saw.

Sweden Coach Tommy Svensson

I'm devastated at what has happened and want to stress that it was obviously a complete accident.

I'm so upset by this that I'm going to find the lad and make a point of saying how sorry I am. I'm absolutely gutted to think that I have broken his nose.

There's no way I would ever do anything like that deliberately and I'm going to explain that to him.

Paul Gascoigne

He's so tiny. I half expected him to come out with a school satchel on his back. If he had, I'd have trodden on his packed lunch.

Wimbledon's Andy Thorn on Middlesbrough's Juninho

I have to accept that the English game is far more physical and if I am going to be successful in the Premiership I need to learn the fighting spirit.

Juninho

Nice as it is for people to admire your skills, I accept that without the fighting spirit that epitomises the game in this country, I could have a problem. I won't shirk a tackle if it means the difference between winning and losing.

I have a free role in the Newcastle side, but it's the critical tackles and the desire to drop back and defend that will win me friends, commitment is vital.

I'm not kidding myself, I know it won't be easy.

David Ginola

David Ginola is a class player. So why does he need to throw himself around so much? A lot of foreign players tend to be like that. But as well as developing a reputation as one of the Premiership's most exciting talents, he risks being known as a diver.

To be fair, the referee wasn't impressed by his theatrics on Saturday, although I wondered why he didn't show Ginola a yellow card because he committed the offence more than once.

Robbie Fowler

My two pot-bellied pigs don't yelp as much as Ruud Gullit.

Vinny Jones after being sent off for a foul on Ruud Gullit

Vinny Jones believes Ruud Gullit is a cheat. The Wimbledon player claimed Chelsea's Dutch superstar took a dive on Boxing Day to earn the Welsh International his third red card of the season.

The football world is getting fed up with Jones. He has now been sent off eleven times, the record of a thug who strives desperately to make up for his lack of ability by throwing his weight around on football pitches around the country.

His only success this season was to get a dismissal against

Liverpool commuted to a caution after an appeal. He is hoping the FA let him off the hook again after this latest episode, but TV evidence suggests referee Dermot Gallagher was spot on.

Jones believes he is a man's man in a tough game. The pathetic truth is that he is the ultimate second rater. The sly elbow, the kick while the player is down, the unforgiveable stamping, the tackle from behind . . . These have all been weapons in Jones's armoury in the past. He is certainly not learning with the passage of time. In other words he hasn't got a football brain.

Ruud Gullit, for one, doesn't need to dive to get the better of Jones. They play football on a different planet. In the passing of time, fans all over the world will recall the quality and triumphs of the famous Dutchman. But there are thousands of Joneses in the telephone directory and our man from Wimbledon will very quickly become Mr Anonymous.

To save confusion, might I suggest he makes an early decision to change his name by deed poll to 'Vinny Who' because this is how we will be referring to him as soon as he retires.

Ken Rogers

I like the English game. It's constant action, they play to win. In France it's stops and starts. There's less pleasure in playing like that.

Eric Cantona

He's not a tackler. I've told him don't bother tackling because you can't tackle. I'm fed up saying that to him. When he does go into tackles he doesn't know how to do it and he ends up getting a booking. I don't think forwards are expected to tackle abroad, you see. You don't see them haring about tackling centre halfs. They conserve themselves for the thing that's most important, scoring and creating.

Alex Ferguson on Cantona

Eric Cantona has a vast amount of flair and quality, I couldn't get near him that day. If you give an international player like him a lot of space he's going to show his quality and he did. He does things off the cuff and when they come off he looks really good. If they don't he doesn't let it worry him too much.

David Burrows, taken from Champions:
The 26 Year Quest for Glory

If Cantona had been playing in my time, 20 or 25 years ago, there were countless hard men who would have done him without even giving a foul away.

They would have sat and waited, and as soon as he started his tantrums they would have copped him – and the referee wouldn't have seen a thing. They would have copped him without even thinking about it, and left him lying there.

Every team had two or three hard lads who you steered clear of because not only were they hard, they were cute about it.

In my day, there were real hard men. They were the likes of Peter Storey, Terry Paine, Ron Harris, Nobby Stiles, Dave Mackay – and the entire Leeds team!

When Cantona gives a foul away, everybody in the ground knows about it. He flicks an elbow out or flicks a heel, and has been shown enough red cards to prove he's not cute about it. In my day you'd get turned over and nobody in the ground knew you'd been done. But that is cute, not stupid like Cantona has been.

But it's not just today's hard men who will go for him. Virtually every other player will try to wind him up, knowing he is likely to flip.

Don't kid yourself that it doesn't go on, because it certainly went on in our day. We would say: 'Let's get him off if we can because we know he's got a sharp temper, so let's have a bit of a niggle at him and pull his shirt and see if he lashes out.'

Emlyn Hughes

Players are bigger today because for some strange reason they think they have to be big and tough. But when you look back at the bad boys, David Mackay, Chopper Harris, Nobby Stiles, they were all midgets.

George Best

Eric's booking spoilt the win. It was the usual Eric red mist but he'd been elbowed in the face by Ruddock.

It wasn't just that, it was the goading too. He kept annoying Eric by pulling his collar down. I was screaming to Eric from the side, 'Leave him, ignore him. We're winning, don't get involved.'

But the moment Ruddock started trying to take the mickey out of him by pulling down his collar he'd had enough.

Alex Ferguson, taken from A Year in the Life: The Manager's Diary

Eric Cantona, with his efforts to control his fiery temper and behave himself, is not half the player he was before he had that little bit of a fiery temperament.

Tommy Docherty

We've had some real barnies and run-ins kicking each other off the ball and swearing at one another. We've both said a few things to each other but it's all forgotten later and I'd like to think we've got a mutual respect.

You can't go on spitting, kicking and having a punch-up these days, but there's still room for a wind-up.

Last season the PA announcer at Anfield, Paul Martin, suggested the ultimate insult would be to turn Cantona's collar down if I got the chance. Well, it wasn't long before we were at it. I fouled him, then he kicked me up the backside so I went up behind him and turned his collar down. He didn't like it and he got a bit narky, especially when I did it a couple more times.

But he can handle the wind-up stuff because he can put the ball in the back of the net and come back and smile at me which hurts more than anything.

Neil Ruddock on Eric Cantona

He's a bit *Swan Lake* isn't he? Ginola.

GMR broadcaster Jimmy Wagg

David has to live with his shirt being pulled, hard tackles and being booed away from home. Lee Dixon didn't play fair but that's the way it is in the Premiership. Sometimes I tell him to take care before a match because the right back is silly or is doing some very hard tackles. If this sort of story works then great, because when he plays there's no one in England can touch him.

Philippe Albert's advice to David Ginola

I would think Kevin Keegan has told him only to go down when someone really clatters him. This has probably all come about because he's collapsed in a heap too easily in the past.

But you can't say when he's been smacked and gone over that it should not for once be a free kick in Ginola's favour.

Alan Hansen

Cantona's problems with the English laws mean referees have something of a downer on him. I'm not helped too much in that respect, either. It's always the main problem.

I'm French and have to prove myself. I have to accept that I'm a foreigner. I try a lot of things that defenders don't like, and they try to stop me. My legs are black and blue after every game.

David Ginola

I'm furious at defenders who commit fouls, point accusing fingers at Ginola and say: 'I never touched him.' In my opinion, that's as much conning the referee as taking a dive in the box.

You can't allow fellow professionals to get away with that. Referees must stamp it out now. I have seen it with my own eyes on four or five occasions away from St James's Park.

He's been accused of diving by rivals when he's totally innocent of any foul play. I've seen defenders lay into him and the referee has waved play on.

That can't be right.

Alan Hansen on David Ginola

Opponents are so terrified of him they are now doubling up on him to stop him. And they still can't. So now they accuse him of diving.

And the mud is starting to stick, as we saw when he was booked for being fouled at Highbury the other night.

There's no doubt that he does have a tendency to make a meal of challenges. When people kick him, he goes down. But all decent forwards do that.

Now he's got to prove he has the strength of character to stand up to soccer's hatchet men. And I'm sure that he will.

Mark Lawrenson on David Ginola

The thing that annoys me is that here you've got a very skilful and very talented player who loves to entertain the public and he's going to get hammered at every opportunity, and he's not going to get any protection. Against Coventry as soon as the boy Ginola got the first pass of the afternoon, the Coventry supporters were booing him like anything. Every player in the Football League should be given protection from referees. What's going to happen with Ginola is that every club that plays against him, the right full back and the midfield players are going to hammer Ginola at every opportunity they get until the referee puts them in the book.

Tommy Docherty

It's the first time I have seen players settling scores with a fist fight.

I was very concerned before the game. But after the fight I felt a team so split could be beaten very easily.

Before the game I told my players they would be up against eleven men ready to fight for each other for 90 minutes. But not with each other!

Spartak manager Oleg Romantseuer after the Graeme Le Saux–David Batty punch-up during the Spartak Moscow v Blackburn European Cup-tie

He was flying through the air when Clarkson came from behind him. I didn't agree with either booking.

I warned Ian – I told him if he wasn't within three inches of Ginola all the time it would give him the chance to dive.

He's got the ball, seen Ian coming, turned to go as the foot came and then just thrown himself over and rolled and rolled. You don't act like that if you're hurt. You just stay down.

Stoke manager Lou Macari after Ian Clarkson was sent off for a foul on David Ginola in the Coca-Cola Cup

How can I stay on my feet if defenders foul me? They don't like it when I keep running past them and sometimes when they can't get the ball they kick me down. My legs get covered with cuts and bruises after every match.

David Ginola

David Ginola has been criticised for diving, but that's the culture that these guys are brought up in.

Terry Venables

I predicted earlier in the season that Ginola's over-theatrical reaction to tackles would do him no favours with opponents, opposing fans or referees.

My fear was that officials would fail to punish offenders who fouled Ginola, and that is exactly what happened at Highbury. Referee Gerald Ashby provided little protection for the talented Frenchman and, in the end, his frustration boiled over.

Much criticism has been heaped on Dixon but, to be honest, what would any professional do in an important Cup-tie against Ginola? Not surprisingly, the Arsenal full back decided to try his luck with an over-aggressive approach and could not believe his good fortune when Mr Ashby allowed him to provoke the winger into retaliation.

One could not condone Ginola's use of the elbow, but his booking for taking a dive was a disgrace. The Frenchman was clearly fouled and had every right to look bewildered, but in this incident his reputation cost him a yellow card.

Dave Hilley

I accept the fact that I can't play in the competition, but I do not accept any guilt and I am disappointed that nothing has been said about the Ancona coach. It could have been me or Paul Tait who ended up in hospital after what happened that night.

Has Cacciatori been cleared of any blame? I'd like to know, I will sit out my suspension because the competition has to come first, but I am innocent.

Birmingham's Liam Daish on his ban from the remaining Anglo-Italian Cup games after the brawl in Ancona

I went in for a tackle and the next thing I knew they were coming at me from all angles. I saw a fat guy running towards me out of the corner of my eye – I thought it was Barry Fry at first – and he screamed 'You're dead'.

It was their coach. Then all hell broke loose. It was happening all over the pitch. I don't think that I have ever played in a match like that before.

Birmingham player Paul Tait on 'The Battle of Ancona'

Ruud Gullit is a squealing, money-grabbing, cockroach.

Vinny Jones

He is a complete twit for what he said about Gullit. He does things and then regrets them.

Wimbledon manager Joe Kinnear on Vinny Jones

German players have turned the dive into an art form.

FIFA General Secretary Sepp Blatter

Players who have come to Scotland from the Continent have brought diving with them. It's quite prevalent abroad. Most times foreign players are tackled they catapult themselves to the ground.

It's now happening in Scotland. Indeed, recently I saw a big-name foreign player dive even before the tackle came in!

Some are trying to con refs into awarding penalties and free kicks, as well as get opponents a yellow or red card. That places added pressure on referees.

Hugh Williamson, former Scottish referee

Yes, I swear a lot. But the advantage is that having played abroad, I can choose a different language to the referee's.

Jurgen Klinsmann

It was the sort of tackle that happens at every match in England. He was sent off for retaliation but in England that is not so much of a problem.

Dutch star Ronald Koeman after Craig Short was sent off for retaliating against a Koeman tackle that left a six-inch gash in his leg

When I was in Brazil I saw Juninho play for São Paolo and he was marked by a beast of a defender who was really dishing it out. But the little man handled it. I've no doubts he can deal with the British style of football.

Bryan Robson

Juninho will move like a gazelle. He will sense when the rhinos are coming. He may only be 5ft 5in tall, but size does not count if you have a football brain.

Many lightly built players in my playing years were great footballers because of their natural talent and timing. Good players know when to make a move and how to beat an opponent.

Wilf Mannion on Juninho

The English play hard, but fair. The only thing that might upset me are those nasty taps on the ankle.

Juninho

The idea that he wouldn't last physically was silly. I watch South American football on television and it isn't just hard, it's actually brutal.

Some of the tackles are terrible. Some of the time their defenders don't even bother to try to make it look as if they're playing the ball, and anybody who can come through that can play in England.

Colin Cooper on Juninho

I can cope with the physical problems. I have faced tough teams and defenders who kick you, but I've not let them intimidate me. I accept that in Europe teams use strength more than they do in South America, but skill is always more powerful than strength and it will always triumph.

Brazil have proved that many times in World Cup competitions and I will prove it in England.

Juninho

The Referee didn't ask for my name. He just made sure I looked at him to know he had booked me.

Juninho on his first booking

Here in England I'm continually being roughed up in every game. But I'll have to adjust to it.

Newcastle's Asprilla after a couple of games in the English League

It is right that fair play should have been adhered to but football is also a physical game; it is a game of fighting as well as beautiful touches and we don't mean brutality by that, but reasonable aggression.

Aggressive tactics have nothing to do with brutality or bad tackles. Brutal tackling and aggressive play are two different things.

Berti Vogts, coach of 1996 European Champions, West Germany

9 'They Know the Rules but They Don't Know the Game'

The referee

I've always hated referees. To me they're all no-marks. Otherwise, they wouldn't be there. Who are they? All the week they're sitting there in offices, scribbling away, scribble, scribble, and on Saturday afternoons they're on the field with all the big men, and they're saying, 'Right, now you do what I tell you or you're going in my little book.' I've seen blokes kicking lumps out of each other, and what's the referee doing? He's wagging his finger and making a great production out of moving the ball three foot back for a free kick.

Tony Kay, taken from The Football Man:
People and Passions in Soccer

I don't know how many players I've sent off. I don't want to know. It's one of the easiest decisions to make, to send a man off. That's not what you're there for. The hard thing is to keep him on sometimes. You do better keeping your voice down. I've run alongside players and said, 'Ee, give over, I knew thee when tha was a good player.' That hurts more than shaking your finger at a man.

I've known a captain threaten to thump one of his own men for arguing with me.

Referee Ernie Crawford, taken from
The Football Man: People and Passions in Soccer

The trouble with football referees is that they know the rules but they don't know the game.

Bill Shankly

A referee has to be firm. Players do not like him any the less if he is. He might be cheerful. He might be sombre, but he must

231

not be weak. The players sort referees out as they sort opponents out. If the referee is 'easy' the sillier ones among them will take advantage. Sillier, I say, because however frustrated a player might become when he thinks the referee has made a mistake he cannot beat the referee. On the other hand if the referee has a reputation for pouncing on anything, serious or trivial, the buzz goes round the dressing room, 'Watch out. This fellow won't stand any nonsense.'

Sir Matt Busby, taken from Soccer at the Top: My Life in Football

I've been booked for showing dissent to a referee. I can understand that. I find it harder to interpret an 'over-robust' tackle. Where does robust become 'over-robust' – particularly when the judge, in this case a referee, has a split second to see the tackle.

Although I cannot always agree with their definitions, I accept that the referees must be the final arbiters. They say no two people see a football match the same way, and that includes the experts, so it must be doubly difficult for an official to define between such hairline things as robust, which is usually fair, and over-robust.

Ron 'Chopper' Harris, taken from Soccer the Hard Way

In those days you could say what you wanted to refs, provided they never heard it.

Francis Lee

Not all officials have the same sense of humour as Willie Reilly of Port Glasgow. When the feet began to fly Willie would say, 'Now lads, behave yourselves – you know I'll have the last laugh.' Willie was an undertaker and local gravedigger.

Jimmy Guthrie, taken from Soccer Rebel:
The Evolution of the Professional Footballer

While we tend to be lenient over what is said, players should always remember that if they use foul language they risk being sent off. George Best, for instance, was sent off once for calling a man a 'wanker'.

Jack Taylor, taken from Soccer Refereeing: A Personal View

In my day, before the game began, in the dressing room the players would have a natter to themselves and ask who's the referee today? We'd get the match programme and it might be, say, Jim Finney from Hereford and you would say right away 'No nonsense, behave yourself because you're off'. An early bath almost immediately if you stepped out of line or started taking the mickey out of him. But he had a lot of common sense, we had a good bit of banter and a bit of fun. You'd say, 'What a referee, you're rubbish.' You'd miss an opportunity in the goal-mouth and he'd say, 'What a flippin wing half.' He'd get his own banter back. They were very, very good. You know yourself the game was a bit slower then, it was harder, fairer, not too many poseurs in those days. But you knew all the good referees. You knew the ones you could take a mile with, you could con some of them, but not too many. They were characters and personalities.

Tommy Docherty

I was involved in an incident with Geoff Hurst, and Jim Finney stopped the game and came across and told us that we would both finish the game in the dressing room if there was any more nonsense.

I respect Jim Finney both for warning and for giving me a chance.

A top referee is an official who treats a player like a man.

Ron 'Chopper' Harris, taken from Soccer the Hard Way

There was a referee called Jack Taylor, and in those days you could speak to referees. I remember turning to him and saying: 'Jack, that wasn't a goal.' He said, 'Brian, look in tomorrow's *News of the World*.' I tell you what, Jack was right, it was a goal. I respected that man very much.

Brian Labone

For one match at Highbury I knew that great tension had been built up by the Press anticipating a battle royal between Arsenal and England centre forward Joe Baker, and Liverpool and Scotland centre half, big Ron Yeats. So I planned my positioning so that I could keep close to that contest. And a battle royal it was, flaring into a fist-fight to which I was close enough to separate them quickly and send them off.

Jack Taylor, taken from Soccer Refereeing: A Personal View

I don't think that there are enough absolutely top-class referees who can command respect from the moment they step on the field. There are some of course – and they do get respect. And the games they control are better for it!

Some are too ready to whistle for petty fouls. They stop the game far too often – much more than is necessary. And all this spoils it for the spectators just as much as it does for the players.

Ron Yeats

It was Manchester United's First Division championship party held at Old Trafford on 13 May 1967 when Stoke City were the visitors and 63,000 people turned up to salute their heroes.

The match itself never lived up to its billing perhaps because nothing was at stake. There was the odd flash of genius from George Best wearing Denis Law's Number 8 shirt, no goals, and what was described by one writer as 'the ugliest clash Old Trafford has seen for many a match'.

That flare-up was to have far reaching effects witnessed as it was by millions of TV viewers who flooded the Football League with complaints and it eventually led to a change in the laws of the game. Yet the most offending part of the whole incident I never even saw. It happened like this: Paddy Crerand and Peter Dobing suddenly lost their heads and had a real go at each other. Fortunately I was right on the spot and I jumped in smartly to drag them apart. Players were jostling for position and I had my arm round Crerand restraining him so that his face was directly over my right shoulder close in. Unknown to me while he was actually leaning over my shoulder he spat at one of the Stoke players, left half Tony Allen. Naturally I couldn't see it – it happened out of my line of vision – but the angle of the TV camera was such that Crerand was in full view.

When everyone quietened down I cautioned Crerand and Dobing for the original incident and restarted the game. No-one mentioned the spitting either then or after the game. I drove home blissfully happy and unaware of the pandemonium which was to be released that night on Match of the Day.

We only had an old black and white telly at the time so Margaret and I popped round to my parents to watch the game. When I saw Crerand's face loom up on the screen I could have been sick. I thought: 'My God, he's been allowed to get away with it.'

Pat Partridge, taken from Oh Ref!

Well, I've had my troubles with British fans, with British players and with British referees. But give me good old British soccer justice any time! There are still some grounds where we come in for a bit of barracking even before the game starts; but that is dropping off now, as people begin to realise that we don't just kick our way through a match but play football, even if it's hard. Maybe even some referees were subconsciously influenced by our so-called reputation as a dirty team, in days gone by – although I'm prepared to admit I could be wrong here, for after having seen at close quarters what goes on in games abroad, I know deep down that the British referee is the most impartial in the world. And I certainly believe that now we have proved, once and for all, that Leeds United are not a team of thugs, but a combination of players who play it hard but fair, and also possess a fair amount of footballing skill. Football is a man's game: and if you can't take a knock or two – I'm talking of fans now, as well as players – then you shouldn't have anything to do with the game.

Billy Bremner, taken from You Get Nowt for Being Second

In Leeds' first season in Europe most of the players had to learn more or less as they went along and to their credit they learned more quickly than most.

Perhaps the biggest problem that English teams face in Europe is the eccentricity of referees.

Most Continental refs, of course, don't accept physical contact as part of the game, as we do in this country, and regard it as an offence even for a player to show his studs in making a tackle. At the same time, they condone shirt pulling and obstruction!

But you never quite know what to expect from these fellows. I mean, I was once booked by a referee for shouting for the ball!

The only time I have ever been sent off was in the first leg of the Fairs Cup semi-final against Zaragoza in 1966.

I was penalised for barging a Zaragoza defender in the back, and as I turned to walk away, he retaliated by punching me on the side of the neck. Incredibly, the referee sent us *both* off.

Johnny Giles, taken from Forward with Leeds

The English style of hard physical challenge was changed to one of sly gamesmanship. A lot has been said in recent years of the 'rough' play. In fact it is not nearly as physical as it used to be. Any League referee or trainer knows this from the relative freedom from serious injury. Not even the targets of the tacklers, the George Bests or Rodney Marshes, were often harmed or out of action. What did increase was the dramatics, with players writhing and agonising only to leap up a second later and dash the length of the field. To see an old-style physical game, which used to be commonplace in England in the days of Dean, or Lofthouse, or Bobby Smith, I have had to wait in recent years to referee an International abroad. A recent match between Hungary and Russia would have made the modern English player wince, and it reminded me of the hard challenge you could see in the forties or fifties. The change to niggling gamesmanship has certainly made it harder for the referee. I tell young referees never to be worried by physical violence. There is bound to be some violence they meet, because football is a physical contact game in which passions can be roused. But it is clear and straightforward and simple to handle. It is the crafty tackles, the behind-the-back aggro, the deliberate play-acting to get another player in trouble, which gives him his problems.

Jack Taylor, taken from Soccer Refereeing: A Personal View

When Osgood played for Chelsea against Norwich City in the

Football League Cup semi-finals, he went up for a high ball with Norwich's centre half Steve Govier, who headed clear. I turned to follow the play and, upon hearing a roar from the crowd, turned around to find Govier lying on the ground, unconscious. I looked at both linesmen, who shook their heads – they'd seen nothing.

In last season's Southampton–West Ham FA Cup third-round-tie, Bobby Gould was injured in a tackle with Osgood. I really didn't believe Osgood had fouled him. But when I got up to Gould, he was shouting, 'I'll kill you, Osgood, you could have broken my leg.' Gould showed me the leg as he was going off at half-time, and it was a mess, black and blue almost up to the knee.'

Gordon Hill, taken from Give a Little Whistle: The Recollections of a Remarkable Referee

Going 'over the top of the ball' is generally regarded as being about the worst foul in the book, and in my view it is rarely attempted. The really bad example of it is when a player gently lets the ball run away from him, and as his opponent comes in he kicks out ostensibly at the ball but in fact he goes over the top and takes the other fellow's ankle or shin bone. It will be appreciated how difficult a foul this is to discern. If the referee is sure in his mind, then not only is it a foul it should also be 'marching orders'.

Just how badly quick judgement is needed is appreciated by any referee when he sees the centre forward in full flight tackled late or from behind by a desperate defender. The question to be decided is, did the defender intend to fetch him down or was he genuinely trying to play the ball? Well, if the defender does succeed in blocking the ball, it must be fair enough even though the forward comes an almighty purler, as he is bound to do if the ball stops suddenly and he goes on – though most home crowds will have a different opinion about it if it is their forward!

Jack Taylor, taken from Soccer Refereeing: A Personal View

Manchester United were playing Huddersfield at Old Trafford and Bestie, who scored United's goal, was having his shirt stretched out of his shorts by Jimmy Lawson. He spun round angrily on the Huddersfield winger and arms were raised. Best pushed off Lawson then reeled back holding his face. I dived in between them and said: 'Don't be two silly little devils. Get on with the game and enjoy it.' I didn't caution either one of them.

The amount of natural God-given ability George Best had was unbelievable. At his peak I put him in the same class as Beckenbauer, Pele and Cruyff. No one can say more than that.

Pat Partridge, taken from Oh Ref!

It is when the defender misses the ball that our real difficulty starts. What did he intend to do? One of the secrets is to get a good look at his face as he comes into the tackle; that will often tell the story. Otherwise we have to judge by the relative position of the two players, their speeds and so on. But no referee can give a foul or penalty unless he is certain in his own mind that the player intended to commit the offence.

Wild kicking at the ball causes difficulty in interpretation. Only the referee seeing the actual incident and the circumstances of the moment can decide whether this is dangerous play, foul play or violent conduct. There is a proper distinction between each that has to be discerned.

Jumping is another matter to cause trouble. It is quite in order to jump at the ball, unless the referee decides it is dangerous play, but it is a very serious offence to jump at an opponent. Close and careful observation is needed. A referee would be quite justified in sending off the field any player who deliberately jumped feet first at an opponent. It would, in fact, be equivalent to kicking an opponent, for which the ultimate penalty of dismissal from the field must be exacted. The referee has no choice. Striking comes into the same category – violent conduct. So does the use of bad language to the referee.

Jack Taylor, taken from Soccer Refereeing: A Personal View

I am afraid that a large percentage of them don't even know when a serious foul has been committed. Too many see only the obvious and are more likely to book you for swearing than for going over the top on someone. I will say now that the standard of officiating in Britain is as high as anywhere in the world. I have been booked unfairly many times but, equally, I have often escaped when I should have been cautioned. The referees I cannot stand are the schoolmasterly types who beckon you to them and then treat you like a naughty school boy.

We are fully grown men earning our living and I wish they would treat us like adults in the way that Gordon Hill used to. He was the best. Swear at him and he was just as likely to swear back at you. A lot of duping goes on with a great deal of appealing and chat. The worst team I have ever come across for this is not Leeds, as you may imagine, but the more recent Sheffield Wednesday side, who have five or six players regularly appealing *en masse* for offsides everytime the ball is played through. It is so regimented that it looks as if they have been specially coached in how to con officials and it must intimidate referees.

Graeme Souness, taken from Graeme Souness: No Half Measures

George Best, like Bremner, attracted trouble which was not always of his own making and therefore demanded protection from the man in the middle.

Players would bait him hoping for a response which would see him ordered off. They knew he had a short fuse and was an easy target for that sort of treatment. He blew hot and cold very quickly and the answer was to try and get in close whenever he was involved because he could snap.

Pat Partridge, taken from Oh Ref!

I have on occasion been advised by other colleagues to 'watch so-and-so on Saturday', but I always ignored such advice.

To my mind it is courting disaster to go on the field with anything but an open mind about either the match or the players participating. If the administrators of the game wanted a players' record to be a factor in how he is treated, they would circulate his record to all referees. I strongly advise referees to treat each player on his own merits in each individual game, for players' reputations are as well known to other players as they are to us.

I have certainly experienced the situation, fortunately, rarely, when such a player is provoked by his opponents because it is thought he will be sure to react strongly and either lose his temper to the detriment of his own play or come into trouble with the referee, or both. Every player on the field is entitled to just treatment and I am happy to think that by and large he gets it.

Jack Taylor, taken from Soccer Refereeing: A Personal View

Andy Lockhead was streaking towards the goal when Nobby clipped him from behind.

Out came my book and Stiles, full of apologies, pleaded: 'It's the floodlights, ref. They shine in my contact lenses and I can't see a thing.' As I was writing Nobby leaned over and said: 'You spell it with an 'I' not a 'Y'.' And he was supposed to have bad eyesight.

It is that sort of thing which I love between player and referee. It is healthy and full of mutual respect. Nobby knew he had to be cautioned and he accepted it. There was no animosity between us and if you could get to that level in other situations half of football's problems would be solved.

Nobby and Tommy Smith are the sort I would always have in my team.

I remember Smithy getting an elbow in the face once as he went to head the ball. He was out cold and we all gathered round. 'Where am I?' he moaned. 'Who did it? I'll effing get 'im.'

'No Tommy,' I said. 'Forget it. He's not as hard as you.'

Pat Partridge, taken from Oh Ref!

The two things I get remembered for are kicking people and a European Cup Final goal. It does sometimes get on my nerves. You don't play over 600 times for Liverpool under great managers like Bill Shankly and Bob Paisley if that's all you can do.

Tommy Smith

Stiles, Smith and Norman Hunter are all the same. You must be around when they put their visiting card in, put in yours, and say: 'Right, who is next?' Hunter and Everton's Colin Harvey clashed so hard one day, fair but like two runaway steamrollers with no quarter given, that I stopped the game to ask if they were both alright and then restarted it with a dropped ball. No foul had been committed.

Pat Partridge, taken from Oh Ref!

In my day referees used to let you warm up. They need to give you five minutes to get your tackles sorted out. In Tommy Smith's case he was given twenty minutes.

Brian Labone

I once sent Derek Hales off at Charlton and no one knew he had been sent off. He hit an opponent and I said, 'Are you going quietly?', and he said, 'Okay.' And off he went. Brian Moore had to rewrite his script the next day for the TV highlights because he didn't know he had been sent off. Neither did anyone else in the ground. There was no fuss from the player.

Players didn't argue as much with the referee in my day. When you gave a decision they accepted it and didn't crowd around the referee like they do today.

Jack Taylor

One of the aspects of the game which annoys me the most is this business of players overreacting to fouls on them, and forwards such as Liverpool's Kevin Keegan and Steve Heighway and Coventry's Tommy Hutchison are particularly guilty of this. I am not saying that they deliberately try to get opponents into trouble – maybe their overreaction is an emotional response but it often has that effect.

I think it is mainly forwards too, who commit the sly, under-hand fouls.

Gordon Hill, taken from Give a Little Whistle:
The Recollections of a Remarkable Referee

This one was bad, I must confess, even considering the brutality I had suffered before I hit back. The referee, whose idea of protecting ball-players from leg-players was to get rid of the ball-players, had me in such a rage with his cowardice that I eventually aimed a boot at him, not to deliberately assault him, but more than anything to show him how it felt to have to suffer that sort of treatment. It was sheer frustration. His answer was to bury his head in the sand even further. Still, it was an unforgiveable act of petulance on my part, and I deserved the £100 fine and five-match ban the FA handed me. The club, as expected, also took disciplinary action against me. But the kickers got away with it, and so did that nonentity of a man whose sort brings all referees into dispute, no matter how unfair that may be.

Willie Johnston on being sent off playing for West Brom v Brighton in the FA Cup, taken from Willie Johnston: On the Wing!

What is not legitimate, and is very dangerous, is the tackle through the legs. That was the one aimed to harm, which referees had to stamp out. But the misleading terminology led some to penalise quite fair tackles.

The 'foot-over-the-ball' or 'over-the-top' tackle can be crippling when the player deliberately goes into the tackle with his studs well over the ball to crunch into his opponent's leg. But in fact I have very rarely seen that happen. Yet so much was the catchphrase used that players fairly felled by a hard tackle, or caught by a mistimed one, were forever yelling, 'What about it, Ref? Over the top!' You need to watch for it, but not be mesmerised into believing that it happens all the time. Over the years you may notice that many of those who shout about it are still prepared to play part of the time with socks rolled down and no shin pads. Would they dare do that if they were expecting 'over-the-top' tackles as regularly as they complain? Sometimes the phrase was used simply to get into trouble players who were too hard and strong for them, like Norman Hunter or Tommy Smith, even when their tackles were fair.

Jack Taylor, taken from Soccer Refereeing: A Personal View

The trouble with Scottish referees is the lack of consistency. Swear at some referees or just appeal to them and they whip out the yellow card and your name's in the book. Others, like young Brian McGinley will answer you back – firmly and politely – and tell you to get on with the game. But he won't book you for run-of-the-mill complaining. I'm always moaning at referees so I know what I'm talking about.

I can't stand referees who play to the gallery by running the length of the park wagging their finger at you. They're trying to show off and usually they're not very good referees anyway. Why should a player have to stand to attention and be dressed down by a referee in front of the crowd? If he is telling me off – why shouldn't I be allowed to speak in my own defence and explain my side of things? A referee who indulges in the finger-waving histrionics doesn't impress any of the players I can assure you. I'm sure he isn't impressing the crowd either.

Derek Johnstone, taken from Rangers: My Team

During a match, there would be this constant dialogue, going on between us . . . we were bollocking one another, going on at one another all the time.

Gordon Hill on Peter Osgood, taken from Give a Little Whistle:
The Recollections of a Remarkable Referee

I swore at referees throughout my first season with Tottenham, but they never booked me because I swore in Spanish. What a difference, though, when my English improved! Only five months into the second season I'd collected eighteen disciplinary points for dissent, only one wrong word short of an automatic suspension; I then took a grip on myself and shut up.

Ossie Ardiles, taken from Ossie: My Life in Football

I swore at players. Now, I've always looked upon swearing quite simply as something that is part and parcel of any emotional involvement, and I constantly used swear words in the heat of a game. I could and did switch it off immediately the game ended, but during the game I could be quite foul.

Gordon Hill, taken from Give a Little Whistle:
The Recollections of a Remarkable Referee

Another clash that surprised me was between Mike Channon

and Peter Shilton in November 1983. Channon challenged Shilton late and unfairly and I gave a free kick.

Perhaps I went into the situation slightly unprepared – Channon and Shilton had been England team mates on many occasions. I thought they were bound to be friendly towards each other, but the atmosphere was decidedly unfriendly. I had to nurse the situation for the rest of the game. The ball had been loose and, in retrospect, it was clear that Channon achieved what he set out to do – and that was to 'clonk' Shilton. I vowed that I would never again automatically assume that players would be on good terms or prepared to forgive and forget simply because they had once played together.

Keith Hackett, taken from Hackett's Law: A Referee's Notebook

They are so inconsistent. One week you will get a really good one, and the next three will be awful. I don't know their names, but I know their faces and which ones are decent.

Viv Anderson on referees, taken from Viv Anderson

I feel so ashamed after being booked, realizing that I've lost my self-control again and failed once more in simple human understanding: in other words, I haven't regarded the referee as someone who can make honest mistakes as easily as the rest of us. Once in a match at either Coventry or Leeds, I can't remember which, my abuse of the referee was shocking. I felt dreadful about it when I came to my senses and I wanted to write to him to apologise. Somehow the letter wasn't sent and I'm still looking for that referee to express my regret personally.

Ossie Ardiles, taken from Ossie: My Life in Football

In England ball-players have a better chance of survival because as soon as they're tackled from behind it's a foul. Up here, you gather the ball and you know that in a split second you're going to get thumped from the back. That's why we see more skilled ball players in England – they get protection.

I just wish referees would get to grips with the petty fouling that goes on quietly when they are unsighted. In Rangers we have some big men to go up to the goal when we get a corner kick – myself, Colin Jackson, Derek Parlane, Gordon Smith. It's a pretty formidable line-up if you're a defender facing them. Yet time and again we're impeded by a defender who times his move well and pretends to stumble into us just as we are set to jump for a header. Referees never seem to notice this malpractice. The defenders are paying no attention to the ball – they're just blocking you. It's a professional foul and it should be punished.

A referee can make or break a good game and I've seen too many of them who get whistle happy and blow for everything and it stops the flow of play. This is how niggles creep in between the players and you can have an explosive situation on your hands.

Derek Johnstone, taken from Rangers: My Team

On the very morning of the game, I picked up the biggest selling Sunday newspaper of all, the *News of the World*, to read the headline: 'I accuse Dalglish.' It was an article by the controversial, publicity-seeking Welsh referee Clive Thomas saying that Kenny was cantankerous and difficult while Souness was a hard man whom he had booked on a number of occasions, and there was a picture of me to emphasise the point.

As far as I am concerned it was a set-up and disgraceful that a current official, as he was then, could provoke such an inflammatory situation. As Kenny and I read it in our Hertfordshire hotel that morning, I said that one of us would be booked for certain that afternoon.

Graeme Souness before the Merseyside derby Milk Cup Final,
taken from Graeme Souness: No Half Measures

One game involving Souness that stands out was an FA Cuptie between Blackburn and Liverpool in January 1983. In the opening minutes Souness committed a late foul tackle on Blackburn's Noel Brotherston. I awarded a free kick and informed Souness that I was going to caution him. His reply was, 'You were at the top of my list of referees, but now you're at the bottom.'

'You are going to be at the top of my list of players right here in the book,' was my retort as I took his name, 'and if you repeat that type of foul again I will have no alternative but to send you off.'

Souness most certainly did not find that amusing. My little quip, designed to ease the tension, backfired. I must add, though, that Souness behaved impeccably for the remainder of the match.

Keith Hackett, taken from Hackett's Law: A Referee's Notebook

There is only one branch of the game in which I believe English referees lack experience, and that is in their control of the early stages of a match. Hardly any referee in Britain is firm enough in the first ten minutes, which are often a free-for-all. English players cherish the notion that no-one is ever sent off in the first minute and they trade on it. The game here will improve rapidly when stricter refs show them they're mistaken.

Ossie Ardiles, taken from Ossie: My Life in Football

Frankly I don't rate the standard of referees in Scotland all that highly. Again it comes down to the overall standard of games here compared to England. There's more high quality football played in England than north of the border and it is reflected in the standard of their whistle men. Every week there are big matches played – it brings out the best in the players and at the same time keeps referees on their toes. This standard is bound to be higher. They have to know their job down there to exist. The same high quality is not sustained in Scotland and I think it shows in the performances of a lot of our referees.

Derek Johnstone, taken from Rangers: My Team

I think it is true that every good side needs one iron man, but sometimes the reputation is far more fearsome than the actual article, and it does not have to be a defender. Referees must not be lulled into the theory that defenders are the real hit men of the game. Often it is the reverse. Forwards can create problems by illegal use of the arms or elbows, by pushing, shoving or kicking opponents and so on.

However, the more renowned iron men have usually been either defenders or midfield players. Jimmy Case, for example. He can be a fairly violent player. That can be seen from the

246

number of cautions he has received over the years, and he must be watched carefully. Gerry Gow was a mighty hard man. But that was his role – to put himself about and put the fear of God into opponents. Billy Bremner and Norman Hunter were recognised as the hard men of the Leeds United side under Don Revie but, towards the end of Revie's reign, Terry Yorath was probably worse than either of them. Tommy Smith, Ron Harris, Peter Storey, Jim Holton and during my time watching Sheffield Wednesday, Tony Kay. These men were all known to be hard. But I do not think they were cynical. Clumsy, maybe, but not cynical. They invariably had the ball in mind.

Keith Hackett, taken from Hackett's Law: A Referee's Notebook

Give the players a good referee and you'll usually get a good game. The Salford referee Neil Midgley is a good case in point.

He was in charge of a game between Liverpool and Wimbledon recently that had all the makings of a really tough one. Wimbledon's FA Cup Final win over Liverpool hardly endeared them to the football purists and there was a lot of pre-match talk about trouble brewing.

But nothing happened. Why? Because Neil Midgley was in command. The players knew it and they responded. Vinny Jones went in just as hard as ever and when he committed a foul he was punished. But there it stopped. I lost count of the number of times I spotted Midgley having a word here and there with players who were getting steamed up. In doing so he took the steam out of the situation and helped to create a good, hard game of football.

Dissent is another problem. Players have always had the odd niggle with the referee. It's human nature. But a good referee will stop things getting out of hand with a joke or a short, sharp reply. What we must stamp out is this mass protesting where virtually a whole team surrounds the referee. They must know they're wasting their time. All they're doing is setting a bad example to the fans and young players. Footballers, like anyone else, must accept authority.

Nat Lofthouse, taken from The Lion of Vienna: 50 Years A Legend

Nowadays, because of television cameras, players have really got to be very careful about what they do on the park. We would not have got away with what we got away with had we been playing today. My mother always said if they kick you, kick them back, 'cause if you don't they will kick you forever. And we did used to kick 'em back. Fortunately for us the cameras were not there. Nowadays I think you would have to think twice before you did that.

Denis Law

This is the first evidence I have seen of the so-called referees' clampdown, which is a follow-on from the strict application of the rules brought in during the World Cup. In my view there's no need for it. There's nothing wrong with our game, so why change it? One of the great attractions of British football is its speed and aggression. It's a man's game and all of us are prepared to give and take a few knocks. Take that competitive edge away and you'll spoil it. There are seven bookings at Wembley and one of those cautioned is Ryan Giggs. That says it all about the new get-tough approach.

Alan Shearer on the 1994 Charity Shield,
taken from Alan Shearer's Diary of a Season

I was at a game yesterday, Nottingham Forest against Manchester City, and there were eight bookings and a sending off. But there was not a bad foul amongst them. The refereeing standards today are abysmal.

Tommy Docherty

It's very hard now. The game is getting less and less physical, contact wise. I think the crowds like to see the 50–50 tackles. But more and more now the referee sees it one way or the other.

Vinny Jones

We have faith in referees in general and they are all honourable people; they are all human beings. But being human beings sometimes they are going to make mistakes. One of the mistakes that all of us do is we always have certain opinions about fellow professionals. When it comes to Wimbledon maybe they think we are a bunch of macho thugs or something? I don't know. But we are not that. It isn't Vinny Jones that we need to concentrate on, it is the whole club and the re-occurrence and frequency of this matter, and it has to stop.

**Wimbledon chairman Sam Hammam on Vinny Jones'
tenth sending off**

I feel that referees are out there and they don't give me the same sort of leeway that they give other players. The minute I do anything it's terrible. If some other players do it, it's not so terrible.

Vinny Jones

I've always told Vinny to be quiet. He made some remark to the linesman telling him to 'keep up with play', or 'he's rubbish' or something like that. The referee was not happy with that statement and books him. But it's hard to take sometimes when referees make poor decisions and costly decisions and it's happened to us on numerous occasions. I've just come back after a six-month ban (from the dugout) for telling the truth. We got robbed of a goal at Newcastle. It has been proved that it was a perfectly good goal, but I got done for calling the referee a little Hitler, because I couldn't speak to him. They're laws to themselves. They're not the best in the country by any means. The referees now are getting too big for their boots. They go unpunished, they go home, they're happy, we pick up the bill. We haven't run out of team spirit. We've got a lot of good players who can play football but unfortunately it's the easiest thing in the world for people in the world to tarnish Wimbledon football club because of what's happened in the past.

Joe Kinnear on Vinny Jones

I've had some delightful moments with Tommy Smith. The one which stands out in my mind was when I refereed Ron Yeats' testimonial match against Celtic at Anfield. Early on in the game, Tommy was involved in a clash with a Celtic player, and pulled his fist back to put one on him. The incident happened right in front of a large selection of Celtic supporters – there was green and white everywhere – and I had visions of the whole bloody lot coming over the top. 'For God's sake,' I shouted to him, 'you'll get us killed.' He immediately put his fist down by his side, and his face bore the startled expression of a man who had suddenly come face to face with a group of Martians.

Gordon Hill, taken from Give a Little Whistle:
The Recollections of a Remarkable Referee

Because I built up a reputation for being a soccer hard man, most people assume my disciplinary record must have been horrendous. The truth of the matter is that I was sent off only twice in a top flight career that covered close on two decades.

I admit that I probably verbally abused referees down the years, but this was simply because I always felt they were on a different planet to the players. We always felt completely misunderstood.

The reality is that the refs in my day had a damn sight more commonsense than their 1995 counterparts. Since the World Cup in America, officials have been using the letter of the law in every instance, which is a recipe for disaster.

There are grey areas in every situation, but modern referees seem unable to give and take. They are under constant pressure from the game's governing body and the end product is that yellow and red cards are constantly being handed out.

I feel sorry for the modern professional footballer. Something must be done – and quickly – to restore some sanity to the situation.

Tommy Smith

Inconsistency is the problem which frustrates footballers most.

At least if we knew that we were going to be booked for one offence and sent off for another – and every referee stuck to the same rulebook – we'd know where we stand.

At the moment we're all over the place.

Different referees apply rules in different ways. It's understandable when players and managers get frustrated.

David Unsworth

The one thing I think about referees is that everything you get you deserve. Because really and truthfully they get kicked from pillar to post by players, by managers, by the crowd and especially by the FA and the Football League. If they haven't got the bottle to stand up and get their own union going, where they can come into the game on a professional basis, I think whatever they get they deserve. While the League and the FA are telling them how to referee they're never going to get any better.

I think they should go professional on a decent wage. I think they should be stood up and be counted basically for every decision they make, rather than hide under the FA or the League rules and say it's not my problem it's theirs. Until they get going and turn professional we are going to get what we are getting now, which is not very good refereeing.

Tommy Smith

Something has got to be done about the refereeing. There were about five fouls on him before he got a free kick. The referee is saying he's diving and this and that. I've seen him in the last eight games and he's brilliant. He's playing with Barmby, who is also only small, and the thing I'm worried about is that they are going to get fouled so many times, it's very difficult for them. These little guys are doing so great in English football.

Malcolm Allison, on watching Middlesbrough's Juninho

Some are bad, and some are even worse. Joking apart, we have to be very careful to referees that we don't drive them all out of football. Starting in Sunday football some are subjected to violence through to the Premiership where some are subjected to verbals in the papers, which we have all done. I think the sooner we can get back to the days when the referee was always right, the better. There seems to be a different respect on the Continent. When I watch Italian football what I do see is a certain respect for the referees. The players just walk away from things and they get on with it. I think we have got to get back to that.

We had two players sent off at Newcastle last year for heavy breathing. So there is an inconsistency about it, but the other side of it is that we've got to get back to giving the referee a chance to get on with the game and do it his way. There's a fellow called Keith Cooper for Wales who I personally think is the best around. He smiles, he has a little word in players' ears and he runs around without too much fuss at all and if you want to model yourself on anyone do it on him. The big secret is he smiles. We can tell when we go in the room to meet the referees before the game by their actual attitude. Quite often the two managers will come out of the room, look at each other and say, 'Oh God, no chance today, five bookings and two sent off.'

Joe Royle

When I used to referee it was a sport and a hobby and I put a lot of professionalism into it on my application on the field of play. If referees became full-time professionals, I'm afraid the sense of humour would definitely go out of the window. Most referees have a job to go to on Monday morning and they look on football as a relief valve to their pressure of work. The way the sport is going at the moment, with money being the prime orientation of it, I'm afraid it's going to go the same way. You would get robots; if you want robots go ahead, go professional.

There's no referee in the world who is going to referee a game the same as another one. Consistency comes down to 90 minutes of football. Everyone is different, the crowd look at decisions differently, referees look at it differently, but at the end of the day the referee has got a job to do and he does it the best way he can, not what the rules say.

Roger Milford

It's a sorry state of affairs when the referee feels he's got equal billing with Eric Cantona. Eric came through his test, I'm not sure the referee did.

**Roy Evans on the referee (David Elleray) of
Eric Cantona's comeback game**

I'm almost speechless about the referee.

Alan Green on the Arsenal v Newcastle Coca-Cola Cup-tie

Managers all over the country were worried about the deteriorating standards and the attitudes of referees and the authorities. The authorities should take a more considered view of what managers want. I wonder how much more we can take before someone listens to what we have to say.

Colin Todd

A lot of young referees are coming through. The ones that used to swear back at you have gone, unfortunately. Referees take it to the letter of the law now. I think the majority of supporters enjoy seeing a good crunching tackle as much as they enjoy seeing a great goal. I think if you take that out of football, which is what's happening, unfortunately, I think you are losing something.

Keith Houchen

What makes me nervous is inexperienced referees. They all know the rules, every one of them. But the inexperienced blokes are having to learn about players and until they become sure of themselves they referee strictly by the book, not letting any little thing go.

They are under enough pressure without this latest business of knowing there's some chap watching everything they do with a pair of binoculars from the terraces.

The result is that you have referees on the edge, and tension all around.

Lawrie McMenemy

I think it's a good idea for ex-pros to be referees. They know how the players think, they know they lose their heads sometimes.

Bernie Slaven

I've always been a great believer that we should have ex-professionals as referees because they know the game inside out, they know when players are taking a dive and when they are fouled legitimately. The one thing that referees can't seem to differentiate between these days is what is a fair 100 per cent challenge for the ball and what is a foul. Players are being yellow-carded and red-carded for very petty things these days and I think it reduces the game. The sooner we get professional referees the better.

Frank Worthington

I know ex-players could be expected to spot the crafty foul quicker than some referees who learn the game by the book, but generally speaking I don't think former players are the right types for good referees. I don't believe they have the right temperament. It takes a strongly disciplined man with a school-master air and deaf to insults. I doubt if ex-players could stand the criticism without answering. There are still plenty of good refs around and I don't really think they would become better by making them full-time professionals.

Take men like Jim Finney, Gordon Hill, Jack Taylor, Leo Callaghan. I had a lot of respect for them. First-class referees. They knew how to use discretion, the quality a lot of refs lack. There are times when the rulebook can be overlooked. Like the time a player takes a free kick a couple of yards from where the foul was given. As long as it's not close to the penalty area the ref should play on.

When a player takes a throw in and pinches a few yards, it's not really a crime, though it's against the rules, but a call from the ref like, 'Don't take the ball home with you' does far more to keep control than irritating players and crowd whistling every little infringement.

Jimmy Greaves, taken from Let's Be Honest

Refs are the same as in my day, except they no longer have commonsense. They should be pros, who are fitter and have the help of a third referee for crucial decisions.

Joe Kinnear

He's the player's referee. One who you can talk with and reason with, but you still know who is in charge.

There is a lot of pressure in football today and there are not enough people around who can smile.

Craig Hignett on referee Keith Cooper

I don't like the way the game's going today with yellow cards being shown straightaway for many things. It seems nine out of ten tackles today are deemed worthy of a booking.

When I played you used to get a wag of the finger from the referee and told to get on with things.

Sometimes you'd get three tellings off before being booked!

Dave Hickson

The game I played when I was young was a man's game.

Referees were firm but fair. It was only if a player committed a serious offence that they were booked or sent off. Now there are too many players getting cards for tackles that are late but not vicious or intentional.

Years ago there used to be only one player at Everton or Liverpool sent off a season, now it can be three or four a fortnight. There should be a full inquiry into the rules which took away referees' discretion on action against foul play.

Merseyside MP Bob Parry, who had trials with Everton as a youngster, on why he backed a 1996 Commons Motion for the reduction in the 'excessive' use of yellow cards

All referees are incompetent. I can't pick out a single one doing a half-decent job.

Ian Wright

It's getting ridiculous at the moment and somebody should look at all the suspensions which people are getting.

The powers that be are taking away the art of tackling. Every time you go in aggressively you're booked.

And some of the refereeing decisions are not helping the game. They're ruling players out of important games and they are costing us money. People should be coming to watch a team fielding its best players but that's not happening because so many players are suspended.

Steve Bould

I've only been booked twice this season. The last one was for doing an impression of the linesman.

When I asked what I had done wrong he said, 'This is for mimicking the linesman.' I just laughed. I looked across at the linesman and he was laughing too.

I really think that referees suffer from a lack of humour these days. They don't seem to understand jokes – just ask Gazza!

I got the other yellow card this season for winking, and I can't do that any more either.

Alan Shearer

Neither the SFA nor the supervisors are the problem. They don't make the laws of the game. They are only carrying them out.

All the rulings about crackdowns and players not being given an inch of leeway are coming from on high. FIFA, the world ruling body, is telling us all what we must do. The SFA and the referees have no choice but to obey them.

I've heard it said often that in my day a referee would have a quiet word in passing with an offender, instead of diving into his pocket for his black book and pencil.

That's true. I did it almost every week myself. But that's not how FIFA want these matters dealt with nowadays. They want a caution, followed by a red card if the need arises, and referees have no option other than to comply with those instructions.

Tom Wharton, Chairman of the Scottish FA Referee Supervisors

The way referees clamp down on the least little thing. I'd spend most of my time in the stand suspended nowadays.

I had all my trouble when referees had a sense of humour. You could still have a laugh and joke with them.

When I saw Paul Gascoigne booked for trying to raise a laugh at Ibrox last week, I could not believe it.

Willie Johnston

Occasionally it is pure anger. Most of the time it is quite rational. The annoying part is when you try to speak to a referee and he won't speak to you. When you are not swearing and you are trying to speak to him calmly and he says, 'Go away, go away,' it's ignorance. They can't speak to you. I don't know whether they have been told not to speak to players, whether they are being assessed as to whether they do that or not. We don't know what their assessors are looking for. It's very difficult.

Matthew Le Tissier

I thought it was a poor tackle. You don't break legs if you go for the ball. These days you can get a yellow card for kicking the ball away and you can get one for breaking someone's leg. It doesn't seem sensible. What happened was there for the whole nation to see on Match of the Day. But if the FA are not going to take any action on video evidence, who is? I know players don't go out to try and break people's legs. I'm sure John Salako didn't. But if it happens with a totally mistimed tackle like this, it should be properly punished. We have lost a player, yet Salako carries on playing.

Liverpool manager Roy Evans after Steve Harkness has his leg broken by a mistimed John Salako tackle, 1996

There's not a bad bone in John's body. He's had more than his fair share of injury and would never deliberately go out to hurt anybody.

Coventry manager Ron Atkinson's response

Shock waves reverberate through the sporting world after a precedent-setting High Court ruling that held referee Mr Nolan from Tamworth, Staffordshire, responsible for the paralysis of a player through his failure to control a game. The *Guardian* reports: 'In the first ruling of its kind, the player, Ben Smoldon – who has been a tetraplegic since being injured during a match in 1991 – won his case against the match referee, Michael Nolan. Mr Smoldon went to court seeking £1 million in damages. The final sum he will receive is to be assessed by the

Court at a later date. One of the country's most experienced football referees, David Elleray, said: 'It may discourage people from refereeing sports, particularly at lower levels. They may think, "If someone gets hurt, I may be sued".' Mr Elleray added that the laws of football had been amended last year to protect referees from just such claims. The new law stated that referees were not liable for injuries during a game, from anything from an icy pitch to dangerous play.

High Court ruling, April 1996

BILL SHANKLY

It's Much More Important Than That

Stephen F. Kelly

'Football is not just a matter of life and death; it's much more important than that'

Bill Shankly was without doubt among the greatest football managers of the post-war era. But to football fans everywhere, Bill Shankly was far more than just a manager: he was a folk-hero whose legend still dominates the game.

Bill Shankly's wit, down-to-earth wisdom and sheer determination set a standard that holds good to this day. This full and frank biography tells his larger-than-life story, and is an inspiring tribute to one of football's most enduring heroes.

ISBN 1 85227 547 2

MOTTY'S DIARY
A Year in the Life

John Motson

John Motson is Britain's favourite football commentator, and he is known and welcomed at every club in every division throughout the land. In 1996 he celebrated 25 years with *Match of the Day* and gave his thousandth football commentary for the BBC.

Now, for the first time, John Motson gives his personal account of all the big events in the 1995/96 season. The thrills and spills of the international game, his own thoughts and comments on the main issues, and an individual view of England's progress towards and during Euro '96 are all in Motty's first-hand story. Here's your chance to find out who Motty thought would win the FA Cup, how he became the voice of football, and where he got that sheepskin coat.

Informed, witty, opinionated and revealing, *Motty's Diary* is a unique record of a memorable season, and a riveting read for every fan.

ISBN 1 85227 620 7

FOOTBALL BABYLON

Russ Williams

It's a funny old game, football. Take that centre forward who was gored to death by wild boars during a game. Or the time there were topless models in the players' bath after they'd won an important match. Cor, some players have been known to take drugs, get drunk, have punch-ups, kill referees and accept bribes. The managers can be even worse, and as for the chairmen, well, you wouldn't believe it. Would you?

Here's your chance to find out. The most astonishing, amazing, abso-bloody-lutely astounding tales of sex, death, bribery, corruption, violence and humour that you'll ever find in the game of two halves. It's a funny old game, football. Isn't it. Eh? Marvellous.

ISBN 0 7535 0046 9

PATRICK COLLINS:
THE SPORTSWRITER
Twenty Years of Award-Winning Journalism

Patrick Collins

For almost twenty years Patrick Collins has written about, analysed and enjoyed sport around the world, from Adelaide to Zimbabwe, via South London and Las Vegas. He has covered five World Cups, five Olympics, numerous Five Nations Championships and countless World Boxing title fights, and on the way he has interviewed key figures in every major sport.

This book brings together the very best of Patrick Collins' writing for the first time and is an essential collection for every sports fan.

ISBN 0 7535 0086 8